"Zakoura..." Leigh whispered into the stillness of the night.

The moon's light reflected off his eyes, making them seem to float in the air above her. "What is it that troubles you?"

"I don't know.... I run from you, and all I want is to be with you. I'm terrified of something, yet I don't know what it is—or why it scares me so."

"Sometimes it is best not to question too closely. Fear has its place. It can protect you."

"Protect me from what? Not from you. I don't need to be protected from you." She said the last with more conviction than she felt. In spite of her desire to be with him, vague doubts were stirring restlessly at the gates of her mind.

When he answered her, there was a heaviness in his voice that bordered on pain. "There are dangers you cannot imagine...."

Dear Reader,

Despite the summer sun shining brightly outside, you'll find yourself a prisoner of the shadows this month as, once again, we take a walk on the dark side of love.

Begin by walking through *The Portal*. Sharon Pape's tale of a woman of our world—our dimension—and the man she falls in love with, a man from somewhere entirely different—and entirely dangerous.

Then move on to Marilyn Tracy's *Sharing the Darkness*, the story of a mother on the run, trying to save her young son, and the enigmatic—and irresistible—man who takes them in. You'll be shocked by the bargain he offers her, but you'll also shiver with desire.

In months to come, look for more of the best eerily romantic reading around as we bring you books by favorite writers such as Jane Toombs, Rachel Lee and Maggie Shayne. And those are only a few of the authors we've got lined up to escort you to the dark side of love. You won't want to miss a single book.

Yours,

Leslie Wainger
Senior Editor and Editorial Coordinator

Please address questions and book requests to:
Reader Service
U.S.: P.O. Box 1325, Buffalo, NY 14269
Canadian: P.O. Box 1050, Niagara Falls, Ont. L2E 7G7

SHARON PAPE

THE PORTAL

Published by Silhouette Books
America's Publisher of Contemporary Romance

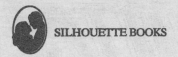 SILHOUETTE BOOKS

ISBN 0-373-27033-X

THE PORTAL

Copyright © 1994 by Sharon Pape

SHARON PAPE

spent a number of years teaching French and Spanish at the secondary level, before finding the time to write her first novels, *Ghostfire* and *The Godchildren*. Even though both stories dealt with the supernatural, romance was an integral part of each.

Sharon lives on Long Island with her husband, their two children, a golden retriever—the laziest dog on the planet—and a horse. When she's not writing, she spends her time reading, working out at the gym, horseback riding and traveling.

For Robin Kaigh, who knows a thing or two about opening "portals"

PROLOGUE

She jerked her head up from the pottery shard she'd been working to unearth. Head cocked to one side, she held her breath, listening. The wind that rumbled through the canyon sounded angrier than usual; in the distance a coyote howled in counterpoint. No other noise intruded on the stillness of the cave. Even so, she was certain that the Indian was back. She felt his presence.

When she finally exhaled, her breath was ragged and her heart, which seemed to have suspended its rhythm while she strained to hear, tripped into an anxious double time. She had to get out of the cave. Grabbing the propane lamp, she ran, awkwardly, stooped beneath the low ceiling and stumbling over the uneven earthen floor. The distance to the one narrow exit seemed greater than she remembered. An illusion caused by her nerves?

Her pulse was drumming so loudly in her ears, she couldn't hear her own footfalls. When she reached the opening, she stopped short—it was dark out. The team never stayed at the dig this late; climbing down the cliff at night was too dangerous. Could they have forgotten—left without her?

She took a hesitant step outside. The wind rushed at her, thick and damp, riding point for an approaching storm. The new moon, which provided a sharp scar of light over the opposite cliff wall, was obliterated by racing thunderheads as she watched, plunging the canyon into a darkness as deep as blindness. Her fingers tightened around the handle of the propane lamp, and she tried to remember how long she'd had it on, how long it would be before it ran out of fuel. But she couldn't seem to place the time they'd arrived at the dig. If it had been early that morning, the light might die at any moment. Panic rose in her like a snake striking, its venom flashing through her chest. Maybe she should wait out the night in the cave. But the cave was a dead end, a trap with one exit. And the Indian was out there somewhere.

Thunder growled menacingly. She had to make a decision, and she had to make it fast. She looked to her left, where the ledge wrapped around the rock face, connecting the cave with the main cliff dwellings. It had always been wide enough before. Now it seemed to fall off into the abyss of the canyon just past the pale circle of lamplight. But if she wanted to leave, there was no other choice. The ledge was the only way back to the rest of the team—if they were still there. The only way back to a trail to the canyon floor that wasn't a drop of sheer rock. She was trying to muster up the courage to step out onto it when she saw him.

He was standing just to her right, motionless, all but the surface of his body merged with the deep shadows of the cliff face, as if he weren't real at all, as if he were a bas-relief carved from the rock.

She opened her mouth to scream, to shout for her colleagues, but her larynx was a knot that grew tighter the harder she strained to make it work. The Indian stepped away from the cliff and came toward her, slowly, as if he knew she wouldn't run. The propane lamp illuminated the long hair that whipped around his face like a cat-o'-nine-tails in the gusty wind; it highlighted the sinewy muscles of his arms and torso and thighs as he moved. In spite of the cool night air, he wore only a breechcloth and sandals.

Logic told her to try to escape, but some other part of her, inexplicably, wanted her to stay.

When he was within a foot of her, he stopped. His eyes were riveted on her, black eyes, underscored by the sharp flare of high cheekbones. He raised his hand and reached out to her, trailing his fingers down the side of her cheek, along her neck, finally cupping her chin in a large, callused palm. With his touch, the trembling that had been fear was transmuted into a trembling of desire, so quickly, yet so subtly, that she didn't know when the one ended and the other began. Why had she been afraid? She searched her mind, but reason eluded her. And after a moment she discovered she didn't care.

As the first ragged spear of lightning cut through the sky to the west, the Indian took the lamp from her hand and set it down beside her. With his other arm around her back, he drew her closer. She moved to him willingly, molding her body against his, circling her arms around his neck. When he bent to kiss her, she opened her mouth and drew his tongue inside. She was stirred by the taste of him. A warmth, liquid and dense, rode through her blood, spilling over and flooding her with a strangely familiar longing. Wherever her body touched his, she was suffused with a heat so intense it seemed capable of melting her into him, so that when he leaned back for a moment to look at her she was surprised to find that she was still whole.

Taking her hand, he led her along the ledge for several yards to the place where it widened, where the cliff face sank back into the hollow of an embryonic cave. His hands around her waist, he lifted her onto a low, rocky shelf as the storm exploded over the canyon.

Leigh Morgan sat bolt upright in the narrow bed to the explosive crack of thunder. The RV was shuddering under the impact of wind-driven rain. Lightning flashed, strobe-like, outside, and thunder boomed in volley after volley. She hugged her knees to her chest, shaking and waiting for her thoughts to untangle themselves. She'd been with the Indian again—for the fourth time in the past few weeks. The recurring dreams were a roller coaster ride between the terrifying and the erotic. But they were never exactly the same. It was as if each were newly scripted and not just a rerun of the last. Of course, the Indian was always there, and she always started off trying to run from him.... What was happening to her? She'd tried analyzing the dreams, using every scrap of information she could dredge up from her memory of undergraduate psychology courses and miscellaneous articles on dream research that she'd read over the years. So far, she'd been unable to fathom their significance. She might feel better if she at least recognized the Indian, if he were someone she'd seen on the reservation. The mind was agile when it came to editing reality into dreams. But she'd never seen him before that first dream. If she had, she would have remembered. His was not a face easily forgotten or mistaken.

Thunder exploded again, the sound waves rocking the RV harder, scattering any lingering fragments of the dream and reminding Leigh of the dangers of being out on the vast flat plain where the only things higher than the camper were a few widely scattered mesas. She'd been through some violent electrical storms in New York, but at least then she'd been surrounded by millions of fellow humans. Here in the Navaho Nation of northern Arizona, she was in a small RV, with one roommate and only a handful of people for miles in any direction. First the emotional tempest of the dream, and now this storm. She'd never felt quite so unprotected before, so utterly vulnerable.

CHAPTER ONE

Leigh glanced across the two feet that separated her bed from Karen Hennessy's. In spite of the violent storm outside, her roommate was still sound asleep, her breathing deep and peaceful. Leigh wasn't surprised. During the six weeks they'd been sharing the camper, Karen had slept through the alarm clock every morning. She'd slept through Leigh dropping an entire drawer of silverware on the other side of the thin wall that separated the bedroom from the kitchen. She'd even slept through Alex hammering up a window shade over her head. Paul, who'd been on several digs with her in the past, maintained that she would sleep right through a scalping. She was certainly the most unflappable person Leigh had ever met.

"After nine years of digging up other people's bones, you gain a different perspective about the trivia of life," she'd said when Leigh asked her the secret of her equanimity. "Why waste time worrying, when it all comes down to bones in the end?"

Until now, she'd been the perfect roommate and mentor for Leigh's first professional field assignment. The perfect emotional ballast for Leigh's more turbulent nature. But at that particular moment, Leigh would gladly have traded her in for a roommate who was awake. She needed conversation, a distraction from the fury outside.

She thought about throwing on her raincoat and boots and sprinting the six feet to the other trailer. One of the three guys was bound to be awake. Paul always complained he couldn't sleep, and Hugh claimed to stay up reading most nights anyway. But the rain was sluicing down the windows with such force that it made the panes rattle. She'd be soaked to the skin before she was halfway there.

She was still debating the idea when she heard the noise. Between the bursts of thunder, beneath the clattering of the rain, something was scuttling around outside. It wasn't a loud noise, but it was strange. It didn't belong in the context of the storm. A moment later she heard what sounded like claws scratching on the side of the trailer—at least four feet above the ground. Whatever it was, it wasn't small. What kind of creature would be out on a night like this? The possibilities that paraded across her mind were all either extinct or mythical. Leigh was unnerved enough to try waking Karen. Then the wind gusted, slamming the thing hard against the trailer door. There was the unmistakable rasp of metal against metal. She gave a sharp hiccup of laughter. The folding chair she'd left outside. Some monster. She was definitely letting her imagination run amok. And just sitting there in the dark wasn't helping.

She crawled out of bed and pulled on a zippered sweat suit and socks. She felt a little better once she was snuggled in the soft fleece lining. The storm had brought a wave of cooler air, and the T-shirt she'd worn to bed hadn't been adequate. But as she moved about the cramped bedroom, she couldn't shake the uneasy feeling that someone was watching her. She glanced at the one window, over Karen's bed. The shade was drawn. Even if someone was out there in such a storm, he couldn't possibly see inside. She really had to get a hold on herself.

She padded into the kitchen to make a cup of hot chocolate. After mixing the cocoa by the night-light over the stove, she set the mug in the tiny microwave to heat, then leaned her elbows on the counter, looking out the black square of the window while the timer blinked its way back to zero. As she watched, a silvery fork of lightning speared the sky, brightening it to midday. For a moment she was staring straight into the obsidian eyes of the Indian. Leigh cried out and stumbled back from the counter until she collided with the table, never taking her eyes off the kitchen window, which now framed only darkness.

The Indian was the same one who stalked her in her dreams. Given the breadth of the counter and the trailer's hull, he'd been no more than three feet away from her. And she'd been trained to observe details and nuances. There wasn't a doubt in her mind. But the certainty was a troubling one. It meant that somehow the Indian had followed her past the threshold of her dreams into reality. The sheer impossibility of it was overwhelming.

When the lightning flared again, she sucked in her breath, expecting to see those foreign, yet familiar, eyes. But all she saw was the empty plain sweeping off to a mesa on the horizon. She had imagined the Indian, the same way she'd imagined that the chair was some monstrous creature. He had simply been a trick of light and shadow. She wanted to believe that. She wanted to believe it as much as she'd ever wanted to believe in Santa Claus and superheroes and four-leaf clovers. But the memory of his face was etched as cleanly in her mind as if her eyes had snapped a Polaroid of him.

The timer beeped, and Leigh jumped. She took a deep breath to steady herself, and started inching her way back to the counter. Her jaw clenched, she leaned close to the window to see if he was hiding below it or to either side. No one was there. Her photographic memory of the Indian notwithstanding, she had imagined him. There—that's all there is to it, she told herself firmly. But when she lifted the mug out of the microwave, her hand was shaking so badly, the cocoa slopped over the rim and onto the floor.

When Leigh stepped out of the RV the next morning, the sun had risen on a placid blue sky that stretched to the far horizon without even a wisp of cloud. The storm was like a fragment of a dream, but she couldn't shake the feeling that something wasn't quite right. That something was lurking just behind the benign backdrop of the day. The image of the Indian in her dream and at her window haunted her.

While she waited for Karen to emerge, she took a walk around the perimeter of the trailer. Maybe there would be some evidence that the Indian had been substantial, not just a product of her imagination, fueled by fear and the storm. Of course, she wasn't entirely sure she wanted to find such evidence, since it would mean that her dream wasn't just a dream anymore. Still, the scientist in her needed to know what was going on.

She walked around the corner of the RV to the side where the kitchen window looked out. Her breath hitched in her throat momentarily, although she knew no one would be there. She'd checked the window as soon as the sky was light. But her nervous system seemed to be functioning on automatic, without any relationship to what logic told her. Yet all she found back there was the folding chair lying on its side, its aluminum frame dented and part of its webbing torn loose. She wasn't surprised. If there were any clues, they would be small ones, not easily detectable. Footprints were out of the question. After the deluge they'd had, not even Bigfoot would have left tracks.

She scoured the area behind the camper, walking back and forth as if she were mowing a lawn. If anyone saw her and asked what she was doing, she'd tell them she was looking for a pen she'd lost the other day.

She was twenty yards from the trailer when she jerked her head up sharply. That discomfiting feeling again that someone was watching her, intense eyes holding her in tight focus. She spun in a quick circle. No one was there. What was going on? She'd never been the type to jump at shadows before. Chastising herself, she resumed her search. Without some hard proof of the prowler's existence, she could never mention what she'd seen to Karen or the others. She wasn't about to admit to four "I'll believe it when I've seen it and analyzed it" scientists that she'd been scared half to death by an Indian Peeping Tom during the worst thunderstorm of her life. Or that, although she'd never seen this particular man before, she'd been dreaming about him for weeks. If *she* thought it sounded ridiculous, *they* were bound to think she'd snapped.

Leigh continued her exploration, head resolutely bent, studying the ground. She still felt like a small creature being watched by a predator, but she refused to look up again to find the cause of her discomfort. No doubt it was as imaginary as the mystery man himself.

After a quarter of an hour, having found nothing, she gave up and returned to the front of the trailer. Karen was standing in the doorway, yawning and blinking in the sunlight like a bear roused from hibernation. Her hair, which was cut into a practical bob, was mashed against her head on one side. "Looks like we got some rain last night," she said, as she and Leigh detoured around two tub-size puddles between them and the other RV.

Leigh laughed and shook her head. It was a relief to talk about mundane things. "Are you sure there aren't any van Winkles in your family tree?" she asked.

"You're just jealous." Karen knocked on the trailer door, sniffing the air appreciatively. "Thank God Hugh has the coffee going."

One of the men yelled, "Enter!" As they stepped inside, they were enveloped in a spicy cloud of sautéed peppers and onions, interlaced with the aroma of strong coffee. Hugh Stafford was in the minikitchen, preparing omelets with the same intense concentration he brought to every project. At fifty-two, he was the old man of the team by a couple of decades, and its supervisor. His graying hair was pulled back into a short ponytail, and he had a dish towel flung over his shoulder on which he alternately wiped his fingers and his glasses.

Paul Delaney was at the table, completing the excavation register and daybook entries for the previous day's work. Karen liked to tease him about having been an accountant in another life. Leigh was just grateful he enjoyed writing up the reports, in all their annoying but necessary detail. Paul yawned a hello and rubbed his eyes with his fists. With his curly mop of brown hair and his large ears, he reminded her of an oversize poodle.

He nodded toward the bathroom, where an electric razor was buzzing on and off. "You hear that? That's Alex. Day and night—he spends so much time manicuring that new beard of his, you'd think he was shaping a whole topiary."

"Well, I like the look," Karen said.

"Ah, I think I detect the signs of another imminent conquest by Alex Bennetti, Mel Gibson of the archaeological set."

Karen glared at him. "Since when is having an opinion on a beard an indication of romantic interest?"

Paul turned to Leigh and whispered, "The lady doth protest too much, doth she not?"

Leigh shook her head. "Give it a rest, Paul. I happen to like the beard too."

"Someone get that table set," Hugh ordered from the stove. His voice was a deep bass that had taken Leigh by surprise the first time she heard it, since Hugh was so thin that he always seemed to be on the verge of drowning in his clothes.

Paul swept the notebooks off the table and into the folder at his feet. Then he opened the drop leaf that made it possible for them all to sit down together. Karen grabbed utensils and mugs; Leigh set the coffeepot, milk and sugar on the table. Alex emerged from the bathroom in time to unfold the two extra bridge chairs. After six weeks of living together in the field, they worked with drill-team efficiency.

Hugh carried all the plates to the table at once. It was a feat he'd learned waiting tables in Las Vegas the summer he turned eighteen.

The room grew quiet as omelets were devoured and coffee cups were filled and refilled.

"Where's the old appetite?" Hugh asked watching the way Leigh was picking at her food.

"The eggs are delicious, really. I guess I'm just a little tired." Which was only part of the truth. She'd learned to deal with lack of sleep back in college. She just worked her way through it. What she couldn't seem to work her way through were the dreams and the dark-eyed stranger. Although reason mandated that he'd never even existed, she kept seeing his face, black eyes boring into her, in that unsettling flash of lightning.

"You look tired," Alex agreed.

"Good one," Karen said. "Just what every woman wants to hear."

"I didn't say she looked *bad*." He forked a thick wedge of omelet into his mouth. "It isn't possible for Leigh to look bad."

Paul laughed. "Nice save."

Leigh felt the color rising in her cheeks. Compliments made her uncomfortable. If people said they liked her outfit, she had to point out its flaws. When she did well in school, she claimed the test had been easy, the teacher too generous. When boys, and later men, told her she was beautiful, she couldn't muster up words at all, she just blushed. She didn't understand what they saw in her. Oh, her eyes were okay, large and dark-lashed so she didn't need to bother with mascara. But the rest of her face was—well, too regular. That was why, when her dentist tried to talk her into having her chipped front tooth bonded, she'd steadfastly refused. She insisted it gave her face character.

"I didn't get much sleep with that storm last night," she said to change the subject.

Hugh mopped up the last of his eggs with a piece of toast. "The weather can get a little hectic here. You'll adjust. By the time we're packing to leave, you'll probably be snoring through the storms along with Karen."

"Snoring?" Karen was indignant.

Leigh ignored the chance to tease her roommate. "You're probably right. I'm sure the Navaho go on about their business, even on a night like last night, just like I would have back in New York." If anyone else had seen her "visitor" last night, now would be the perfect time for them to mention it.

Hugh shook his head. "All the Indians I've ever known have a healthy respect for nature. We Anglos are the ones who think we can defy the gods."

"If the Indians have such a healthy respect for nature, what happened to all the Anasazi?" It was Paul who asked the often-debated question. "The way they disappeared, you'd think they had a major falling-out with one deity or another."

Hugh rose and put the milk back in the refrigerator. "Speculation is the pastime of sluggards," he said to cut off what promised to be another lengthy discussion. "Off to the salt mines, children."

They obediently swallowed last mouthfuls of coffee and started clearing the table.

"There," Leigh thought, lecturing herself, as she collected the dirty dishes and stacked them in the sink. "No one else saw your Peeping Tom. And that's probably because there was no one out there to see!"

She followed the others out to the Bronco, determined not to dwell on what had to be a product of her own imagination.

The site they were excavating was a small Anasazi cliff dwelling that dated back to the eleventh century. Although the site was within the cliffs of Canyon de Chelly, they'd chosen to set up camp on the rim in order to facilitate propane and water deliveries and to avoid having their temporary homes become the focus of tourist attention. To reach the excavation, they took the dirt road that led into the canyon, then followed the rutted Chinle Wash. The river that had once flowed there had been reduced over the centuries to a narrow stream that weaved restlessly back and forth between the canyon walls. Gorged on last night's rainfall, it had swelled, stretching several feet across in some places, and every time Hugh had to recross it, another layer of mud spattered up the side of the Bronco. Karen suggested they go exploring for an Anasazi car wash, and Alex beaned her on the head with the empty artifact bags he was holding. Everyone started laughing and throwing out comments. Leigh wanted to participate in the lighthearted banter, but she was troubled by how loud and irreverent their voices sounded in the early-morning stillness. She knew that in a little while the tourists would start to arrive, and the noise level would be higher, but at that moment it was as if they were wantonly violating the quiet sanctuary of a church.

Although she'd made this trip nearly every day for the past month and a half, today, for the first time, she felt like an intruder. As they passed beneath the ancient red cliffs, she felt hostile eyes peering at her from every shadowy fissure. Even the peaceful little Navaho summer farms scattered throughout the canyon suddenly seemed like a facade for a more sinister reality. Leigh shook herself mentally. This would never do! Her imagination was running wild, because she'd given it free rein. Well, that was going to stop right now! The canyon was no different today from what it had been every other day.

By the time Hugh parked at the base of the ruins, she'd managed to sweep the anxieties from her mind and she was genuinely looking forward to the day's work.

The multistoried stone structures they were excavating had been built into a huge cavern in the cliffside, which meant they had to climb seventy feet from the wash to the cavern floor. The first day, when Leigh had frozen at the prospect of the climb, Hugh had assured her this one was "nothing." Ten years ago he'd excavated a cliff dwelling so inaccessible, "one of the requirements for joining the team was having mountain goat in your lineage." Leigh had laughed, relaxing a little, and Hugh had promised to stay right behind her. Now she was as adept at making the climb as any of them, but she still didn't like it.

Adjusting her peaked cap so that it shielded her face from the sun, she swung her knapsack onto her back and started up the cliff behind Paul, who had the lead. Each of them carried a knapsack with a tape recorder, a trowel, a dustpan and a whisk broom, various sizes of bags in which to deposit the artifacts they unearthed and a kitchen ladle with which to sift dirt out of small, deep holes. For working around delicate objects like skeletons, they also had pocketknives, artists' spatulas, dissecting needles, paintbrushes, atomizers and spoons. Alex carried the camera equipment, since he was in charge of principal photography. Hugh and Paul took turns carrying the foam cooler with the team's lunch, which Hugh packed every morning before fixing breakfast.

For most of the ascent, they were able to walk upright, using jagged outcroppings of the cliff face for handholds, but in several spots the incline was too steep and smooth. There they bent over, crablike, throwing part of their weight forward onto their hands in case their feet slipped out from under them.

Leigh found the trek easier if she reminded herself that the Anasazi, young and old alike, had scaled these cliffs without benefit of hiking boots or Nikes, carrying the heavy stone blocks with which they built their cities.

She was immersed in thoughts of the canyon's original inhabitants as she scrambled up the last stretch of weather-polished rock. A hand reached down to help her up to the cavern floor. She grasped it, expecting to see Paul crouched above her. Instead, she found herself looking up into the dark, narrow eyes of Sergeant Carlos Tsosie, one of the Navaho police working out of Chinle. Carlos smiled at her as he hoisted her up, but the smile stopped at his jawline. His eyes remained impassive, as blank as shuttered windows. His inscrutable expression always made her uncomfortable, as if she were being viewed through a one-way mirror.

Murmuring a thank-you, Leigh let go of his hand as soon as her feet were on solid ground. Paul was standing behind Carlos, one eyebrow hitched upward in anxious curiosity. Most of the police on the force had visited the dig at one time or another. A few had a genuine interest in archaeology. But Carlos had made it clear from the beginning that he disapproved of the project and considered the team's presence intrusive. He'd stopped by a dozen times already to monitor their activities. He'd wander around the site without a word, picking up bits of pottery to study, always replacing them exactly where he'd found them. Before leaving, he'd remind the team that every artifact was the property of the Navaho Nation and must be properly accounted for.

Karen had dubbed him "the inspector general." But they treated him with a deference born of necessity, since permission to excavate this site was completely at the indulgence of the Navaho people. And Carlos Tsosie didn't seem like the kind of man you wanted for an enemy.

Hugh had pulled himself up beside Leigh. Setting the cooler down, he held his hand out to Carlos.

"Didn't see your truck down there, Sergeant."

Carlos shook his hand in a single firm downswing. "I left it at the rim and climbed down."

Paul whistled. "That's quite a climb."

"This was my playground when I was a boy." The policeman's tone was proprietary.

A picture instantly filled Leigh's mind—Carlos as a young boy, clambering over these ruins the way Leigh and her friends had climbed jungle gyms and hung from monkey bars. While they'd been digging for treasure in their suburban backyards and finding bones their dogs had buried, Carlos had been playing in an archaeological treasure trove.

She wanted to ask him what artifacts he and his friends had found back then, but she decided he might consider the question accusatory.

Karen and Alex joined them on the apron of the cavern. They, too, looked concerned to find Carlos there.

"Is there a problem?" Alex asked in his straightforward manner.

"No," Carlos said, "not that I can see." He smiled that discomfiting smile again, and Leigh had the distinct impression that he wished he could find something wrong, some reason to request that the tribal council revoke the team's permit. She could tell from the way Hugh's jaw was working that he, too, understood the unspoken motive. But age had mellowed him, given him an appreciation for diplomacy.

"Good, good," he said, picking up the cooler. "We'll be getting to work. We have a long day ahead of us. If there's anything we can help you with, just ask."

Alex gave the policeman a friendly slap on the back as he walked past him. "Glad you stopped by." His tone was sincere, but Leigh knew that sarcasm lurked behind each word. Judging by Carlos's expression, he knew it too. His lips had compressed into a thin, angry line that seemed on the verge of being completely sucked into his mouth.

"*I* am not the visitor here," he said, slipping on the mirrored sunglasses he'd been holding. To Leigh, the effect of the glasses was redundant. His eyes already masked whatever else he was thinking.

Hugh sent Alex a chastening glare, then turned back to Carlos. But he couldn't think of anything to say that didn't sound obsequious. Instead, he raised his hand in farewell, and he and Karen headed for the kiva, descending into the underground ceremonial chamber by the collapsible ladder they'd installed the first day.

Carlos didn't acknowledge the gesture. He stood with his hands on his hips, the right one cupped over the top of his holster, and watched the scientists disperse.

Alex and Paul headed toward the main building, which they'd named the "condos," where they'd been digging in what had once been adjacent rooms.

Since the cliff dwelling occupied most of the area within the cavern and was divided into numerous small rooms, there was little open space for the elaborate gridwork an excavation generally required. With the exception of Hugh and Karen, who were working in the comparatively large kiva, the team members worked alone, laying out small grids within individual rooms.

Leigh was excavating a storeroom they'd discovered in a natural cave fifty yards away from the rest of the buildings. To reach it, she had to follow the ledge that curved around the cliff face, the ledge that had been so daunting and unnavigable in the darkness of her dream. She steeled herself again to the memory. Dreams might be able to unnerve her at night and interfere with her sleep, but she wasn't about to let them sabotage her work.

As she approached the place where the cliff curved to the right and would cut off her view of the other buildings, she glanced over her shoulder. Carlos was no longer there. She walked on to the cave. As she was lighting her small propane lamp, she heard the muted roar of an engine starting up, and the grinding of tires over rock and scrub. At least she didn't have to worry about the policeman stopping in to watch her work today. He'd done so only once before, but the experience had been nerve-racking. The cave, which had seemed so large in her dream, was in reality not much more than a six-foot square, and it had been hard to ignore his presence. When she'd tried to ease the awkwardness with conversation, he'd let her ramble, answering questions with a single word. Finally she'd given up, allowing a silence as thick as a mudslide to fill the cave. By the time he'd left, she was having trouble breathing, as if the air had actually been displaced.

Leigh unpacked the rest of her equipment and tried to settle down to work. After the first week of cataloging, photographing and bagging those basket fragments and pieces of pottery close to the surface that had not been looted over the years, she'd been able to get down to the part of archaeology she liked best. Using a trowel and a whisk broom, she sifted through the earth, layer by layer, searching for pieces of history. With each shard of pottery, each petrified kernel of corn, there was the pleasure of discovery. And with each scoop of the trowel there was the possibility that she might find a definitive clue to the Anasazi's disappearance. Sometimes she felt like a little kid being paid to dig for treasure at the beach.

But not today. Today she couldn't seem to lose herself in the work. The cave, which was always cool, seemed cold and damp, as well, with a stale, metallic odor, as if the rock were sweating minerals. She couldn't find a position that was comfortable for more than five minutes, and after half an hour she was stiff and chilled to the bone. All the result of fatigue, no doubt. The harder she tried to concentrate, the more her impatience betrayed her. Twice she walked out of the cave to stretch her legs and clear her head. And each time she had the same disquieting sense of vulnerability she'd had in the dream. She felt as if she were being stalked. She returned to her work more agitated than she'd been before.

For the first time since starting the excavation, she wished she were working out in the open, with the others in sight. Maybe she just needed a change of environment. She could switch with someone—Paul had shown an interest in the storeroom. Or she could just put the cave on hold while she excavated one of the "condo" rooms. With so few of their walls intact, they were open and light. She'd speak to Hugh about it this evening. The decision made her feel somewhat better, and she was able to work through the next hour, until she heard the crunch of footsteps on loose gravel. She looked up, grateful for the company, waiting to see which of her colleagues would appear in the low doorway. But the footsteps stopped short of the cave entrance. Trowel still poised for her next sweep of the soil, Leigh waited and listened. A minute passed. Then two.

"Okay," she called out playfully. "I know someone's there. Who is it?"

No response. Not even the sound of feet shifting position.

"Whoever's out there, come in and stop trying to scare me."

Still no response.

"Paul, is that you?" The amusement was gone from her voice.

The footsteps started to recede. Leigh dropped the trowel and jumped up, determined to catch whoever was playing games with her. She ducked out through the doorway, swinging her head in both directions, although she was fairly certain the noises had come from the left. It couldn't have taken her more than three seconds to exit the cave, yet no one was in sight. There were no sounds of footsteps running away, and there was no place in the immediate vicinity for the prankster to have hidden.

Too curious and frustrated to go back to work, Leigh turned off her lamp and walked back to the main buildings. She could hear Karen's muffled voice filtering up through the opening in the top of the kiva. It would have been impossible for either her or Hugh to have climbed back down there without Leigh spotting them. She walked on to where Paul and Alex were working in adjacent rooms, a two-foot-high wall remnant between them. They both looked up. No smug smiles, no shortness of breath.

Alex was labeling a small bag holding a piece of corncob. "What's up?"

Leigh forced a smile. "Nothing. Just out for a stroll. I was beginning to feel like a mole in that cave."

She plopped down in a corner of the dirt floor, across from where Alex was working. They talked about the Anasazi's diet, about the stream that had once been the lifeblood of the canyon. Then the conversation turned to Carlos Tsosie.

"Why do you feel the need to tweak his nose like that?" she asked.

Alex dusted off a small, triangular wedge of pottery and studied it. "I've never been good with authority figures. They bring out the worst in me. Just ask my father."

"Just ask Hugh," said Paul. "I'd say you're scheduled for a lecture on the proper way to treat a host on whose good graces our continued work depends."

"Carlos is just one cop. Our permit doesn't depend on him, unless he catches us committing some atrocity while we're here."

Paul shook his head. "I think you're underestimating how tight these people are. Relationships are everything. I'm sure Carlos has an uncle or a cousin or two on that council."

Leigh listened to the two men debate the issue for several more minutes. But, as important as the matter obviously was, she couldn't stop thinking about her mysterious visitor. Walking back to the storeroom, she went over the possibilities again. If not one of her co-workers, could it have been Carlos? Unlikely. Why spy on them, when he could observe whenever he cared to? When he could inspect their personal belongings to see if they were trying to smuggle out artifacts that hadn't been accounted for in their records? No, as uneasy as Carlos made her, she didn't think he was sneaking around the dig. Then, in spite of herself, she thought about the Indian she'd seen during the storm. Well, if he hadn't been real, then maybe the footsteps she'd heard today hadn't either. She laughed a nervous rattle of a laugh and chided herself for worrying too much. In all likelihood, the noises had been real—the scurrying of a small animal across the pebble-strewn surface of the ledge, amplified by the acoustics of the surrounding cliffs.

Leigh had just decided that that explanation was as valid as any when she heard another set of footsteps. There was no question of an animal making the noise now. The muted grinding of rubber-soled shoes on the gravelly dirt of the ledge was unmistakable. She stopped in her tracks for a moment to make sure that she wasn't just hearing the reverberations of her own footsteps. In certain spots, the canyon walls could produce eerie echos. But the footsteps continued, louder and closer with every stride. Whoever was wearing those shoes was coming toward her from the direction of the cave, but was still well out of sight around the bend of the cliff. Her anonymous visitor again?

Leigh resumed walking, taking slow, deliberate steps to make as little noise as possible. The rhythm of the approaching feet continued unchanged. The odds were that the other person hadn't heard her, which gave her a distinct advantage.

Two feet from the curve, she stopped and pressed herself into a shallow depression in the cliff face. Her heart was pounding, although logic told her she didn't have any reason to be afraid. Unless, of course, Carlos had hired some thug to scare them off. Or her hallucination was stalking her. She'd definitely seen too many horror movies when she was a kid.

Rubber soles grinding into gravel—only a few yards away now. A shadow bent around the corner, as if scouting ahead for its master. Leigh tried to take a deep breath, but her chest felt weighted, unable to expand properly. If a stranger came around that bend, and if he had a knife or a gun, she'd have only a second or two to react. To lunge and push him off the ledge.

A moment later, she found herself face-to-face with Karen, who instinctively jumped back two steps at the unexpected meeting.

"You scared me half to death," Karen said, but her voice was as calm and steady as ever. "What are you doing there?"

By contrast Leigh's voice was high and tremulous. "I, uh...I got a cramp in my leg. I just stopped to work it out." She massaged her left calf for effect. She couldn't very well tell Karen that she'd been hearing noises and suspected someone might be after her. Even to her ears, such a story screamed "paranoia." She put her left foot down tentatively and moved away from the cliff face.

"Were you looking for me?" Thank goodness her voice was returning to normal. Karen didn't seem to have noticed, in any case.

"I wanted to borrow your pocketknife. I can't seem to find mine."

"No problem. You could have taken it."

"I did." Karen held up her right hand with the knife in it. "Thanks."

"You didn't come by earlier, did you?"

Karen shook her head. "Why?"

"Nothing. I thought I heard someone outside."

"You think maybe we've disturbed a ghost?" Karen's eyes twinkled with mischief.

"I hadn't thought of that, but thanks so much for bringing the possibility to my attention," Leigh said wryly, trying to decide whether she preferred the idea of a ghost to that of a hallucination or a dream come to life.

"Oh, come on now, you're a scientist. You don't believe in that kind of nonsense, do you?"

Leigh agreed that she certainly did not. But when the two women separated and she continued on to the storeroom alone, she couldn't help thinking that if ever there was a place that could turn a skeptic about the supernatural into an acolyte, this was it—this isolated, barren land that plunged unexpectedly into deep canyons and erupted into awesome mesas and monoliths of stone.

She shivered in spite of the warm July sunlight. Time to get back to work and to some discipline of the mind. She had never believed in ghosts as a child, and she wasn't about to start now.

She was turning to enter the cave when she saw the Indian atop the opposite canyon wall. He was standing beside a stunted juniper tree, its shadow rippling over him as if he were nothing more than an image reflected in a lake. Although she couldn't see him clearly, she had no doubt that his face was the one that had been branded on her mind by that brilliant burst of lightning. The one that had both frightened and seduced her in her dreams. And despite the width of the chasm that separated them, she knew that his eyes were focused on her. A cold tremor skittered up her spine and set her limbs tingling with apprehension.

She shut her eyes tightly for a moment to see if he would vanish as he had during the storm. When she opened them, the shadow was empty, as if he had dived into its depths and out of sight.

CHAPTER TWO

Leigh stood to one side of the bedroom window. Lifting the corner of the shade, she held her breath and turned her head just enough that she could glance outside; she wanted to see, but not too well—a throwback to her childhood, when she'd watched horror movies with her fingers splayed across her eyes. No one peered back at her. The night was still and dark, a void blacker than space, since not even the stars were visible from inside the camper.

She let the shade drop back into place and made her way around the bed where Karen was sleeping peacefully and on into the living room, where she repeated the procedure. Again no one was there. But since this window faced west, she could see the other RV dimly illuminated by the low-wattage bulb over its doorway. She and Karen had a similar light over their door in case anyone needed to go from one vehicle to the other during the night. No light shone from inside the men's camper. Apparently even Hugh had taken off his reading glasses and retired. According to Leigh's watch, it was after 2:00 a.m.

She crossed to the kitchen on knees weak with fatigue and nervous energy. She could feel the adrenaline pumping into her blood in rhythm with the ragged tattoo her heart was beating. Even if tonight proved to be yet another false alarm, she'd never calm down sufficiently to fall back to sleep before the alarm clock rang at 6:00.

It had been almost a week since the storm, and she had yet to sleep through a night. She'd crawl into bed and immediately fall into an exhausted sleep, only to awaken in the wee hours of the morning. If she dreamed at all, she didn't remember. But each night when she awakened she was gripped by a vague, restless terror. She'd lie in bed, torn between the need to check the windows and the fear that she would see the Indian staring back at her if she did. Inevitably she would drag herself out of bed to make what she had come to think of as her "rounds," going from window to window, because there was no hope of closing her eyes again until she was convinced he wasn't out there.

Leigh paused before the kitchen window. This one was the most difficult, not only because it was through this window that she had first seen him, but also because she had to confront it head-on, since the counter and cabinets stretched along the rest of the wall. There was no shade, but she'd pulled the thin voile curtains together as best she could. No one seemed to be out there. She pulled the curtains back to be sure. Only the night pressed against the window, reflecting her own image back at her in the wan glow of the stove's night-light.

The last window she had to check was actually the windshield of the camper. Here there were no shades, no curtains that could be drawn. Leigh had been stymied for a few minutes that first night after the storm, wondering how she was going to cover such a large surface. Then she'd remembered the cardboard foldout they'd brought along to block out the sun's heat during the day. Except for a border of several inches, it had proven to be an adequate solution.

She left the kitchen area and moved toward the front of the RV. Squeezing between the passenger seat and the door, she peered around the edge of the cardboard. No other eyes stared back at her. She exhaled a wobbly sigh of relief.

If Karen wondered about her sudden compulsion to cover all the windows after dark, she didn't mention it. Paul was not as kind.

"Alex been up to his old tricks again?" he'd said teasingly one morning over breakfast.

Alex had looked up from his French toast with the defiance of a child who knows that for once he's not guilty. Leigh just appeared confused.

Paul tried to keep a straight face, but a grin was tugging at his lips. "The way you've been covering up your windows, I assumed you'd seen a Peeping Alex."

Alex grabbed the squirt bottle of maple syrup and aimed it at him. "Watch it, Buster. I'll have you know I've never gone in for spectator sports."

Leigh forced a smile and debated telling them about the mysterious man who seemed to have leapt from her dreams into her life. After all, she *had* seen him a second time. But from their remarks it was clear that no one else had seen him. And apparently she was the only one who suffered from the unnerving sensation of being watched. In the end she decided she didn't want to be the object of anyone's concern or the butt of anyone's jokes. Once the laughter had died down, Hugh mercifully changed the topic, and no one probed further.

It was two-thirty when Leigh completed her window patrol and snuggled under the covers to try to find her way back into sleep. But when dawn started to fade the black rim of night around the window shade, she was still wide-awake. Too restless to remain in bed a minute longer, she dressed in jeans and a sweater, pulled on her work boots and let herself out of the camper.

The sky was a dusky gray, the sun like a giant saffron bubble boiling up out of the horizon. Turning in one quick circle, Leigh was able to assure herself that she was completely alone. The land was nearly even here, the few mesas and rocky towers resembling eerie modern sculptures in a vast, desolate park. Aside from their vehicles, the only structure that hadn't been erected by nature was a small hogan. The first time Leigh had seen it from this distance, it had looked to her like an overly symmetrical rock. It hadn't been until she walked halfway to it one evening that she'd seen enough detail to realize it was a human habitation. Beside the hogan were a makeshift corral enclosing a dozen sheep and a couple of poles with laundry strung out on the line between them. Having come from a city of eight million people, Leigh was genuinely amazed that it was possible to live in such utter isolation. Sometimes the idea appealed to her—an uncluttered life in mind-clearing stillness—but more often it was simply too foreign a concept for her even to imagine.

She started walking, stretching her legs and enjoying air that smelled sweet and clear after the mustiness of the tiny bedroom. She kept her eyes on the ground as she walked, because the sun's light was still oblique enough that some snakes might not yet have taken refuge from its heat.

When she'd gone half a mile, she stopped and climbed up to rest on a low rock formation that looked like a mesa aborted by nature early in its development. Daylight was sweeping away the hiding places of night, and across the flat land the campers looked deceptively close. In the distance, a dog barked, a series of sharp, throaty bursts ending in a comical howl. Leigh pivoted on the rock to see if the animal was in sight—and found herself staring into the eyes of the Indian.

She jumped, her heart knocking as if someone had jolted it with an electrical charge, but she didn't make a move to leave. She stayed where she was, trapped in his gaze like an animal ensnared in the paralyzing glare of oncoming headlights. He was barely twenty feet away, dressed in the same breechcloth and sandals he'd worn in her dream. Across his forehead was an intricately embroidered headband, and hanging from his neck, a magnificent silver thunderbird inlaid with bits of turquoise.

Somewhere inside her head, a voice screamed for her to get going, get on her feet and run. But the voice seemed to be coming from far away, the distance damping its urgency.

She didn't know she'd been holding her breath until it burst from her lungs and she was forced to gulp down fresh air. That involuntary action helped focus her mind again, and she realized how precarious her position was up on that plateau. She started to back down slowly, afraid that any sudden movement might spark some reciprocal action from the stranger. But he remained where he was, his expression impassive, only his eyes following her.

Once her feet were on the ground, Leigh felt safer, and curiosity started chipping away at her fear. If he came after her, she'd have a head start. The odds were that he could catch her, but probably not before she'd covered at least half the distance back to camp and alerted her colleagues. Besides, she wanted to know who he was and why he'd been spying on her. She might never again have the chance to find out. She hesitated, worried that words would act like a gunshot, shattering the stillness that stood like a fragile barrier between them. She'd have to be careful, use exactly the right tone. As she studied him, wondering what that might be, she was struck by the poise and grace with which he held himself; it was the posture of one born to a privileged class. And yet he also had the look of a man who understood physical labor. His body was lean and strong, evenly muscled, as if from years of hard work.

Her eyes traveled back up to his face. Unaccountably, interwoven with her curiosity and her fear was a startling thread of desire. A desire she remembered all too vividly from her dreams. But what was possible, even understandable, in the chaotic logic of dreams, was unacceptable in reality. Fear was something she could comprehend under the circumstances. But although he was arrestingly handsome, exotic, she had no business feeling this sudden attraction for a man she didn't know, a man who was the source of her nightmares, who haunted her waking and sleeping hours.

Her voice trembled badly when she finally managed to speak. "Who are you?"

He didn't reply. She wondered whether he'd understood her. But all the Navaho she'd encountered spoke English, and there was no sign of confusion on his face.

"What do you want?" A growing sense of frustration gave her voice a harder edge.

He came toward her. The dream flashed in her mind, and along with it a momentary thrill of anticipation that scared her even more. The memory was overwhelmingly distinct in detail and sensation—the heat of his mouth on hers, the hard pressure of his body... If he had some kind of power over her in her dreams, would he have that same power over her now?

She started backing away, her feet stumbling over scrub and rocks. His strides were longer, surer, than hers. The distance between them was closing quickly. Good sense dictated that she turn and run back toward the camp. No, she was not going to be intimidated. She was not going to run away without finding out exactly who or what he was.

Why she dreamed of him. Why he followed her and spied on her. She stopped and stood her ground.

She remembered her father's frequent warning that her stubborn streak would someday be her downfall. Well, today might just be that day. She drew herself up straight, her jaw set tightly with determination, and tried to ignore the way her heart was lurching.

The Indian stopped when he was within arm's reach of her. He was easily eight inches taller than she; she had to cock her head to look him in the eye. He returned the gaze with an intensity that made it difficult not to look away.

"I want to know who you are." She'd intended to make the words challenging, but they emerged as a hoarse whisper.

He didn't respond immediately, but seemed to be weighing a decision. Leigh waited, anger building inside her. When he finally did speak, she was momentarily startled.

"If you must have a name, Leigh, it is Zakoura." His voice was even, self-assured, its timbre rich and deep.

"How do you know who I am?"

"Such things are not difficult to know." He had a peculiar way of speaking. The words were right, but the cadence was off, as if he were accustomed to another language, with a different rhythm.

He raised his hand to her face. She flinched, rocking back to avoid his touch. Maybe she couldn't resist him in her dreams, but she'd be damned if she'd put herself in the same position while she was awake. She waited for his reaction, ready to run if he persisted. But he dropped his hand to his side. She could see a fierce struggle raging in his eyes, emotions shifting so quickly that she couldn't distinguish a single one. The turbulence lasted only a moment. Then an ironic smile curled his lips.

"You are right. This must not be." He turned away abruptly.

Leigh knew she should be relieved to see him go. All her instincts told her this man was dangerous. But what she felt was a troubling twinge of disappointment that only served to fuel her anger. How dare he just walk off, when she still didn't know why he'd been watching her, following her? Finally, spurred by the thought of more sleepless nights, she found the courage to call out to him.

"Wait a minute."

He kept walking.

"What is it you want?" she shouted, dismayed by the plaintive note she heard in her voice.

He didn't stop, or even look back at her. She stood watching him go with a helpless sense of frustration, until the dog barked again, closer than before. She turned. Now she could see the animal, a black-and-white blur racing toward her from the left. Great. She hoped he was friendly, because she wasn't ready to leave quite yet. She found a baseball-size rock near her foot, just in case, then glanced back toward the Indian. He was gone. Not receding into the distance, but gone. The logical part of her mind told her that he was most likely hidden behind one of the other mesas, but she couldn't shake the dizzying notion that he had melted right back into the landscape from which he seemed to have sprung.

She didn't have time to speculate on it for long. The dog was close enough that she could see his tongue lolling out one side of his mouth. To her relief, a boy followed closely behind him. She heard him calling to the dog, but couldn't make out the words. When the animal reached her, he danced around her a few times, then came to a stop, alternately panting and sniffing her feet. He was big and hairy and looked to Leigh like a cross between a Border collie and a Lab. Once it appeared that she'd passed whatever test the dog used to differentiate friend from foe, she held out her hand and waited for it, too, to be sniffed and approved. Then she scratched behind the dog's ear, which seemed to suit him just fine.

A minute later, the boy joined them, as breathless as the dog. "Rowdy," he scolded, "you're s'posed to come when I call you." He grabbed a fistful of fur at the nape of the dog's neck and looked up at Leigh.

"I'm sorry, lady. He's s'posed to be watching the sheep, but he likes people better." He was trying to tug the dog away from her, without success. Leigh guessed that Rowdy had a good twenty pounds on the boy, who looked about ten, but was small and wiry.

Leigh smiled. "That's okay. He's not bothering me."

The boy let go of him and stuck out his right hand. "I'm Jimmy," he said. "I live down that way." He nodded in the direction of the hogan Leigh had seen earlier.

She shook his hand. "Hi, Jimmy. My name's Leigh."

"You're one of those archaeologists, right?" His dark eyes twinkled with intelligence and interest.

"That's right."

"Mary Yazzi—that's my grandma—she doesn't think you oughta be here. But I think what you're doin' is neat. I like playin' archaeologist."

"Your grandmother lives with you?"

"Yeah… I mean no, I live with her. My mom's dead, and my dad, he left the reservation pretty soon after I was born."

"So it's just the two of you?" Leigh asked, finding it hard to imagine how an elderly woman and a young boy could eke out an existence on this barren land.

"Yup. Us and Rowdy. Could I come down to watch you dig sometime? My grandma told me to stay away. But she doesn't know how nice you are. And if you say I can, then..."

"Absolutely. Come down whenever you like, and I'll give you a personal tour. You just get your grandma's permission first."

"All right!" Jimmy's smile spread until it covered half his face.

"Can I ask you something, Jimmy?" While they'd talked, it had occurred to Leigh that if the boy had lived here all his life, he might know who this Zakoura was.

"Sure."

"I've seen a man around here who doesn't dress or act like a Navaho. He says his name is Zakoura, but I don't know if that's true. He's big, tall and broad-shouldered, and his hair is really long. Do you know who he is?"

As she described him, she saw Jimmy's eager smile fade, his burnished skin pale. He looked down at the dog and started picking burrs out of his fur.

"I don't know anyone like that," he mumbled, without looking up. "Nobody like that lives around here."

A prickly chill raised the flesh on the back of Leigh's neck and along her arms. Jimmy knew the elusive stranger and was afraid of him, that much was clear. She didn't want to press the child further. But if she had any lingering doubts about Zakoura being a hallucination, Jimmy's reaction had put them to rest. At least she wasn't on the verge of a nervous breakdown. That should have made her feel better, but it didn't. There were too many other unresolved questions, not the least of which was her attraction to this mysterious man.

Leigh repeated her invitation to the boy, stroked Rowdy's head one last time and headed back toward camp. The others were probably ready to get to work by now and wondering where she was. She decided she'd have to pay Jimmy's grandmother a visit one day soon. Whatever Jimmy knew, she would certainly know, and more.

CHAPTER THREE

She raced toward the light, toward the sun setting behind the ridge that ran like a dinosaur's spine along the western horizon. She had to reach the light. Behind her, night was swallowing the world; in minutes it would outdistance her. And so would the Indian. Zakoura. She'd stood her ground against him and demanded his name. Then why was she running now? She had to reach the light. Reach the light. The phrase drummed in her head in rhythm with the hammering of her feet across the jarring scrub plain. Her knees ached as if she'd been running forever. Reach the light. She'd be safe there. Her mouth was so dry she couldn't swallow. Her throat burned from the dust and the effort of pulling enough air into her lungs. Reach the light. Stiletto pains sliced into her sides. She couldn't go much farther.

The sun was dying, sucking the last of the light from the sky. She wanted to look behind her, see how close he was, but she knew she'd lose time that way. Night slithered around her feet, snakelike, as if it might strike her ankles and fell her. Reach the light. Any moment now, Zakoura's steely fingers would close upon her arm. The apprehension was draining her, turning her legs rubbery and unresponsive. She couldn't stand it—she glanced over her shoulder. He wasn't there. Confusion made her stumble, but she didn't dare stop. Reach the light. Surely she would see him if he was close enough to grab her. Maybe there was still time after all. Willing a final thrust of energy through her legs, she turned back to the sun. The last of its rays were coruscating off the craggy ridge. And there, surrounded by the brilliant flashes of light, stood Zakoura.

She didn't hesitate. She ran straight toward him. As the sun plunged behind the horizon and the last beam of light blinked out, he opened his arms, and she flew into them as if he had been her destination all along.

He held her against his chest with one arm, the other hand slowly stroking the length of her back. Gradually her breathing became more regular. She closed her eyes and marveled at the rich sense of relief she felt. Moments ago she'd been racing from him in sheer terror, certain her life depended on escaping him. Now she was at peace, nerves relaxed, muscles unknotted, as if she were immersed in a luxurious tub of warm water. This was where she wanted to be, even if it made no sense at all. Yet one small, insistent part of her mind kept probing, needing to understand the inexplicable transformation.

She raised her head to look at him, but he seemed to have merged completely with the darkness around them.

"Zakoura," she whispered into the preternatural stillness that had descended with the night.

He inclined his head, and the moon's light reflected off his eyes, making them seem to float, disembodied, in the air above her. "What is it that troubles you?"

"I don't know.... I run from you, and all I want is to be with you. I'm terrified of something, yet I don't know what it is . . . or why it scares me so."

He didn't answer her immediately, and when he did, there was a heaviness in his voice that bordered on pain. "Sometimes it is best to accept and not question too closely. Fear has its place. It can protect you."

"Protect me from what? Not from you. I don't need to be protected from you." She said the last with more conviction than she felt. In spite of her desire to be with him, vague doubts stirred restlessly at the gates of her mind. She wanted to be assured that they were without substance.

"There are dangers you cannot imagine."

"How do you expect me to avoid these 'dangers' if I don't know what they are?" She wished Zakoura would speak more plainly. She wanted hard facts, not riddles with cryptic meanings.

"Fear is intuitive. The smallest prairie dog seeks refuge from the mountain lion."

"I'm not a prairie dog." She sighed with frustration. "I need to know why."

"I have told you what you need to know. Trust me in this. And let it be." Zakoura's tone had become commanding. Where there had been a hint of vulnerability, now there was a firmness close to anger.

Leigh bristled and tried to pull away. "Don't do this, Zakoura. Don't treat me like a child, and don't give me orders." But even as she struggled against him, she was aware that her own anger was strangely muted, several degrees removed in intensity. It was as if she were working as hard to maintain her indignation as she was to break free from his embrace.

Zakoura held her securely within the circle of his arms.

"Take it not as an order, then, but as a plea. My own fears overpower my good sense."

The conciliatory words surprised her, and she felt the anger ebb from her body as effortlessly as the terror had earlier. This was, she suspected, the closest thing to an apology she would ever hear from him. In any case, she was grateful that he had broken the tension and provided the means for her to stay. All too often, her stubborn pride produced knee-jerk reactions, and she'd never quite learned how to reverse the process once it started. This might easily have been one of those times. Not only did she want more than anything to stay with him, but, looking around her, she realized she wasn't entirely sure where she was anymore, or where she would have gone had she left. Even the frail light of the waning moon had faded, hidden behind a monolith or obscured by clouds. The darkness was so absolute, she couldn't pick out any features in the landscape. Every mesa and tree, even the massive ridge on the horizon, had vanished as if the sun had absconded with it all and left nothing but the piece of ground on which she and Zakoura stood.

She laid her cheek against his hard, bare chest again, feeling safe in spite of his dark warnings. Running her index finger around the worn edges of the thunderbird pendant, she listened to the strong rhythm of his heart and tried to clear her mind. She wanted to do as he'd requested, stop questioning, accept. But one thing he'd said kept flashing in her brain as if it were written in neon. She didn't want to provoke another argument. She knew she should forget it . . . but she couldn't. She'd never been able to let a question go unanswered, or unexplored.

"What fears do you have, Zakoura?" She tensed, expecting him to lose patience with her. But he only shook his head. She didn't see the movement; she felt it transmitted through the muscles of his neck to his chest.

"There are things beyond the comprehension of your science."

Her curiosity piqued more than ever, Leigh started to ask what he meant by *her* science, but he put his finger to her lips. "No. I will talk no more of this," he said evenly. If he was angry with her, he was controlling it well.

Before she could protest further, he lowered his mouth to hers, drawing her more tightly against him. Then he moved his lips to her temples and found the pulse there. Her blood responded, pounding through her body to the point of contact. He kissed her eyelids, the outer shell of her ear, the corners of her mouth. His tongue weaved a cool, wet trail down her neck to the hollow of her throat. Leigh dug her fingers into the thick hair that fell below his shoulders, grateful for the surge of passion that drowned out the torment of questions and reason.

When he stiffened suddenly and jerked his head upward, she gasped as if her supply of oxygen had been cut off. For several elongated moments, he stood motionless, and she could tell by the way he held himself that he was listening. She hadn't heard whatever it was that had caught his attention, and although she strained to, she heard nothing now. She started to ask him what was wrong, but before the words could clear her lips . . . she found herself alone in her bed.

The transition was so abrupt that she couldn't think clearly at first. Barely formed thoughts burst like soap bubbles as soon as they surfaced in her mind. When lucidity finally returned, it brought with it more questions and more bewilderment, and a coterie of disturbing emotions. But the turbulence existed only within her this time. No storm had awakened her. In fact, she didn't feel as though she'd been awakened at all; she felt as if she'd been released. Which only added to her disquietude.

She closed her eyes against the sun that was squeezing past the window shade and tried to settle her roiling emotions. The remembered terror of her flight from him still had the power to shoot adrenaline through her body. But even more powerful was the tactile memory of his hands and his mouth upon her, the deep, aching warmth they had left in their wake. And there was the anger. Anger at the unexpected, unacceptable surge of disappointment that had come with the end of the dream. Anger at having allowed this man to insinuate himself into her life, into her subconscious. Like a dog chasing its tail, she came back to the conundrum: She had dreamed of Zakoura before she'd ever seen him, ever heard of him. Before he'd existed for her. Yet he was no mere fantasy, no fabrication of her mind. He was real. Jimmy knew him.

Leigh opened her eyes in frustration and stared at the bright scarves of light that the sun had flung across the RV's ceiling. It was all impossible. Then she thought of her mother, and her lips quivered into a smile. As far as Nina Morgan was concerned, nothing was impossible. She would no doubt tell Leigh that it was just a simple case of precognition. Her mother believed in keeping an open mind, in "possibilities," as she liked to call them, which included anything that hadn't been scientifically disproved, including alien abductions, ghosts and Nessie.

Leigh had always preferred proof to "possibilities." She wasn't sure if she'd inherited her scientific inclinations from her father, David Morgan, D.D.S., or if they were just a rebellion against her mother's predilection for the supernatural. Right now she wished she could be a little more like her mother. Ascribing her dreams to a sudden psychic awakening might have brought her some peace. She toyed with the idea, but after ten minutes it was clear that her mind would have none of it. There had to be a more logical explanation, and she intended to find it.

She looked at the clock on the table that separated her bed from Karen's. The alarm should have rung fifteen minutes ago. She jumped up. She hadn't overslept since they'd arrived in Canyon de Chelly. She was about to shake Karen awake when she remembered it was Sunday. She sank back onto her own bed with a groan. Hugh had a strict policy of no work on Sundays, which had less to do with any religious belief than with the belief that rest empowered work. But today work would have helped take her mind off Zakoura. Now the day stretched ahead of her like the barren expanses of land that stretched in all directions around the camper. At least there was the weekly trip into Chinle to buy supplies and do the laundry. It would probably do her good to get away from the canyon for a while and be among other people. She could use a good shot of normalcy in her life right now. Once Canyon de Chelly had enchanted her with its ancient mysteries, its peaceful isolation. But Zakoura had added a frightening and confusing dimension to it—emotions beyond the bounds of control, riddles beyond the bounds of logic. Shadows were no longer just shadows. Dreams were no longer just dreams.

She showered and dressed in shorts and a sleeveless shirt that she'd brought along specifically for her days off. She wouldn't be "playing in the dirt" today, which was how her older brother, Gary, liked to characterize her chosen profession.

When she was ready, Karen was still asleep, so she went outside to see if any of the men were stirring. Alex was between the two RVs, exercising with a set of weights.

"Just in case we find some really heavy bones?" she asked as he grunted through the end of a set.

"Or someone needs rescuing." He dropped the barbell to the ground. She could feel the vibration right up through her feet. "Someone afraid of climbing cliffs, for example."

"Touché," she said. But "rescuing" didn't bring cliffs to mind anymore, it brought Zakoura. In the dream she'd been running away from him as if her very life depended on it, at least until the last moments. It made no sense at all. But since when were dreams supposed to make sense? she thought, chastening herself. She really had to stop dwelling on them, on him!

"Anyone else up?" she asked, trying to banish him from her thoughts.

"Hugh's writing out his grocery list, and Paul's figuring the budget." Alex stooped to lift the weights again.

"Are you going into Chinle today?" she asked.

"Wouldn't miss a trip into the big city for anything."

The "big city," population 5,100, had churches of several Protestant denominations, a video store, a Taco Bell and a pizza parlor, a motel, a grocery and a few other stores that provided the basics of life. To find a movie theater or a restaurant with table service you had to drive two hours into Gallup, New Mexico. Still, after a week in the virtual isolation of Canyon de Chelly, Chinle represented civilization, and Leigh always looked forward to the outings. What she would gladly have forgone was the trip itself, most of it bouncing over the pitted terrain or the dirt roads forged by Navaho pickup trucks.

Between the ride along the rocky wash to the dig nearly every day and the ride into Chinle on Sunday, she'd suffered with constant stomachaches and backaches for her first few weeks in the field. Hugh had assured her it was simple muscle soreness. Her body wasn't used to the jostling it was taking. As she had with the cliff climbing, she'd adjusted, but she still didn't like the way her insides felt when the Bronco was negotiating the unpaved roads. Only Paul seemed to mind it more. He usually spent the entire round-trip cursing each and every bump. But that day Paul was staying behind to catch up on the paperwork, and Hugh was stretched out on a lounge chair beneath his striped beach umbrella, determined to relax.

"Low tide today," Karen observed as she carried the laundry bag past him to the truck.

"Yeah, but none of those pesky jellyfish," he said, rubbing sun block on his toes. "Don't forget the lemon pepper."

Karen climbed into the driver's seat of the Bronco. It was her turn. Driving around here was on a strict rotation basis. Everyone coveted the seat, with the steering wheel to hold on to. Leigh slid in beside Karen, leaving Alex to occupy the back seat alone.

"Bennetti alone in the back seat?" Paul called out to them. "What is this world coming to?"

Alex found an empty water bottle on the floor and chucked it through the open window at him, missing by inches, as the Bronco lurched away.

"So, are we calling the boys today?" Alex inquired after they'd been driving for several minutes. "Leigh?"

Karen tapped her arm. "A question from the peanut gallery."

Leigh swiveled around as much as the seat belt would allow. "I'm sorry, Alex. I must have been daydreaming." What she'd really been doing was scouring the countryside for Zakoura. Although she'd vowed not to spend the day thinking about him, ever since they'd left camp she'd had that peculiar feeling again that she was being watched. It was patently ridiculous, of course. He had no way of knowing where she would be at any given time. And she certainly didn't believe in ghosts who could simply materialize at will. Still, she found herself searching every rock formation they passed, every deep shadow sculptured by the sun, expecting to find him. This time the knot in her stomach had nothing to do with the jouncing ride. She wasn't even sure how much of it was dread, how much anticipation.

Alex repeated the question. "I asked if you were calling the boys today."

"Of course," she said, laughing at his choice of words, relieved to concentrate on something else for a while. "If I don't call, Butch and Sundance might forget me."

"Trust me," said Karen, "golden retrievers have better memories than that. They won't forget you, even if they are enjoying the good life up in Connecticut with your folks."

"Besides," Alex said glumly, "you'll be home plucking dog hairs off your clothing again before you know it. Labor Day is less than six weeks away."

"Don't remind me—we hardly have enough time to scratch the surface here. Pun intended." Karen jerked the wheel sharply to the right to avoid a yawning pothole that had appeared after the last storm.

"Hey, Annie Oakley," Alex groaned, "slow down and plan ahead, would ya?"

Leigh faced forward in her seat in case there were any more road surprises ahead. A couple of weeks ago she would have been as upset as her colleagues that their time in the field would soon be coming to an end. But she was beginning to think that the only way she would be rid of her obsession with Zakoura was to leave this place. She tried to ignore the unexpected pang that accompanied the realization.

"It all comes down to money in the end," Alex was saying. "The university's hurting, federal grants are drying up. Hugh had to beg, borrow and practically steal to come up with the funding for this summer."

They were passing a monolith that reminded Leigh of a Stone Age spaceship. Movement flashed in her peripheral vision. Anxiety tightened her chest. She turned—nothing but the rock, its shadow looming like a gantry at its side. She scanned the rough surface for a niche where he might have hidden, craning her neck around as the car moved on. Great—now she really *was* seeing things. They were a quarter of a mile down the road when she glanced back in the sideview mirror and saw a raven swoop out from behind the rock. She nearly cried out with relief. She hadn't been imagining things, at least not this time. But the fact remained that she needed to exorcise Zakoura from her mind, and the only way to do that was to find out exactly who he was. Right now her curiosity was playing with the idea of him the way a cat played with a ball of string. If she eliminated the mystery, unraveled the ball down to the simple twine, she was sure she'd be able to let go of him.

She was so preoccupied with her thoughts that she didn't notice they'd reached the two-lane road that would take them into Chinle until the tires glided onto the smooth macadam. A few minutes later, they were slowing to a crawl behind a line of cars and RVs headed for the motel and campgrounds owned and operated by the Navaho. Tourist season was in full swing. A quarter of a mile past the congestion, they entered Chinle itself.

In contrast with the mesas and ridges, which provided a magnificent backdrop, Chinle was a bleak little town without gardens or cultivated lawns. Whatever grass or flowers grew there grew at their own whim and at their own peril. There were always several horses, branded but untended, who roamed the streets, grazing on whatever caught their fancy. The first time Leigh had seen them, she'd been coming out of the grocery store and had almost run smack into one in the parking lot. Amazed, she'd watched them ambling through town all day while the Navaho went about their business without so much as an interested glance. She could barely imagine the pandemonium a horse would cause wandering around the parking lot of a mall back home. But now she, too, paid them as little attention as she would have a couple of stray dogs.

Karen blasted the horn and came to a sudden, screeching stop.

"What the hell—?" Alex started to complain. "Oh, old Graffiti."

A swaybacked chestnut was crossing the street directly in front of the Bronco. Hugh had named the horse their first day in town based on the half-dozen brands that decorated the animal's left flank.

"That horse must be deaf," Leigh said, watching him make his way calmly across the street.

Karen shook her head. "He knows we won't hit him, because we'd have to spend the day filling out police forms."

A few minutes later, with Graffiti safely nibbling weeds on the other side of the street, they pulled into the strip mall that comprised most of Chinle's commercial district.

They all emerged from the Bronco stiff and stretching. Alex hauled the laundry bag out of the back seat. Karen found the detergent. While the clothes were being washed and then dried, they took turns walking around the town. When it was Leigh's turn, she found a public phone and made her weekly call home.

On her way back, she took a detour, as usual, through some of the side streets she hadn't yet explored. The street she chose appeared to be much the same as the others she had seen. Small, boxy ranch houses sat on randomly sized lots. All the homes were in need of major repairs. Roofs sagged, broken windows were covered with cloudy plastic, and entire exterior walls were stripped down to tar paper that hung loose in places, flapping in the wind like hungry black tongues. If anything set this street apart, it was the extent to which it appeared deserted. No children played on the dusty ground. No dogs came running out to sniff at her. No radio or television sounds leaked out of open windows.

Leigh wasn't sure if it was just the abandoned atmosphere of the street that spooked her, but she was suddenly convinced that not only was she being watched, she was being studied at close range. The sensation was so intense that she wouldn't have been at all surprised to find that she was caught in the tight focus of a pair of high-powered binoculars, or even in the sights of a rifle.

She scolded herself for letting her imagination ride roughshod over her common sense. But in spite of her efforts to remain calm and not surrender to senseless panic, her pace automatically quickened. Her eyes darted nervously from the black maw beyond a partially opened front door, to the shadowy interior of an old car, to the darkened slits between boarded up windows—there were far too many places for someone to be hiding. Far too many places where she wouldn't see an assailant before it was too late.

By the time she reached the main road again, her knees were quaking badly and a clammy sheath of perspiration covered her body. She had to make a conscious effort to slow her breathing and her gait. She'd expected to feel safe in Chinle. It was to have been her sanctuary. Now even that had been taken from her. But who could have been watching her? Although Zakoura was the first one who came to mind, she couldn't picture him wandering the streets of the town in his breechcloth. Nor could she picture him wearing the jeans and Stetsons she saw on the Navaho men. He didn't belong in Chinle. He belonged in the canyon. She believed he would stay there. Then why couldn't she shake the notion that he had been the one watching her?

She was enormously relieved when the Laundromat came into sight at last. She covered the three blocks to it, struggling to compose herself so that neither Alex nor Karen would ask why she was so distraught. She didn't want to have to explain that she'd been the target of an unseen and unknown adversary. The farther she got from that lonely little road, the sillier the whole idea sounded, even to her.

"So, how about Mexican?" Karen asked after they'd deposited the clean clothing in the Bronco.

Alex shook his head. "I'm going to grab some burgers on fry bread back at the motel. Any takers?"

Karen declined. She'd had a craving for burritos all week. Leigh wasn't hungry enough to care, but she'd decided she had to talk to someone, at least about Zakoura, and Karen was the likeliest candidate. She'd keep the conversation superficial, leaving out the dreams and her paranoia. Maybe she'd even discover that Karen had seen him, too. That would definitely make her feel better.

Alex took the truck, saying he'd return for them in half an hour. Leigh and Karen filed into the Taco Bell two stores down from the Laundromat. It was identical to the one Leigh had sometimes frequented in Connecticut, but she didn't find the sameness comforting. It seemed as though fast food places were popping up all over the world. The archaeologist in her rebelled against the way the world was becoming homogenized, all of its unique aspects whipped into one ugly, dull uniculture. A millennium from now, there would be no point in leaving your hometown. Every place would be the same.

She and Karen placed their orders. Except for one table occupied by a young Navaho mother and her two children, they had the restaurant to themselves. They took a booth and spread the assortment of burritos, tacos and nachos out between them. After considering several openings Leigh decided to start the conversation with a casual, indirect approach. She didn't want to make Zakoura seem too important to her.

"I met the little boy who lived in that hogan we can see from camp," she said. "He and his grandmother live alone there."

"I think I've seen him out there. Always has a big mutt with him?"

Leigh nodded, swallowing a bite of taco that was oozing salsa. She blotted her chin with a napkin. "He's a nice kid. Seems really interested in archaeology, so I promised him the VIP tour one day."

"It must be lonely for him. Not many other kids nearby."

That was the opportunity Leigh had hoped for. "Not many people, period, especially up on the rim." She let a few moments pass while she drank her soda. "Have you seen anyone besides the boy?"

"Just a woman hanging out some laundry—must have been the grandmother you mentioned."

She waited to see if Karen would turn the question back to her. But Karen was more interested in dipping nachos into the runny cheese sauce, so Leigh plowed ahead. "I've seen a man a couple of times." She wondered if Karen could detect the anxious edge that had crept into her voice. "Once when I was working in the cave, another time on the rim, when I was taking a walk."

"Navaho?"

"I don't know. He was dressed strangely. Actually, he was hardly dressed at all—just a breechcloth-type deal and sandals."

Karen smiled around a mouthful of nachos. "Probably some townie trying to have a little fun at our expense. You know—" she lowered her voice menacingly "—'Beware, there are still wild Indians out here.'"

"I didn't get that feeling."

Karen's smile turned sly. "Exactly what feeling did you get?"

The remark triggered a full-blown memory of being pressed against Zakoura in her dreams, the woven breechcloth across his groin hiding nothing from her imagination. She tried to force the memory out of her mind, with only partial success.

"Come on, what I meant was that he seemed completely comfortable, as if he always walks around practically naked. As if he belongs out there in the canyon. And I don't mean in a little hogan, either."

"I think you're reading into this. Why wouldn't he be comfortable? It *is* summer, and there really isn't a heck of a lot of difference between a loincloth and a Speedo."

Leigh wanted to tell her more, to make her understand how different he was, how dangerous he might be. "I talked to him briefly, and his English was... I don't know, kind of peculiar. All the Navaho I've ever met sound the same as you and I."

Karen shrugged. "That could just have been part of the game he was playing. Do you want the last taco?"

Leigh shook her head, defeated. What more could she say without telling her about the erotic dreams that had preceded Zakoura and continued unabated? Without telling her about the mysterious way he seemed to appear and then vanish? Without telling her about the feeling that she was being watched?

She'd been counting on Karen for some solid, logical input unaffected by emotions, and that was exactly what she'd gotten. If that opinion didn't seem particularly valid, it was because she'd told Karen only half the story. If she was to tell her the unedited version, would she be forever diminished in her colleague's eyes?

Karen was pushing the cardboard container of nachos across the table to her. "Do me a favor and finish these. I think I've had enough cornmeal to last me a month."

When they left the restaurant ten minutes later, Alex was already waiting for them in the parking lot.

"Look who's keeping an eye on us," Karen remarked as they made their way to the Bronco. She tipped her head in the direction of the video store. Leigh turned and saw Carlos leaning against the doorjamb of the store. He had his sunglasses on, so it was impossible to tell exactly where his eyes were focused, but she had a pretty good idea.

"How long has he been there?"

"I noticed him when we came out of the Laundromat."

Leigh knew she should be relieved to find out that it wasn't just her imagination working overtime today. If Carlos was watching them now, he could easily have been watching her earlier. But, although she didn't like the idea of being under the policeman's scrutiny, something else kept nagging at her.

"Why do you think he's keeping tabs on us?" she asked.

"Waiting for us to step one toe over the line. He'd love nothing better than to send us packing."

Alex leaned out of his window. "All aboard, ladies. Next stop—the gourmet delights of the Chinle supermarket."

As they pulled out of the lot, Leigh couldn't resist one more glance back at Carlos. He'd left the doorway and was sliding into the squad car parked at the curb. Now that they were leaving, so was he. He didn't even seem to care how obvious he was about it. Her stomach turned in a sickening wave. That was it—that was what had been bothering her. Carlos wasn't trying to hide the fact that he was watching them. No slinking around in shadows for him, no peeking out of shuttered windows. Open harassment was his game. Had Carlos been the one following her through town, she would have known it.

CHAPTER FOUR

On the trip back from Chinle, Leigh made up her mind—
she was going to visit Jimmy's grandmother before another day passed. If anyone could tell her about Zakoura,
it was Mary Yazzi. She didn't doubt for a minute that the
old woman knew all there was to know about him. The only
question in her mind was whether she would be willing to
impart this information to Leigh. In Leigh's somewhat
limited experience, the older Navaho were not generally
disposed to speak freely with Anglos. She would have to
work at earning Mary's trust. After her disturbing walk
through Chinle that afternoon, she hoped it wouldn't take
too long.

When they arrived back in camp, the sun was arcing toward the horizon, but there were still a couple of hours of
daylight left. Hugh and Paul had already eaten, and they'd
left them the remainder of a meat loaf. But although she
hadn't eaten much earlier, Leigh wasn't hungry. Besides,
she didn't want to waste what was left of the day. Claiming
she needed to stretch her legs after the ride, she set off in the
direction of Jimmy's hogan, grateful that none of her colleagues was a big fan of hiking.

She was only halfway there when Jimmy spotted her
from the corral where he'd just finished putting the sheep
in for the night. He came pounding up to meet her. "Dr.
Leigh! Hi!" He fell into step beside her.

"Hi. Where's your buddy?"

"You mean Rowdy? He's digging up a prairie-dog hole he found out back. He's pretty dumb—he got his nose bitten the last time. Where're you going?"

"Well, I was out taking a walk and I thought I might pay your grandmother a visit. How does she feel about company?" It couldn't hurt to find out what she'd be up against.

Jimmy pursed his lips like an old man and thought for a moment. "She likes it, mostly... company she knows."

"I see. She doesn't like strangers, huh?"

"I don't think so. We only had a stranger come by once. He was here from California to see the ruins. He wanted to talk to my grandmother and look inside our hogan. He even wanted to pay her to let him take pictures. He had three different kinds of cameras—you shoulda seen them. But she wouldn't let him in, wouldn't even talk to him."

Leigh thought of the countless strangers who had come to her door during her life: salesmen, charity fund-raisers, Jehovah's Witnesses, Girl Scouts selling cookies and high school bands selling candy bars and oranges by the crate. In all of Jimmy's memory, only one stranger had come to his home. She was struck again by the isolation of the canyon and the vast differences between her life and the way Jimmy and his grandmother lived. Maybe she'd been too optimistic in believing she could win Mary's confidence; the gulf between them might be too wide. She might not even make it into the hogan. Her only hope was that her friendship with Jimmy would provide an adequate bridge.

"Do you think she'll mind if I stop by to see her? After all, you know me, so technically I'm not a stranger."

Jimmy shrugged in a way that Leigh took to mean "Oh, she'll probably mind, all right, but if you want to try, go ahead. I'm not gonna say anything that'll mess up my chances to go to the dig with you."

"Well, even if she isn't in the mood for company, you and I are still friends, right?" she said, hoping to reassure him that their relationship didn't depend on his grandmother's attitude.

He looked up at her and smiled. "Yeah, we're friends."

They were almost at the hogan by then, and Rowdy had apparently picked up Leigh's scent and decided to abandon the prairie-dog hunt. He came tearing around the rear of the little house, taking the corner like a motorcycle leaning into a mean curve. Once he was on a straight course for her, he stretched out his legs, doubling his speed. It didn't look like he'd made any provisions for stopping in time. Jimmy thrust himself in front of her, taking the brunt of the impact and hitting the ground with a bone-rattling thud.

Rowdy didn't even pause to see if his master was hurt. He hurtled right over him to reach Leigh, then sped in circles around and around her, tail wagging furiously. Finally he stopped so that she could scratch him, lavishly licking her hand and arm in return for the favor.

Leigh couldn't help laughing. She didn't have just one ally, after all, she had two. And she would make Mary the third, she told herself firmly. They walked on together. Rowdy led the way, checking over his shoulder every few seconds to make sure they were still following.

Jimmy's hogan was much like others Leigh had seen in the area. Hexagonal in shape, it had been built from stripped logs that were notched to fit into one another, like a log cabin. Adobe filled in the chinks between the logs. Smoke was puffing from the chimney hole in the center of the roof. Pungent wood smoke—it wafted down to Leigh, carrying the dense aroma of simmering meat.

To one side of the hogan was a crudely fashioned open-sided shelter in which strips of bloody mutton had been hung from crossbeams to dry. To the other side was the weathered wood corral, which had been divided in two. The sheep were in one section, huddled in the lengthening shade provided by two stunted juniper trees. A bay mare, which Leigh hadn't noticed before, occupied the other. Half a dozen chickens scuttled in and out of the enclosures, pecking at the ground for insects.

Leigh stopped several yards from the front door, which faced east as prescribed by Navaho tradition. Beside the door were a neat woodpile, an old three-legged stool and a dented bucket. There was no sign of Mary Yazzi outside. Judging by the smells that were rising through the chimney hole, she was most likely preparing dinner. Rowdy, who had also determined that food was in the air, headed straight for the door. When he reached it, he turned back to them with a look of confusion—weren't they going in?

Jimmy made no move toward the door. He stood next to Leigh, waiting, as if he, too, were a reluctant visitor. He'd grown uncharacteristically reticent as they neared the hogan, and Leigh had the impression that he was dreading this encounter. Her own apprehension clicked several degrees higher. Mary was her only readily available source of information about Zakoura, and Jimmy's obvious anxiety was making her doubt once more whether she would ever learn anything from the old woman. She was also beginning to worry that Jimmy might be punished for bringing her here, even though he was completely innocent. If she succeeded in nothing else, she'd have to make it clear to his grandmother that the idea had not in any way been his.

They'd been standing outside for several minutes, and still Jimmy made no move to invite Leigh inside. She realized she was going to have to take matters into her own hands.

"Do you think I should knock, or do you want to tell your grandmother I've come by to say hello?" She tried to keep her voice upbeat and positive, although she was becoming more uncomfortable by the moment.

"I guess I'll go tell her you're here," he said, without much enthusiasm. He opened the door and followed Rowdy inside.

Leigh strained to hear what was going on. It should have been easy—the hogan was hardly soundproof. And the canyon area, which was always quiet except for occasional animal sounds and the susurrations of the wind, was now absolutely still, as if even the air was holding its breath to hear what was happening. Yet not even the muffled hum of voices penetrated the log walls. She thought of just walking away. Letting Jimmy off the hook and going back to camp. But giving up didn't come easily.

It had only been five or six minutes when Jimmy emerged again, but to Leigh it seemed like an hour. During that time, she had run out of optimism, and she fully expected to read defeat on his small face. But, although he still wasn't smiling, there was a triumphant glow in his eyes that told her that, in spite of the odds, he had succeeded.

"Please come in, Dr. Leigh," he said formally, moving to one side of the doorway to let her pass.

Leigh stepped into the hogan, silently vowing to do her best not to say anything that might antagonize Mary or offend her. No matter how much or how little she was able to learn from this meeting, Jimmy would not be sorry he had gone so far out on a limb to help her.

She was surprised at how bright the interior was, until she realized that the one window faced west and the sun, which was by now quite low in the sky, was providing almost a spotlight effect in the single room. The white insulation board that had been fitted in the spaces between the wall beams helped refract the light, too, adding an airy quality to the room.

Mary Yazzi was seated beneath the window at a primitive-looking loom that had been constructed on a frame of two upright poles connected along the top by a crosspiece. The first third of an intricately patterned rug covered the upper portion of the loom, and Mary's hands flew deftly over the dyed wool beneath it.

As Jimmy led Leigh across the earthen floor, she tried to take in as much as she could without seeming too nosy. There was a wrought-iron bedstead against one wall, covered by a magnificent Yei blanket in which red ceremonial figures danced across a white background with a single thick border of black. Sticking out from beneath the bed Leigh could see the edge of the pallet on which Jimmy probably slept.

On the wall above the bed hung an old cradle board made of wood and rawhide, the decorative patterns on it all but erased with wear. Jimmy had likely been carried around in that cradle board as an infant, and perhaps his mother had, as well.

Aside from the chair on which Mary was seated, a small table and two other chairs completed the room's furnishings. A potbellied stove squatted in the center of the room, a kettle simmering on it, scenting the air with the rich smell of mutton. Rowdy had curled up next to the stove in anticipation of dinner. He thumped his tail against the floor as Leigh walked by, sending up a cloud of pink dust, the motes glittering like a swarm of iridescent gnats in the sunlight.

Shelves on one of the walls were stocked like a pantry, and there were a couple of old cupboards that probably held dishes and glassware. Lined up on the floor along another wall were half a dozen cardboard boxes in which Leigh could see neatly folded clothing.

They came up beside the loom, and Jimmy waited until Mary looked up from her weaving. Then he took a deep breath and introduced Leigh.

Mary's expression was hard to read. The light behind her was casting her face in shadow. Even so, the eyes that peered back at Leigh were polished chips of onyx, bright with intelligence. A deep net of lines radiated from them, continuing down her cheeks like the rutted branches of the Chinle Wash. Her gray hair was pulled back in a tidy knot, held fast with the customary string of white wool.

"It's so nice to meet you," Leigh said, trying frantically to remember whether the Navaho shook hands. Deciding to err on the side of foolishness rather than rudeness, she extended hers.

Her face still impassive, Mary placed her hand in it briefly. "Dr. Morgan. My grandson likes you a lot. He talks about little else."

Leigh wasn't sure if the last remark was meant to be sarcastic, but she smiled anyway. If this meeting wound up being a disaster, it wasn't going to be her fault. "He's a great kid. But I'm sure you already know that."

Mary nodded. "Would you like to sit down?" Although the words were polite, Leigh could hear the unspoken wish that she would decline. But, as much as she didn't like to stay where she wasn't welcome, she had no intention of giving up now.

"Thank you."

Before she could help herself to one of the chairs, Jimmy had fetched it for her. Once she was seated, he plunked himself down on the edge of the bed and made a big show of playing with several Star Wars figurines. But, although he was trying to look casual and unconcerned, his tension was apparent in the stiffness of his posture. He was alert to everything being said across the room.

Leigh cast about for a neutral topic with which to start the conversation and decided on the rug Mary was weaving. Completely inept at any type of craft herself, she'd always been fascinated by the ability of others to create things that were at once beautiful and practical.

"The colors in that rug are wonderful," she said with real enthusiasm. "The red is aniline, right?"

Mary nodded.

"If you don't mind my asking, where do the others come from?"

Perhaps Mary had sensed that her interest was genuine, because when she answered, her tone was somewhat less guarded.

"The yellow comes from rabbitbrush, and the pink from cedar roots. The black, the gray and the white are natural colors of the wool."

Leigh asked several other questions and received answers that were polite but succinct. Mary's rugs could be purchased at the Hubbell Trading Post at Ganado, as well as the Upper Greasewood Trading Post. Her mother had taught her to weave when she was eight. The designs had been in her family for generations, although she had added some variations of her own.

Mary didn't make any remarks or ask any questions in return, which made the conversation seem more like an interview. Leigh didn't know how much longer she could keep up this lopsided dialogue. She could already see a flicker of impatience in the older woman's eyes. How was she going to segue gracefully to the topic of Zakoura without it being too obvious that that was the real reason she had come?

"You are very interested in the Navaho," Mary said finally as the silence in the room became increasingly awkward.

Leigh thought she detected some hostility behind the words. But she also saw the opening for which she'd been waiting.

"Unfortunately, I haven't had the opportunity to meet many of your people. Sergeant Tsosie, a few of the other policemen, and, of course, Jimmy. Oh...and Zakoura," she added, as if it were an afterthought. The mere act of saying his name out loud agitated her, sending a cloudy mixture of excitement and anxiety pumping through her body. Across the room, Jimmy had let the figurines fall and was chewing on his lower lip, openly listening to the two women now.

Mary's reaction was immediate, too. Her hands bunched into fists in her lap. Her eyes narrowed, sinking deeper into the seine of lines around them, and her voice took on a razor sharp edge. "He is not Navaho."

Leigh was surprised that Mary hadn't denied knowing him, as her grandson had. What was more, fear had no part in her reaction. In spite of her best efforts to conceal it, Mary seethed with anger, and a bitterness so potent that it curled her lips when she spoke. Yet her only comment was that Zakoura wasn't Navaho.

Pretending not to notice the change in Mary's demeanor, Leigh continued on in a casual tone. "I just assumed he was Navaho because he lives here on reservation land."

Mary stood abruptly, as if the rage roiling within her wouldn't let her be still. She was small and stocky and, in spite of her advanced age, looked as if she could stand her ground in a good-size tornado. She walked past Leigh to the stove, her gait stiff from arthritis, or perhaps from tension.

"Zakoura Kree is not Navaho, and he does not live here." Her words were clipped, as if she had bitten off the end of each one. Picking up a wooden spoon, she stirred the mutton stew with hard, angry strokes.

"Zakoura Kree," Leigh murmured. He hadn't told her his full name. And there was a lot more she didn't know. Why he came to her in dreams, why Jimmy was terrified of him, why Mary hated him—and the list went on. But her time there was almost up. She half expected a buzzer to sound, bringing it to an end. She stood, also, so that Mary would know she didn't intend to outstay her welcome. But she couldn't resist asking one last question.

"If he's not Navaho, what is he?" Probably too blunt, but this was her last chance.

Mary turned, and now the sunlight was directly upon her face. Leigh saw the shadow of something more than anger move within her eyes—she saw a deeply etched and enduring pain.

"He is poison," Mary said, her voice gravelly with emotion.

"I don't understand."

"Stay away from him. There is nothing else you need to know."

Leigh wanted to question her further, but she suspected such persistence would not be tolerated. Remembering her silent vow to Jimmy, she swallowed the words before they could reach her lips.

"Well...I guess I should be going," she said. "I've kept you too long already. Thank you for taking the time to see me, Mrs. Yazzi."

Mary nodded and added some salt to the meat.

Leigh smiled at Jimmy, who managed a weak smile in return. "See you soon, kiddo." She didn't say goodbye. The Navaho didn't bother with hello and goodbye; they simply arrived and departed without fanfare. That much she remembered.

She let herself out of the hogan. The sky was beginning to blaze with the pinks and reds of sunset. Dwarf piñon and juniper trees splashed elongated shadows across the ground like puddles of night. If she didn't hurry, it would be dark before she reached camp again.

She walked quickly, sifting through the few things she'd learned. Zakoura wasn't Navaho, and he didn't live on the reservation. Karen had been wrong on both counts. Her own intuition had been right—he was different. But, of course, Karen hadn't met him or dreamed of him. She'd learned his full name, too. Zakoura Kree—it was unlike any Indian name she'd ever heard before. She had hoped that speaking with Mary would answer her questions, and in so doing quiet her fears. But the little she'd learned, along with Mary's patent anger, had only served to produce more questions and intensify those fears. She needed to return there and talk with her again. It wasn't likely that she'd be welcome, but she'd probably try anyway. Zakoura Kree was swiftly becoming an obsession. When Mary had called him "poison," maybe she hadn't been too far off the mark. Leigh already felt as if her mind were tainted by him.

An owl hooted nearby, causing her to jump. Whirling around, she found the bird sitting on an upper branch of a juniper she'd just passed. Its huge eyes, catching the last of the sun's rays, seemed to be hanging in thin air like the grin of the Cheshire cat. Glancing beyond the tree, she noticed that a police car had parked nose in to the corral; Carlos was standing beside it. She'd been so lost in thought that she hadn't even heard the engine. How strange that he should be visiting Mary barely five minutes after she'd left. No doubt he knew the family and came to check on them regularly. She wanted to believe that his arrival was just a coincidence, but she couldn't forget the way he'd been watching them in Chinle. She was relieved to see that he wasn't looking in her direction. Following his line of sight, she realized what had captured his attention. She froze. Everything inside her stopped dead with apprehension. Off to her far left, a figure stood atop a high slab of table rock. Although he was no more than a dark silhouette against the flaming sky, she knew it was Zakoura. With his hair flying wildly around him in the wind and his stance wide, hands at his hips, he looked both regal and menacing. She felt his eyes boring through the darkening sky to reach her. Felt their raw power on her skin. For a moment, every scientific precept she'd ever held fast to was blown away. Looking at him up on that mesa, Leigh found herself wondering whether Zakoura Kree was indeed a spirit, or perhaps an ancient god.

CHAPTER FIVE

She finished wrapping the sandwiches—tuna salad with celery, onion and herbs, made according to Hugh's recipe—and set them in the refrigerator. Lunch was her job today, since she was the one designated to stay behind and wait for their gas and water delivery. As Hugh had pointed out the first week in the field, it made no sense for him to get up earlier to make lunch on a day when someone had to hang around camp all morning anyway.

Leigh washed the plates and utensils she'd used and wiped down the counter so that Hugh wouldn't complain. For a man who left clean and dirty clothing lying in random heaps beside his bed, he was a fanatic about keeping his kitchen clean. When she was certain everything was spotless, she gathered up the writing paper and pen she'd left on the table, pulled on her Yankees cap and went outside.

The day promised to be one of the hottest since they'd arrived. Although it was not yet ten o'clock, objects in the distance shimmered in a haze of heat. When Leigh looked out toward Jimmy's hogan, it was strangely warped and wavy, as if she were seeing it on a television with poor reception. She could have waited a while longer inside the RV, which was still fairly cool from the previous night, but she'd felt trapped in there, like Tweety Bird locked in his cage with Sylvester on the prowl. At least outside she had an unobstructed 360-degree view. She just hoped there'd be nothing unexpected for her to see.

She set up a folding chair just beyond the campers and settled down to wait. The "delivery watch," as Paul referred to it, was enforced leisure, a good time to catch up on whatever you'd let slide. Leigh had planned to use her free morning to draft some letters of inquiry to various schools. Although she'd completed her doctorate over a year ago, she still hadn't been able to find a teaching position. The country was between baby booms, and with fewer eighteen-year-olds applying to schools, the universities were cutting back on course offerings, laying off instructors and professors whenever possible. The job market was as awful for an archaeologist as it was for anyone else.

Twenty minutes later, all she had to show for her efforts was a page and a half of writing, all of it crossed out. She couldn't concentrate. It was too hot, the wind was tugging at the paper, and the chair kept rocking from side to side on the uneven ground, and...and...dammit, he was out there somewhere. Okay, she admitted it. Her mind wasn't wandering because of the weather, or the chair; the problem was Zakoura. She kept remembering him up on that mesa at twilight, looking as if thunderbolts might erupt from his fingertips at any moment. She'd thought she'd regained her senses, her scientific reason, after her brief slide toward the paranormal that night. Apparently she hadn't. She still expected him to appear out of nowhere, although such a thing was impossible. And what would she do if he did show up now? Now that she was completely alone, with no one around even to hear her scream?

She stood abruptly, stuffing the papers and pen into her pocket. Maybe exercise would calm her. It had worked back in college and grad school. Whenever she'd been stressed out, she'd taken refuge in the gym. Since there was no

Stairmaster within a few hundred miles, she started walking, her gait long and fast, arms pumping. She headed in the opposite direction from the Yazzi hogan, away from the places she'd seen Zakoura in the past. No sense in taking unnecessary chances.

She covered a hundred strides, counting out loud to keep her mind occupied. It wasn't working. The more distance she put between herself and the camp, the more agitated she was becoming. She had to get back. On this flat stretch of land, she wouldn't miss seeing the delivery truck's arrival, but it had suddenly occurred to her that the RVs provided the only safe haven in the area. The locks on the doors were flimsy affairs, but the kitchen was well stocked with knives. What was she thinking? Walking turned to jogging. For a moment it seemed as if she were back in the dream, trying to escape Zakoura. She wanted to run now, her legs itched with the need, but she refused to give in to panic. He wasn't behind her. He hadn't even been behind her in that crazy dream.

By the time she reached camp again, perspiration was weaving down her forehead and her shirt was pasted to her body in clammy patches. She slowed to a walk. What she needed was a plan, a way to fill the time until Hugh returned for her. Okay, she'd find his umbrella, pour herself a big glass of lemonade and relax with the new Sidney Sheldon book she'd brought along for just that purpose. Okay. She felt a little better already, a little more in control.

She was almost at the men's camper when something came flying out from behind it, heading straight for her. At first all she saw was form and motion. In that split second, her body clicked into survival mode, panic flashing along every neural pathway. But before she even had a chance to run, she was knocked to the ground.

Rowdy stood over her, his four sturdy legs imprisoning her body, his sandpaper tongue rasping her face. All she could do was lie there and laugh hysterically, the relief was so great. Jimmy found them still in that position when he came running around the corner of the camper a minute later.

"I'm sorry, Dr. Leigh, I'm so sorry," he said, trying to pull Rowdy away without causing the dog to step on her accidentally. "He knows he's not allowed to jump on people. He knows that." Jimmy sounded truly aggrieved.

Leigh slid backward until she was no longer between Rowdy's legs, then pushed herself to her feet. Her stomach hurt from laughing so hard. Jimmy was scolding the dog, who was lying with his head on his front paws, an appropriate expression of remorse on his face.

"It's okay, Jimmy," she said, still giggling. "He just caught me by surprise."

"He didn't hurt you?"

"All body parts present and accounted for. To tell you the truth, it was kind of nice—I have two goldens back home that I wrestle with from time to time, and I've been missing them. Besides, your timing is perfect. I can sure use some company right now."

Jimmy relaxed instantly. His mouth spread into a cheek-splitting grin. "Then you're not mad?"

Leigh shook her head. "Not one bit." She was glad to see that he wasn't still upset about her visit the other day. She'd been worried about him.

"And you'll still give me a tour of the dig?"

So that was the source of his concern. "Absolutely. You pick the day."

"Today," he said, his eyes shining. "I pick today."

"Well . . . all right." He'd caught her a bit off guard, but since she'd only be working half a day, this might just be the best time to take him along. "Are you sure you've cleared it with your grandmother?" The last thing she needed was to irritate Mary unnecessarily.

"You betcha."

"Hugh should be back for me in about an hour."

Jimmy nodded. "After the delivery truck."

"Not much gets past you."

"Mondays before twelve. Except last week they were late."

"How about some lemonade for you and me, and a bowl of water for my furry friend?"

Leigh served up the drinks, and Jimmy set up the umbrella and another chair. He seemed so capable, so mature, that it was hard to think of him as only ten. But then, he was probably responsible for all the chores his father would have handled. The raw nature of life here had thrust him into quasi-adulthood while most Anglo children were still mastering the intricacies of Nintendo.

Once they were settled in the shade of the umbrella, she answered his questions about becoming an archaeologist. Then she asked him about school, what subjects he liked best, what sports. She avoided any questions about Zakoura, even though the topic was out in the open now, and still uppermost in her mind. Children had a way of putting their fears in a box and burying them; she didn't want to dredge Jimmy's up again.

The delivery truck came at eleven and was leaving just as Hugh pulled up in the Bronco. Leigh introduced him to Jimmy, who was so excited about joining them that he was hopping from one foot to the other.

"One rule, pal," Hugh said as he helped Leigh load the cooler in the truck. "You can't touch anything, because it's very important that we know exactly where and how each artifact is found."

"I know," Jimmy said solemnly. "Dr. Leigh already told me."

"Good. And, much as I like Rowdy, he can't join us."

"We'll drop him off on the way." Leigh opened the back of the truck, and Rowdy bounded in.

"He's gonna be disappointed," Jimmy whispered to her as he climbed in the back seat.

"I know, but he doesn't understand about rules."

Mary Yazzi was outside grooming the mare when they arrived at the hogan. The animal stood dozing in the heat, his tail rhythmically swatting at flies while Mary brushed him with firm downward strokes. In spite of the heat, she was wearing a purple velveteen blouse with long sleeves over a blue flounced skirt.

When the Bronco stopped, she looked up, and Leigh raised her hand in greeting. With an almost imperceptible nod, Mary turned her attention back to the horse.

"She doesn't seem to share the boy's enthusiasm for us," Hugh murmured while Jimmy tried to coax Rowdy out of the back.

"How would you feel if a bunch of Navaho descended on a place you considered sacred and started digging it up?"

"Whoa! Don't preach to the choir. I never said she didn't have a right to be annoyed, even hostile. I'm just kind of surprised her grandson grew up without that prejudice."

Jimmy wasn't having any success with Rowdy. No amount of ordering or cajoling worked. Finally Hugh got behind the dog and pushed while Jimmy tugged at his collar. Admitting defeat, Rowdy jumped down and went to sit beside Mary. He watched them drive off with a look of betrayal as eloquent as any words could have been.

As they drove down into the wash, a muddy Navaho pickup splashed by them, returning from a guided tour of the previously excavated ruins. Eight tourists armed with cameras, camcorders and binoculars were crammed onto benches in the open bed of the truck, mesmerized by the red sandstone cliffs rising on either side of them.

Looking up at the rim of the canyon, Leigh counted a dozen heads peering over the guardrail. There were easily another dozen people following the trail of switchbacks that led down the five hundred feet to the canyon floor. The Bronco had just passed the turnoff to Canyon del Muerto and was coming up on the White House, the only site tourists were permitted to hike into without a Navaho guide.

Hugh was swearing gruffly under his breath as he braked repeatedly for people who were so intent on crossing the Chinle Wash without getting too wet or muddy that they didn't even notice the Bronco bearing down on them.

"They oughta just build a damned overpass for them," he muttered, swerving around a couple of children who'd decided that playing in the water was preferable to looking at the ancient buildings.

Leigh shook her head and grinned. Mondays were always the same. Hugh should just send someone else back to camp for the midday run, someone with more patience. Personally, Leigh had never been bothered by the tourists. And today she was especially glad to see them. Zakoura would never make an appearance with this many people around. She wasn't sure how she knew that. Maybe it was the dreams. She was always alone with him in the dreams.

Once they were past the White House there were no more tourists traversing the canyon floor, although Leigh could still see a good number observing from the overlook points on both the north and south rims. Now Hugh only had to contend with the uneven terrain, the course of the widening stream and an occasional sheep straying from one of the Navaho summer farms that were a more common sight as they drove deeper into the canyon. He stopped once, to avoid splashing a group of tourists riding by on a guided horseback tour.

"That's the right way to see the canyon," Leigh said with a sigh. "Trucks and four-wheel drives don't really belong down here."

Hugh shook his head. "If we relied on horses, we'd get to the dig in time to leave every day. Besides, do you want to listen to Paul complain about bouncing around on a horse?"

"I ride Skywalker down here sometimes," Jimmy said. He'd been silent until then, perhaps worried about bothering them.

"Is that the horse your grandmother was grooming?" Leigh asked.

"Yeah. Her real name's Lucy, but I call her Skywalker most of the time. It doesn't matter all that much, 'cause horses hardly ever learn their names."

Leigh asked him how he'd learned to ride and what kind of care a horse required. Jimmy eagerly told them everything he knew. They passed Sliding Rock Ruins, the Window and Spider Rock, the junctions at Bat Canyon and Monument Canyon. They were more than halfway to the dig. It struck Leigh that she was using these incredible landmarks to measure the trip, the way she would have used a building or an intersection back home.

They passed the last of the overlook points. From here on, the rim road had to swing farther south, beyond the smaller branch canyons. No more tourists. Leigh found herself scanning the patina-streaked escarpments that towered above her. "You're not alone," she reminded herself, as her heart started hammering harder and louder. "Hugh and Jimmy are here." She tried to wet her lips, but her tongue was dry. Of course it was dry. It must have been ninety degrees, and they didn't have the AC on, because it ate up gas too quickly.

She couldn't see the base of the cliffs anymore. Stands of cottonwood trees growing in the sandbar along the shores of the wash blocked her view of what lay beyond. *Who* lay beyond. "You're not alone." The words were like a mantra. If she repeated them long enough, would they bring her peace of mind?

Hugh and Jimmy were having a lively discussion about baseball. Apparently Jimmy had a cousin who lived in town and had a television, complete with satellite dish. Leigh tried to focus on the conversation and forget about playing sentry, but her eyes kept roaming uneasily up and down the canyon walls, even as she was comparing the Yankees to the Mets.

When they reached the site, they found the rest of the team gathered in the shade of the cavern, drinking lemonade and waiting for their lunch to arrive. Leigh introduced Jimmy, and they all sat together eating the tuna sandwiches. Afterward, Hugh and Karen went down into the kiva and Alex and Paul went back to the rooms where they were working. Leigh had received Hugh's permission to start excavating another room near them in the "condo," but when Jimmy heard them talking about the cave, his eyes lit up with excitement, entreating her to take him there. Leigh acquiesced. On a hot day like this one, the cave was sure to be cooler and more comfortable. Besides, she felt that she owed Jimmy a favor for introducing her to Mary.

She led the way along the ledge, telling herself that since she wasn't alone, Zakoura wouldn't come to call. Jimmy followed with her knapsack, which he'd insisted on carrying "to feel like a real part of the team." When they reached the cave, Leigh paused, glancing warily across at the opposite cliff. The last time she'd been here, she'd seen Zakoura on that rim.

"Is this the cave?" Jimmy asked impatiently. "Aren't we going in?"

Leigh took a deep, bolstering breath and turned back to him. "Of course we are. I just have to light the lamp—it's pretty dark in there."

Jimmy loved the cave. He thought it would make a great secret hideout. "Of course, I'd never use it for that," he added quickly, seeing the disapproval register on her face.

"Not even when we leave for the winter?" No point in telling the boy they wouldn't necessarily be back next year. It was important to keep everything as pristine as possible for any archaeologists who might follow.

He shook his head soberly. "I know it's important not to mess things up. But maybe when the excavation's all done?"

"Maybe, but that could be a long time, you know."

"I know." Jimmy seemed satisfied with the deal he'd forged. He settled down to look through the tools and implements in Leigh's knapsack and to watch her work. She explained proper procedure as she dug up pieces of a basket in which food had once been stored. Soon Jimmy was handing her items like a well-trained nurse in an operating room—trowel, spoon, whisk broom, artifact bag, pen, tape recorder. But after an hour with no major discovery, his interest started to flag.

"I'm gonna take a walk, okay?" he said, standing up.

She'd been crazy to expect a ten-year-old to sit still for so long. "Don't wander far away. I'm responsible for you while you're here." It wasn't that she was concerned that he'd get lost or into trouble. He'd grown up with the canyon as his backyard, after all. But Hugh would have her head if they had to waste time looking for him.

"I won't," he said, already scooting through the low entrance.

It wasn't until he'd left that she realized she'd wound up exactly where she didn't want to be—alone in the cave. She tried to bend her concentration back to her work. The last sweep of the trowel had uncovered something that glinted in the lamplight. She dug around it gently with a spoon. Probably the tip of a pottery shard. She spent fifteen minutes removing layer after layer of the dirt that surrounded it, and still most of it remained buried. Ordinarily she wouldn't have noticed the time, or the way her knees ached from kneeling, or how slow her progress seemed to be. But today she noticed all of it. The pungent, earthy smell of the cave was beginning to make her queasy. Her stomach rode in uneasy waves; her head felt wobbly. She needed some air.

Outside the cave, the air smelled cleaner, but it was hot and thick, without a breeze to stir it. Jimmy wasn't in sight, which didn't worry her. The way the ledge followed the curves of the cliff, it was difficult to see more than a few yards ahead in most places. More importantly, no one stood on the opposite rim, no strange footsteps echoed in the canyon. Her head and stomach quieted. She was thinking she should go back to work when Jimmy came tearing around the ledge from the right.

"He's here, Dr. Leigh. He's here. I just saw him." The boy's voice was thin and constricted, as if he were having trouble forcing it through the muscles of his throat. He grabbed her hand and tried to pull her with him, back toward the main buildings.

Leigh knew who he meant, but she heard herself asking anyway. "Who is, Jimmy? Who's here?"

"Zakoura. Zakoura's here. I lied about not knowing him. Please, just c'mon."

Leigh stood her ground. Jimmy's hysteria had a strangely calming effect on her. If he was the child, she had to assume the role of adult. "Where did you see him?"

Jimmy was still tugging at her. "A few turns back. He's coming here. I'm sure of it."

She wriggled her hand free of his hold. "Go into the cave and pack up all the equipment. I'll be right back." She'd been terrified of seeing Zakoura again, but now that he was here, she knew that she had to confront him. She wasn't going to let him rule her life for one more minute.

"No, don't go after him." There was a desperate edge to Jimmy's voice. Tears welled up in his eyes and trembled on his lower lashes. "You don't understand, Dr. Leigh. You can't go after him."

She tried to assure him she was not in danger, although she suspected that it might not be true. The boy's terror was genuine. He wasn't the type of child who cried easily, and certainly not in front of an outsider. Even Mary, who hadn't shown any sign of fear about Zakoura, had warned her to stay away from him. Leigh hesitated, her resolve weakening as Jimmy stared at her with troubled eyes. She could let it go, pack up and rejoin the others. But there was an inherent challenge in Zakoura's coming here, and she'd never been able to walk away from a challenge. Like the deserted house when she was growing up. All the kids had said it was haunted. She'd argued that it couldn't be, since there were no such things as ghosts. To prove her point, she'd gone inside alone and come back out ten minutes later without mishap. In spite of her convictions, her knees hadn't stopped shaking for two hours. She'd learned the power of the imagination. Well, Zakoura was that haunted house all over again. She had to face him. Maybe then she could dispel the power he seemed to have over her.

CHAPTER SIX

He wasn't beyond the first bend, or the second. Each time Leigh came around another curve of the ledge, she steeled herself for the confrontation. Either Jimmy was wrong about where he'd seen Zakoura or the Indian hadn't been coming in their direction after all. She couldn't very well waste the entire afternoon looking for him, but neither was she inclined to give up, especially when she might be so close. She followed the rocky ledge another thirty yards, and then she found him.

He was sitting on an outcropping of rock, carving a piece of sandstone with a strange-looking knife. Even from where she stood, Leigh could see that the blade was made not of steel, but of highly polished stone. The only places she'd ever seen knives like that were museums and books and archaeological research centers. Logic dictated that he'd found the knife at one of the many ruins in the area. Thousands of such precious artifacts had been taken by the local inhabitants over the years. Any other explanation for the knife in his hand was far too incredible to consider.

Zakoura tossed away the rock he'd been working on as if he'd only used it to pass the time while he waited for her, as if he'd known without question that she would come. The decision to go after him had been hers, yet now Leigh felt like a subject who'd been summoned to court against her will.

He didn't say anything, just sat there looking at her with the same impossible mixture of intensity and reserve as the first time they'd met. The angle of the sun delineated the sharp planes of his face so that he looked as if he, too, had been chiseled from the sandstone that surrounded him. Only the subtle movements of his eyes indicated that he was anything more than a superb sculpture.

In spite of Leigh's determination to remain rational and in control, she was once again ambushed by her attraction to him. Like an arrow, it wedged itself between the fear and the anger and refused to be dislodged. And on it rode the memories of the dreams—the cool imprint of his lips on her heated skin, the texture of his hair, dense and smooth, laced between her fingers. She fought them back furiously, horrified at the thought that she might blush in front of him.

She saw comprehension flash in his dark eyes, as if he sensed her turmoil and knew its source. Humiliation made her anger billow like a sail catching a fresh wind. She wasn't even sure with whom she was angrier—Zakoura for being able to see straight into her soul, or herself for being so damned transparent. In any case, the rage helped restore her equilibrium. She clung to it like a fighter clinging to the ropes at the end of an exhausting round. Although neither of them had spoken a word yet, it was as if they'd been sparring for hours.

"What do you want?" she asked without preamble, resolving to take control of the encounter. She was pleased with the calm crispness she'd managed in her tone. Better, much better.

"I am sorry you came," he said, as if he hadn't even heard her.

"Oh, really? Then maybe you'd like to explain why you've been waiting here?" She wasn't going to let him take the initiative away from her. She'd pursue the other question later.

He didn't answer. Instead, he stood up and took a few steps toward her, stopping while she was still out of reach.

"To see if you would," he said finally. "To satisfy a curiosity."

No, not curiosity. Curiosity implied a lack of knowledge. Zakoura hadn't been the least bit surprised when she showed up. He'd waited because he wanted to see her.

"Why have you been following me?" she demanded, feeling for the first time that she had the upper hand.

His mouth curved into a rueful smile that lasted only a moment. When it was gone, his expression was as impassive as before. "Some lessons are harder."

"I don't understand. If you want to talk to me, you're going to have to forget the riddles. I don't have the time or the inclination to play that kind of game."

"It is not for you to understand."

It occurred to Leigh that the Zakoura she'd conjured up in her dreams spoke in the same maddeningly vague way. Her subconscious had it down perfectly. Perhaps a little too perfectly. She didn't at all like where that line of reasoning was headed. And she didn't have time to dwell on it now. If she didn't get back to the cave soon, Jimmy would be certain that something awful had happened to her.

"Listen, I don't care what the reason is, or what you think I can or cannot understand. Just stop following me." She put as much force behind the words as she could muster. "Or I'll report you to the Chinle police."

"I doubt that I am within their jurisdiction." There was a mild sarcasm in his voice that sounded as if it stemmed not from bravado, but rather from a knowledge of the facts. Leigh was stymied, unable to come up with an appropriate rejoinder. She wasn't even sure exactly what he'd meant by that remark. Before she could question it further, he crossed the space between them in one long stride. He took her chin in his hand and lifted it, inclining his head so that his mouth was only inches away from hers. She thought he was going to kiss her, and she knew she should pull away. Later she'd tell herself she'd stood her ground to prove that she couldn't be intimidated. But even she didn't believe that. She'd stayed because she'd wanted him to kiss her. Wanted to find out if her response would be as intense as it was in the dreams.

At the last moment a silvery glint of rage flared in his eyes; his jaw clenched. He let go of her and drew himself up straight.

"You would do better to fear me," he whispered roughly. Raising the hand that held the knife, he pressed the sharp tip of it against the delicate hollow of her throat. If she moved a fraction of an inch, the blade would rip through her skin. Before Leigh had time to absorb what was happening, he withdrew the knife and left her there, disappearing quickly beyond the next curve of the canyon.

She stood frozen where she was, too stunned and confused to react immediately. One minute she was surrendering to a romantic dream, the next her life was being threatened. She stared at the place where he'd been standing, as if it might hold a clue to what had happened. Slowly the riptide of emotions receded. Indignation replaced desire, the one as heated as the other. How dare he? How dare he play with her like that? Just who the hell did he think he was? The words reverberated in her head with such force, she wondered if she'd said them aloud. But even as she railed at him, she knew it was her own disappointment she was condemning, the miserable longing that twisted inside her. She didn't for a moment believe that it was a game to him. The anger and frustration she'd seen him struggle with during both of their encounters were real. There were fierce demons that haunted him, and she couldn't begin to guess their names.

When she returned to the cave, Jimmy was gone. All her equipment was still scattered about, the way she'd left it. He hadn't packed up, and he hadn't waited. For someone so desperate to please her, the boy was acting completely out of character. Or she had badly underestimated Zakoura's impact on him. She tossed everything haphazardly into the knapsack and headed back to the main buildings as fast as she dared along the rocky ledge.

Almost at once she ran into Alex, who caught her in his arms as they collided coming around a blind curve. Hugh was immediately behind him, a trowel gripped in his hand as if it were a sidearm. Jimmy and the others were following closely after them.

"Leigh, are you all right?" Alex held on to her until he was sure she was steady on her feet. "The boy had us thinking we'd never see you again."

She nodded. "I'm fine." She looked past him at Jimmy and saw relief wash across the child's face. His eyes were streaked with red, and tears had carved ragged lines through the smudges of dirt on his cheeks. He lowered his eyes to the ground, ashamed to be seen in such a state now that the danger had passed. Leigh wanted to put her arms around him and comfort him, but she knew she'd only wind up embarrassing him more.

Hugh waited until they were back in the shade of the main cavern and Leigh had been provided with a glass of water before he opened the discussion.

"Jimmy was awfully agitated when he came running back for us. He seemed convinced you were in real danger. But he wasn't too clear about this Zakoura fellow."

"I figured he might be the same guy you mentioned to me," Karen put in. "So I told them what you'd said about him."

Leigh nodded. She was looking at Jimmy and thinking that he didn't look the least bit sheepish about having sounded a false alarm, which probably meant that he still didn't see it that way. To him the danger had been real and, in spite of the outcome, remained undiminished. Like the odds of flipping a coin and winding up with tails—they were the same, no matter how often you played. Any encounter with Zakoura could end in disaster.

She turned to Hugh, trying to figure out how much she should tell them. After the incident today, she could hardly ignore the fact that Zakoura Kree might be as dangerous as Jimmy and Mary believed. And, if he was, she owed it to the team to share the limited knowledge she had. On the other hand, her dreams and her emotions were her own business, and she fully intended to keep it that way.

"I don't know much more than what Karen's already told you. All I can add is that I've seen him a couple of times. Once I caught him looking in the kitchen window of our camper."

"Ah," Paul said, as if he'd just made a major discovery. "The window shades."

Karen grinned and elbowed him in the ribs. "Now that's the kind of deductive leap that makes you so invaluable."

Everyone laughed, and as the tension in the group ebbed, Leigh started to relax. She actually did feel a little better now that they all knew about Zakoura.

"It worries me that you're the only one of us who's seen him," Hugh said, serious once again. "I wonder if it's purely coincidental or by design."

Leigh didn't have an answer, but she suspected that Zakoura wasn't the type to leave things to happenstance.

"So—can we cut to the chase here?" Alex demanded. "Was this guy where Jimmy said or not?"

"He was there." Leigh paused, pretending to need a sip of water. She knew she'd have to say more, but the words wouldn't come immediately. She was still having trouble sorting through their encounter, and trying to describe it on a nonemotional level was going to be difficult.

"I asked him what he wanted, but he didn't really answer me. He doesn't say much, and when he does, well...he doesn't make a lot of sense. I don't even know if it's possible to have a linear conversation with him."

"Then you just talked, and he didn't harm you in any way?" Hugh asked.

"No, he didn't harm me." But he had threatened her. She could still feel the pressure of the knife at her throat. She wondered why she didn't reveal that bit of information. Was it because, in spite of the menacing undertone, the words had been somehow strangely personal, even intimate? In choosing to omit them, she knew she was protecting him. And that made less sense than anything else.

"Well, I'm glad nothing happened and you're all right," Hugh said grimly. "But I think I'm going to ask Carlos what he knows about this guy."

Leigh thought of the policeman watching them from the doorway in Chinle. "I don't know if I'd trust anything Carlos has to say." The idea of letting him into their lives in even the smallest way made her stomach turn.

"I've gotta agree," Karen said. "The less we have to do with that man, the better."

"I'll be very circumspect."

Leigh didn't bother to argue the point. Once Hugh made a decision, it was easier to change the rotation of the earth than to change his mind.

Hugh pushed himself to his feet. "I think we can get in a couple more hours before the storm hits," he said, effectively ending the discussion.

When she heard him say "storm," Leigh looked up. She'd been too preoccupied before to notice the changing weather. Although the sky directly overhead was still clear, an army of bloated gray-green nimbus clouds was closing ranks over the far canyon rim. A slow chill crawled up her spine. They were in for another heavy thunderstorm.

She spent the remaining time working in the "condos," trying to ignore the uneasiness that had settled in the pit of her stomach with the weight of day-old fry bread. She didn't know if she'd ever want to go back to the cave. Jimmy seemed content to stay where they were, dividing his time between her and Alex and Paul, his wanderlust at least temporarily sated.

Two hours later, when they dropped him off at his hogan and returned to camp, the clouds had advanced, over-running the remainder of the sky. They hung in dark, heavy folds, like bunched curtains, obliterating the sun and producing an eerie green twilight that gave everything a sickly glow.

Hugh fixed a light dinner of pasta with broccoli in garlic and oil, Leigh's personal favorite. But she couldn't eat more than a couple of mouthfuls; her stomach was already filled with apprehension. Thunderstorms and Zakoura were irrevocably linked in her mind. She moved the food around on her plate, hoping no one would notice how little she ate. Where was Rowdy when you needed him?

By the time day finally passed into night, the clouds appeared to be throbbing, their blackened underbellies expanding and contracting, but still the storm held off. Leigh was grateful for the darkness. It was a relief from the unnatural cast of the light.

They played poker in the men's camper for a while, betting with sunflower seeds, but no one had much enthusiasm for the game. The air pressed against them, hot and still, stagnant beneath the cap of clouds. Wolves and coyotes, anticipating the storm, howled in a continuous chorus that set everyone's nerves on edge. Finally they decided to go to bed and get an early start in the morning. With any luck, they would sleep through the worst of the deluge.

Leigh didn't even bother getting into bed. She was far too restless and nervous to sleep. She sat at the table with her book and a glass of diet soda while Karen snored softly in the bedroom. She finished the first chapter and then had to reread it. She couldn't even keep the names of the few characters straight in her head.

Around 1:00 a.m. the wind picked up, suddenly gusting through the open kitchen window and sending the flimsy curtains flying. The air was refreshingly cool, but Leigh jumped to shut it out. The curtains had to stay in place. If Zakoura was out there tonight, she didn't want to know it. Confronting him in daylight was one thing. Peering into those enigmatic eyes at night was something else entirely.

The storm started all at once—rain, thunder, lightning—as if in uniform response to some celestial conductor. If possible, it was worse than the last storm had been. Each successive bolt of lightning seemed to be striking closer to the camper, brightening the interior like the noon sun. The acrid stench of ozone penetrated the closed windows.

Leigh sat at the table and tried to control the trembling that gripped her body. She'd never allowed her fears to get the better of her before, and she'd be damned if she would now. The storm was only a storm—a rip-roaring hell of a storm, but a storm just the same. And Zakoura was just an

Indian, perhaps from another tribe. No, she still wasn't buying that one.

When the explosion rocked the camper, she assured herself it was just a particularly concussive clap of thunder. Until she saw the flames through the window. They were close, way too close. The men's RV? She threw open the door, Zakoura temporarily forgotten. The other camper was bathed in the fierce glow of the fire, but was still unscathed. Twenty feet away, the Bronco burned like a huge metallic bonfire.

The rain was battling the blaze without success, hissing and sputtering on the superheated body of the truck like grease on a frying pan. The wind blew directly toward the campers, carrying the black smoke, with its detritus of charred vinyl and plastic. The smell seared Leigh's nostrils and choked off her breath.

Hugh flung open the door of the other RV and stumbled out into the storm, Alex and Paul right behind him, all of them barefoot. Karen squeezed into the doorway beside Leigh. For one frozen moment, they all stared at the fire as if trying to comprehend what they were seeing. Then Hugh started shouting orders.

"Get your shovels! We've gotta try to smother it! Move!"

Leigh was the first one back outside with her shovel. That was when she saw Zakoura. He was standing on the other side of the Bronco, his face pale and wavering in the flickering light, his black eyes as wild as the flames reflected in them. As her eyes met his, he backed away, fading quickly into the night.

Then everyone was running toward the Bronco, and she was running with them. The fire was all that mattered. They had to stop it before it could reach the RVs. For the next hour they shoveled dirt onto the burning carcass of the truck, oblivious of the scorching heat of the flames, oblivious of the storm that plastered their clothing to their skin and cascaded down their faces. Oblivious of the lightning that snapped from the sky to the ground like an endless series of whips. Oblivious of the screaming of exhausted muscles. And, during it all, Leigh kept remembering Zakoura's face through the flames.

Later, after they'd changed into dry clothing and collapsed around the table with a pot of Hugh's strong coffee, she finally had time to think. Why had Zakoura been there? Perhaps it was just coincidence that had put him at the scene of the explosion. But less than twenty-four hours earlier he had told her that she should fear him. Had he blown up the truck to scare her, to enforce that threat? Mary's warnings echoed in her head: "He is poison." "Stay away from him."

Paul was inhaling the steam from his coffee mug. "I don't think I'll ever get the smell of dying Bronco out of my nose."

"Lightning must have struck the gas tank," Alex said. "The damn explosion knocked me right out of bed."

"I can't imagine what else it could be, myself," Hugh agreed. "But I still want a good look at the remains in daylight."

Leigh knew she had to tell them that Zakoura had been there. They had a right to know. That explosion could easily have cost them their lives.

"The Indian was there—Zakoura," she said, feeling strangely as if she were betraying him. "I saw him near the truck. It was just for a second, and of course the fire was distorting everything..." She stopped herself in midsentence. She was making it sound as if she weren't sure she'd seen him, when there wasn't a doubt in her mind. What was wrong with her?

Hugh's brows drew together, sending a sharp crease up his forehead. "What was he doing?"

"Nothing. Nothing I could see, anyway."

"Was this after the explosion," Karen asked, "or before?"

"After. It was definitely after," she said, grasping at this single fact as if it provided Zakoura with an unimpeachable alibi. She wasn't at all surprised when Alex challenged it.

"What does that prove? Just because she didn't see him before, that doesn't mean he wasn't out there messing around. I don't like the sound of this. He may have been hoping to use the storm as a cover for sabotaging us. He could be some Navaho fanatic trying to protect the canyon."

Leigh had her own set of concerns about Zakoura's motives, but that wasn't one of them. "First of all, he's not Navaho. And if he was trying to scare us off, he could have given me an ultimatum either of those times I spoke to him. But he didn't."

Paul shook his head. "So you've become his champion now?" His voice was testy.

"I'm just trying to interject some reason here," she replied sharply, annoyed by the implication. "Jumping to conclusions won't do us any good." Reason—exactly what right did she have to talk about reason, when she was clearly having trouble separating the Zakoura of her dreams from the Zakoura who actually roamed the canyon and seemed quite capable of having blown up the Bronco?

Karen held up her hands. "Okay, guys, neutral corners. I think we're all a little overtired, and if we're not careful we're going to wind up saying things we don't mean."

"Let's just count ourselves lucky that it wasn't the generators that exploded," Hugh said, "or we might not even be here having this discussion."

Paul mumbled an apology, to which Leigh added hers. Alex made an attempt to restart the conversation along safer lines, but no one was inclined to pursue it. They finished the coffee immersed in their own thoughts.

Shortly after dawn, they trooped outside to look at the wreckage. The smell of burned fibers and plastics still muddied the air around it. The bottom of the truck, where the gas tank had been, was completely ripped open and gutted; the side with the gas tank door was gone, exposing the warped skeleton. Most of the roof had been blown off, as well, and the interior was covered in the shroud of dirt they'd shoveled to extinguish the blaze. The hood and grill of the truck were badly buckled, giving it the look of a snarling beast that had been flash-fried.

They were still congregated around the burned-out shell when Carlos drove up. He climbed out of his car and circled the Bronco before coming to stand beside Hugh.

"Morning," he said. "Damn shame about the fire."

Hugh nodded. "I imagine you could see it from town."

"Sure could. I came out to make sure you folks were all right."

"We're fine, thanks," Hugh said evenly.

Leigh wanted to ask the policeman why he'd waited four hours, if he was so concerned, but she kept her mouth shut.

Alex leaned closer to her and whispered, "Great response time." She almost laughed, in spite of the grimness of the situation.

"That was a bad storm last night." Carlos stooped to pick up a chunk of blackened metal that had fallen away from the rest of the charred hulk. He turned it over in his hand as if he were examining it for clues, then tossed it away. "Lightning hit her?"

"That's what we think," Hugh said. "There's no other logical explanation for a truck to explode like that."

"Unless someone tampered with it," Paul said.

Carlos turned to him. "Did you see something?"

Leigh decided it was time for her to show where her true allegiance lay. Besides, she wanted to see how Carlos would react. "I saw someone near the Bronco shortly after the explosion," she said, watching him carefully.

Although his eyes were hidden as usual behind sunglasses, she could see his eyebrows hitch upward in surprise. "Bad night for someone to be out. Can you describe this person?"

"Tall and muscular, long hair held back by a headband. Oh, and he was dressed strangely—just some kind of loincloth.

The policeman's jaw tightened. "I've never seen anyone like that around here." He laughed, an abrupt, humorless laugh. "Are you sure you didn't imagine him?"

Leigh ignored the question, refusing to dignify it with an answer. "I've been told his name is Zakoura Kree."

A muscle twitched in Carlos's cheek. "Zakoura Kree?" He repeated the name as if he were hearing it for the first time. Then he shrugged. "No, sorry."

Leigh had seen the policeman staring at Zakoura on that mesa two days ago. But she couldn't accuse him of lying, couldn't risk making him more of an enemy than he already was. Besides, although catching him in a lie would give her some satisfaction, it wouldn't help her learn what she really wanted to know. Why had he denied knowing Zakoura? She had detected neither fear nor anger in his response, just dissimulation.

"I would have thought you knew everyone who lives around here," Karen remarked.

"Apparently I don't," he said stiffly. "But I advise you not to make accusations against anyone, unless you have some concrete proof. Just seeing someone near the scene isn't enough. This is Navaho land. Our land. And we can come and go as we please."

"It was an observation," Leigh said, "not an accusation."

"Of course it was." Carlos turned to Hugh. "I'll have Bill Dijolei come out and search for any evidence of criminal intent. I wouldn't want you thinking we don't take arson and *observations* seriously around here."

"Thanks, we appreciate it. We're all pretty shook up by the whole thing."

"Understandable," Carlos replied, but his tone didn't soften any.

"Listen, I could use a ride back to Chinle, if you're headed that way. I need to make a couple of phone calls and see about getting us some new transportation."

"Always glad to help."

After the police car left with Hugh in the passenger seat, everyone agreed they needed a few hours' sleep. And with no way to reach the dig, there was little else to do.

Too tired to change, the women just kicked off their shoes and fell onto their beds.

"I don't get it," Karen said. "It always seemed to me that Carlos wanted us out of here. So wouldn't it be to his benefit to let us believe that the explosion was a vicious, premeditated attack instead of an act of nature?"

"I know. I was wondering the same thing. I expected him to tell us that Zakoura was a psycho or something. Really lay it on thick and make us want to run for our lives. But he denied even knowing him. In fact, he would have liked me to believe I'd imagined him altogether.''

"Unless maybe he put Zakoura up to planting the explosives, so he had to avoid establishing any link with him.''

"But if he planned that explosion to convince us our lives are in jeopardy, then why was he so quick to blame the lightning? No, there's something more going on here.''

"You're the only one of us who's seen or spoken to Zakoura. What's your take on him?''

Leigh had to think about her answer for a while. It was a question she'd been wrestling with ever since her first encounter with him, and she hadn't worked it out to her own satisfaction yet. The man who dominated her dreams was not the same man she'd dealt with in her waking hours. Clearly her subconscious had taken her physical attraction to him and rewritten his character and motivations to please her. As much as she liked the fiction, she knew she mustn't allow herself to be fooled by it. The real Zakoura Kree was stony and aloof, with unnerving eyes that barely concealed a raging inner turmoil.

"He's impossible to read,'' she said finally. "The only thing I'm sure of is that he scares me.'' She hesitated for a moment. When she spoke again, her voice had dropped almost to a whisper, as if she were afraid that he could hear her. "He doesn't strike me as the type to work for someone else. But I think he could be responsible for the explosion.'' There—she'd admitted her fear out loud. Maybe now her mind would be done with him. Done with weaving romantic fantasies around a man capable of arson or worse.

"I guess he's probably not just a townie having a little innocent fun at our expense, after all.'' Karen sighed. "So much for my intuition.'' She didn't say anything else, and after a few minutes her breathing slipped into the peaceful rhythm of sleep.

Leigh closed her eyes. She was physically exhausted and weary of thinking. All she wanted right now was sleep, a deep, dreamless sleep. But as soon as she drifted off, Zakoura was waiting for her, even as he'd been waiting for her in the canyon.

CHAPTER SEVEN

Zakoura kissed her with a gentle urgency that spoke of longing and denial, of crossing forbidden boundaries, aware of the consequences, yet unable to turn back. He caught her hand up in his, interlacing their fingers as if he would never let her go again. Though the only points of contact were with his mouth and hand, every nerve ending in her body was responding, straining toward him. She was standing at the edge of a fire, and all she wanted was to jump in and be consumed by it.

When he finally drew back from her, his lips curved upward in an unexpected smile. Leigh wondered if the smile was one of happiness, or if he was just amused by the effect he had upon her. She didn't know him well enough to be certain. The thought that he might find her desire for him nothing more than an entertainment embarrassed and angered her. As he leaned toward her again, she pulled her hand away and stood up. Was that disappointment she saw flash in his eyes, or merely surprise? There was so much she needed to know about this man. Wanting him was not enough.

She walked away from him, out to the lip of the cavern, her head barely clearing the low ceiling. Hundreds of feet below, the Chinle Wash wound through what appeared to be one of the smaller canyons that branched off Canyon de Chelly. Leigh didn't remember climbing up here; nor did she know if Zakoura had brought her there, or if he had been waiting for her. More important, she didn't remember having run from him this time.

When she turned around again, he was still seated, watching her with an expression of mild curiosity. He held his hand out to her. She shook her head. As long as she maintained her distance, her mind was clearer, and she intended to keep it that way until he'd answered some questions.

"I want to know why you left so suddenly the last time," she said.

"There are other considerations," he replied, as always managing to raise more questions than he answered.

"What other considerations?"

"Matters I cannot discuss with you."

Leigh knew she was in danger of losing her temper again, of letting emotion, rather than reason, choose her words. Nothing would be gained from that.

"Cannot, or will not?" she asked, her voice taut but even.

"The result is the same."

"Sometimes it's the intention that matters most."

"My intention is to keep you from harm."

She was surprised that he'd answered her so plainly. But exactly what was he trying to protect her from? If she was to believe Mary, Zakoura himself was the danger.

"You should not be visiting Mary Yazzi," he said, as if responding to her unspoken thoughts. His tone was conversational, his expression neutral. Coming from anyone else, the words might have sounded like nothing more than friendly advice. Coming from Zakoura, Leigh suspected, they were a command.

"Why shouldn't I?"

He stood, head bowed beneath the ceiling, and walked up to her. "Because you do not understand that the truth is a cloud reshaped by every passing breeze."

Leigh had always held the truth to be above subjective interpretation, immutable. If there was no pure truth, there was no solid basis for anything. The scientist in her recoiled at the idea. But this was not the time to debate the issue. There were more immediate questions to be answered.

"What harm are you trying to protect me from?"

"This I cannot tell you, since it is in the telling that the danger may begin."

Leigh felt as if she were lost in a maze of dead ends and paths that circled back upon themselves. There didn't seem to be any means of finding the answers she sought. Unless invoking Mary's name could provide some leverage.

"If you don't want me to believe Mary's truth," she said, "then you're going to have to tell me yours. Who are you, Zakoura?"

"I am what you see before you." He reached for her hand, and before she could object, he had brought it to his mouth and pressed his lips to the center of her palm. She stepped toward him, pulled as if he were the opposite pole of a powerful magnet. Another step and she would be lost, drawn into the warm circle of his arms, from which she would never be able to leave. The prospect was so appealing... hardly a choice at all... She pulled back with such force that she stumbled and nearly lost her balance.

"No... no, that's not good enough." Her voice trembled from the ferocity of her internal battle.

"Will you not let it be?" Zakoura asked, his dark eyes pleading with her. For a fraction of a second, she saw in them the mirror image of her own uncontrollable longing.

The power he had over her was not one-sided after all. The realization gave her strength.

"I can't. There are things I need to know."

"You make this impossible then." Although he tried to mask it, the frustration in his voice was palpable. It bounced off the sandstone walls, agitating the air around her.

"*I'm* not the one making it impossible." They were building an unbreachable wall between them, and even as she said the words she felt the loss of him as keenly as if it were a physical wound. But unless he could convince her otherwise, she was going to abide by Mary's truth. And Mary had told her to stay away.

The safest descent to the canyon floor seemed to be down a series of natural ledges that began six feet below the cavern on the right side. Without saying another word, and trying to forget how much she hated heights, she started toward it.

"Leigh, wait." Zakoura came after her. He grasped both of her hands and pressed them tightly against his chest. His eyes revealed a passion that was frightening in its intensity. "This should never have happened—this way I feel about you. I have spent so many days struggling with it, and yet I cannot bend it to my will. Nothing in my life has ever been as difficult for me. Coming to you, even in this way, is wrong." His voice was strained with emotion, as if he'd wrenched the words right out of his soul.

Though he hadn't answered her questions, he'd given her a glimpse inside his heart. And her own heart responded, melting her resolve. She was no more able to stop it than she would have been to stop the spring melting the snow. Surely Mary and Jimmy had never seen Zakoura this way, had never been allowed past the formidable facade he presented.

She freed one hand from his, and with her finger traced the arch of his brow, the thrust of his cheekbone, the hard line of his jaw. She raised herself up on her toes to kiss him, and he met her halfway, scooping her into his arms so that her feet skimmed the ground. Caught in his embrace, she felt that time itself had stopped. When he finally set her down and she opened her eyes again, she gasped. The canyon as she knew it was gone.

Zakoura was still holding her, and they were still standing in the same cavern. But below her a full and vital river ran where there had been only the dry wash. Instead of the stunted cottonwood, piñon and juniper she was accustomed to seeing, towering trees of every variety grew in a wild profusion of greens from the banks of the river to the base of the cliffs. Birds by the hundreds filled the air and perched in the trees, from tiny hummingbirds to raucous blue jays to eagles with enormous ink-black wings. As Leigh watched, a hawk swooped low over the river, and in a flash of sparkling water and sunlight caught a silvery fish in its talons. Leigh was amazed to find that she could discern each iridescent scale on the fish, each sleek feather on the hawk, each droplet of water suspended in the air like a perfect crystal.

Somehow everything seemed clearer, in sharper focus, as if the world she'd known had only been a copy of the original, and a poor one at that. Colors were denser now, more vivid, more radiant. Sounds were rounder, fuller, from the burbling of the river to the cracking of a branch. And the air was cleaner, softer, as if a storm had just swept through.

In spite of the magnificence around her, Leigh's heart was hammering with a primitive terror. What was this place? Where was the world she knew? She looked up at Zakoura, her senses too overloaded to speak. She saw with some relief that his face was placid, none of her fear or confusion reflected there. Gradually her pulse slowed from its wild gallop.

Zakoura smiled at her with a mixture of love and regret.

"You want so much to know about me. This is all I can give you. I pray you will not suffer for it. Only do not ask any questions. I will not answer them."

Questions were all she had. They ricocheted off the walls of her mind like buckshot in a metal bunker. But Zakoura's tone made it clear that he would not be swayed from his position. She'd already pushed him further than he'd ever intended to go. She didn't know the full extent of his powers—or of his tolerance. And she could hardly forget that he had brought her here, and that he was her only way back to the world she knew.

"It is not now that you need to fear," he said. "As we are, you are safe here."

Leigh had no basis for believing him, other than his admission that he cared for her. Surely attraction and desire were not the best tools for character assessment. But she wanted to trust him. She needed to.

With Zakoura leading the way, they climbed down the cliff to the canyon floor and made their way to the edge of the river, through thick groves of peach and plum trees. Leigh could smell the fruit ripening on the branches, and found she could easily distinguish one from the other, as if their individual scents were carried on different currents of the air.

When they reached the dirt path that bordered the river, Zakoura turned west, toward the canyon entrance. Leigh walked silently by his side, trying to ignore the fear that lay coiled stubbornly in the pit of her stomach, in spite of his assurance that she was safe. There was too much that was strange—the same and yet so different. Too much that made no sense to her.

Zakoura took up her hand, enclosing it in his as if he knew what she was thinking. She felt a warmth spread from his hand to hers, different from the sexual heat his touch usually engendered. It penetrated her skin and radiated throughout her body like the infusion of a drug. Within moments, the fear was diminished, tempered by a feeling of peace and well-being. She had no idea how he had brought about this transformation in her. She could only add the question to a growing list for which she was determined to find the answers someday.

No longer suppressed by fear, Leigh's innate curiosity quickly reasserted itself, and she was able to concentrate on the myriad bits of information she was receiving through senses that seemed enhanced and more finely honed.

They had come to a place where the canyon widened and large tracts of land had been cleared and cultivated. Leigh recognized cotton, alfalfa, beans and squash among the crops growing there. But there were other plants, as well, plants she hadn't seen before. In the distance, several men were at work in the fields. They were naked to the waist, which was unusual for the Navaho. What Leigh found even more curious was that she and Zakoura hadn't passed any hogans. Nor were there any in sight now. Where did the farmers live?

When they reached the junction where the smaller canyon joined Canyon de Chelly, she had her answer, and it stopped her dead in her tracks. Instead of the tumble-down structures and remnants of ruined walls she'd expected to find there, she saw a thriving village with a population of a hundred or more, the stone buildings meticulously maintained, the Anasazi inhabitants going about their daily business as she had so often imagined them.

Had Zakoura taken her into the past? Or was this the afterlife? Although she'd never believed in the possibility of time travel or in the idea of life after death, neither could she come up with a reasonable explanation for what she was experiencing.

As she stood there, trying to stabilize her already reeling senses, she wondered why Zakoura made no effort to hide her. He certainly wouldn't want anyone to see her if she wasn't supposed to be here. Yet he didn't seem concerned, or even particularly anxious to hurry her along. After a few minutes she understood why. Although she could see the Anasazi, apparently they couldn't see her. She felt like a tourist at some archaeological Disney World. But not even Walt himself could have done justice to this intensity of colors that made objects shine as if they were wet with pigment, this vibration of tones that made simple language resonate like music, or the buoyancy of this air as it filled the lungs. Even walking felt somehow different, smoother, as if there were less friction.

Leigh wasn't sure how long she stayed there watching. Time itself seemed slower, elongated. She was caught up in the rhythms of the village. People came and went, scaling the nearly sheer cliffside the way she would have climbed a staircase. Adults worked and children played; they gathered to talk and socialize in the large open plaza formed by the top of the kiva. There was a sense of purpose among them yet there was no urgency, no tension. Rather, there was an almost visible aura of harmony, like a web interconnecting all the members of the community.

As she watched, a young woman came to the edge of the plaza and, looking straight at her, waved. Leigh was startled. How was this one person able to see her? But then Zakoura raised his hand in return, and she realized she was as invisible as ever. It was Zakoura the girl was greeting. Leigh studied her with renewed interest and an unexpected stab of jealousy. She was young, seventeen or eighteen. Her hair, arranged in squash-blossom fashion at the sides of her face, was as glossy as an eagle's wings. Her only garment was a fringed apron tied around her tiny waist, emphasizing the fullness of her breasts and the perfect proportions of her legs. Even from this distance, Leigh could see the adoration gleaming in the girl's dark eyes. She glanced at Zakoura to judge his response and was inordinately pleased to find he was not looking up at his admirer, but off to the left, where half a dozen horses were grazing in a thicket. Something about the horses bothered Leigh, but for several minutes she didn't understand why. Then it hit her— there had been no horses in the Americas at the time of the Anasazi. Did this mean then, that Zakoura had not taken her into the past?

"Come with me," he said, holding his hand out to her. "There is a place I wish you to see, and a horse will make it easier." He led her toward the herd, stopping when they were still twenty yards away. The lead stallion lifted his head for a moment, alert to their arrival, then went back to eating. The other horses didn't even bother to look up.

Zakoura gestured for Leigh to stay where she was, and he continued on to the herd alone. Leigh couldn't see any brands on the horses, or rope halters. Nor were there any fences to enclose them. They seemed to be roaming freely.

As Zakoura entered their perimeter, the stallion looked up again. He started toward the man, head low and wary, ears drawn back. He didn't stop until he was barely a foot away.

Zakoura said something in a language Leigh had never heard before. The stallion snorted, eyes wild and nervous, pawing the ground in warning. He wasn't behaving like any domesticated horse Leigh had ever seen.

Moving practically in slow motion, Zakoura raised his hand, reached out and stroked the animal's muzzle. The stallion flinched, but didn't pull away. Then Zakoura did something extraordinary. He leaned toward the stallion and blew in his face. The horse seemed to calm almost immediately. Zakoura repeated the action. The horse nickered and stood absolutely still as Zakoura circled him, running his hand along the animal's body. Then, grabbing a hank of the mane, Zakoura swung up onto his back. Leigh stiffened, expecting the stallion to rear and buck, but he did neither. Leaving his herd behind without hesitation, he carried Zakoura to where she was waiting.

Zakoura helped her mount, then pulled himself up again, behind her. He folded his arms around her waist, sitting so close that his chest was pressed against her back and his thighs enclosed her hips. His breath was warm and feathery through her hair.

Using his legs to guide the horse, Zakoura urged him into a lope in the direction of the Chuska Mountains. Leigh had ridden only a few times in her life, and never bareback, but after the first few strides her body moved in a natural rhythm with the stallion, as if they were communicating on some basic level. She could feel the powerful muscles moving beneath her, yet the motion was so smooth, it was like Hollywood special effects. They seemed to be standing still while the mountains came toward *them.*

The plain they were crossing was not the harsh desert scrub on which she and the team had encamped; this land was covered in short, sturdy grass punctuated with wildflowers of blue, lavender and purple. Small groups of horses grazed leisurely upon it, few of them even bothering to look up as the stallion raced by. As in the canyon, there were no Navaho hogans. There were no sounds of car engines. No tire tracks cut through the sweep of green. And although Leigh should have been able to pick out Chinle's buildings in the distance, she saw no sign of the town at all.

This potent reminder that she was well beyond the world she'd known should have filled her with renewed apprehension, but the security of Zakoura's arms around her, the pleasure of having his body in close contact with hers, had transformed fear into wonder. Wherever they had traveled in time or space, she had no desire to be anywhere else.

When they reached the base of the Chuskas, they dismounted, and Zakoura led her into the mountains on foot. Leigh wasn't sure how long they hiked up through the steep, rocky passages. Her watch didn't seem to have any relationship to actual time here. It would indicate the passage of only five minutes, when she was certain that more than an hour had gone by. But, judging by the sun's progress toward the horizon, it was clear that substantial time passed before Zakoura finally stopped.

In spite of all the beauty Leigh had already encountered in this place, the scene before her had the power to make her gasp with delight. They were standing at the edge of a waterfall that hung like a sparkling curtain from an awning of rock high above them. At the base of the falls was a shimmering green lagoon, kept at a constant depth by an underground stream that siphoned off excess water. Exotic flowers in liquid, bright colors crowded the shores of the lagoon and spilled out of the crevices in the surrounding rocks and cliff faces, scenting the air with their subtle, individual perfumes.

When she looked up at Zakoura, he was smiling at her reaction, his ebony eyes glowing with an inner luminescence. This time she knew he wasn't mocking her. What she read in his eyes was genuine happiness, and the tenderness of love.

"This pleases you," he said.

Leigh nodded. There were no words adequate to describe this place, or how she felt being here with him. There were only questions, and these she could not ask.

Zakoura put his hand under her chin, tilting it so that he could look into her eyes. "If it were possible, all that I know would be yours to know."

"Someday," she said, hoping to wrest from him a concession that there would be an end to the mysteries, that eventually all her questions would be answered.

"No, you must not think that such a day will ever come." The sadness she'd seen before rose like a veil in his eyes, dimming their light, but he fought it back, and a smile returned to his face.

"We have this place, in this way, and it will be enough," he said, so fervently that it was clear he was trying to convince himself, as well as Leigh.

He guided her around the lagoon to an area where the rock wall was scooped out like a band shell and a thick, spongy layer of moss blanketed the ground. He slipped off his sandals, and Leigh untied her sneakers and pulled off her socks. They waded barefoot into the cool, shallow pool behind the curtain of water. A mist from the falls hung in the air, so fine that it didn't feel wet, but rather effervescent. Zakoura turned Leigh to face him and drew her into his arms.

"I know I'm not to ask any questions," she said, looking up at him. "But this is different." It had been nagging at her since they'd stopped at the cliff dwelling and, unlike her other questions, refused to be laid aside.

"What is this different question?" A smile pulled at his mouth, as if he already knew what was bothering her. Leigh felt the color rising in her cheeks, but she forced herself to continue anyway.

"That young woman who waved to you back at the village—are the two of you . . . were you . . . involved?"

"Involved? What a curious word to use. If you want to know if we were lovers, the answer is yes. Do I love her? Not in the sense that you mean."

Leigh was unreasonably troubled by his first response. She certainly hadn't assumed this man lived a life of celibacy. But the fire for him that she had seen in that girl's eyes was unmistakable. How could he dismiss it so easily?

"I think she's in love with you."

"She believes that she is. But she is young, and with time she will learn the difference. It is, as with all things, a matter of levels and growth."

Before Leigh could ask what he meant, he kissed her, taking the words from her lips and the questions from her mind. He kissed her softly at first, his mouth barely brushing hers. Then again, with increasing passion and intensity. And again. And again. He kissed her for an endless time, playing with her tongue and her teeth and her lips until she felt dizzy with need and her body ached for his touch. She ran her hands over the hard, ropy muscles of his arms, across his wide shoulders, through the long, thick hair that hung down his back, wanting to feel his hands on her and not knowing how to tell him.

When she couldn't stand it another moment, she drew her head back, away from him. "Zakoura." Her voice was as thin and breathless as if she'd just run six miles.

"Patience. There is much to be gained with patience," he whispered, covering her mouth with his again.

When he finally slid his hand down the small of her back, across her buttocks and up across her belly to her breasts, her knees threatened to give way. Her shirt, saturated from the moisture in the air, clung to her body like a second skin, and she could feel the roughness of Zakoura's palms abrading her swollen nipples as if she were naked.

He peeled off her wet clothing and threw it onto the edge of the lagoon. Then he untied the string at his waist and added his breechcloth to the pile. When Leigh took him in her hand, he was hard and wet with desire, and he shuddered at her touch. She drew his tongue into her mouth and sucked hungrily on it, wanting more of him inside her.

He moved his mouth to her breast and slid his fingers between her legs, and this time her knees did buckle under her. Zakoura caught her and, with his hands beneath her, lifted her, thrusting himself inside her in one smooth movement. A muted groan vibrating deep in her throat, Leigh curled her legs around his hips and clasped her arms around his neck. He held her like that, moving so slowly that her heart seemed to stop, waiting for the next exquisite stroke of pleasure to sweep through her body. When he suddenly withdrew from her, her senses were so confounded that all she could utter was a whimper of protest.

"A moment, my love." He picked her up in his arms and carried her out of the water, laying her on the carpet of moss. Moving between her legs, he entered her again, but with a swiftness and a force that took her breath away. In contrast with the slow gentleness of their earlier lovemaking, the intense power and heat of this coupling quickly sent her tumbling over the edge, wave after sweet wave of sensation crashing through her. Seconds later, Zakoura let out a cry that was close to anguish, and she felt the spasms of his body vibrating deep inside her, echoing and magnifying the turbulence already shaking her.

When at last they lay quietly in each other's arms, he kissed her again, softly, like the first time, and brushed the hair back from her face, murmuring words she didn't understand. She opened her eyes, intending to ask him what they meant, but Zakoura was no longer there. Instead, Karen was looming over her, eyebrows gathered together with concern.

CHAPTER EIGHT

"Are you all right?" Karen was studying her as if she were a science project gone awry.

Leigh was far from all right. She was like a diver who'd been submerged for too long and had surfaced too quickly. But she managed a nod anyway. The last thing she wanted was to have to explain to Karen what she'd just experienced. She was having enough trouble explaining it to herself. Her brain still felt as if it were caught in limbo, somewhere between reality and the dream. The dream. Was that all it was? The evidence seemed to confirm it, since here she was in bed. No waterfall, no green lagoon, no Zakoura. But she couldn't possibly have imagined all of that—the details had been too intricate, the emotional and physical reactions too powerful. No, her imagination just wasn't that good. But what if Zakoura was capable of manipulating her dreams? An ugly fear scuttled up her spine. What if he was creating this fantasy in her mind to blind her to the danger Mary had spoken of? Oh, Lord, she really was beginning to think like her mother.

"It's not like you to sleep through all the racket we've had around here," Karen was insisting. "Are you sure you're not sick?"

That was another thing—when had she ever outslept Karen? She'd always been a light sleeper. If the dogs yawned in the next room, she would awaken. Leigh dragged herself into a sitting position, hoping the movement would also drag her wild thoughts back into some kind of order.

"What racket?" she mumbled. It was difficult to form the words properly, as if someone actually *had* scrambled the circuitry in her brain while she slept.

"Hugh's been in and out a couple of times since we got back, and Paul's been in, too, looking for some receipts. Let me put it this way—neither one of them would last long working in a library."

"Being awake all night, then sleeping during the day, must have played havoc with the old circadian rhythms," Leigh said. There—that sounded much more coherent, even scientific. Why wasn't she buying it?

Apparently she was convincing enough, though, because Karen stopped hovering. "Hop in the shower and I'll get you a cup of coffee. Hugh's called a meeting in half an hour." She shook her head. "If he doesn't collapse first. He's working on pure adrenaline."

Leigh stumbled into the shower on rubbery legs that could have been on loan from someone else. But after a few minutes under the invariably cool, spitting spray, her head was clearer and her body was once again responding to commands from her brain. What she couldn't straighten out was her perspective on the dream. Other dreams dissolved upon waking, like fog before the sun. The fabric of this one was different, denser. It remained as crisply clear and realistic as it had been when she was asleep. For all its otherworldly quality, her memory of the dream was the same as her memory of other, more mundane events in her life. She had no explanation of the anomaly, but she suspected that any answer had to start with Zakoura Kree. The reactions he caused in people varied, but were almost always extreme. Mary hated him, Jimmy was terrified of him, Carlos denied even knowing him, and she was drawn to him beyond all reason. She had to find out who he was. Mary was wrong. Knowing that he was dangerous wasn't enough. She couldn't fight what she didn't understand.

Even as she was deciding that she had to speak to Mary again, Zakoura's warning came back to her, as clearly as if he were still standing beside her. "You should not be visiting Mary Yazzi."

"Well, that's just too bad, because that's exactly what I intend to do," she said fiercely, surprising herself when she realized she'd spoken out loud. She hoped Karen wasn't back with the coffee yet.

Once Leigh was dressed and bolstered by the caffeine, she went outside. A Jeep with police markings was parked near the other camper. Bill Dijolei was on his knees, sifting through the remains of the burned truck. Carlos had made good on his promise to investigate the cause of the fire, and more quickly than Leigh would ever have anticipated. Hugh must have caught a ride back with Dijolei, because Leigh didn't see any other vehicle around.

The others were waiting for her in order to start the meeting, but she figured that five more minutes wouldn't be critical. She wandered over to where Dijolei was working. She'd seen him at the excavation a couple of times. One of the youngest men on the police force, he'd joined eight months ago, following his graduation from the University of Arizona in Tucson. He'd studied some archaeology there and had a genuine appreciation for the work Leigh and the rest of the team were doing.

He stood when she came up beside him, his tall, lanky body unfolding like a figure in a pop-up book.

"Please don't stop. I don't want to interrupt your work."

Dijolei brushed the dirt from the knees of his pants. "That's okay, Dr. Morgan. I needed a break, I was getting pretty stiff."

"Have you found anything?"

"Nothing out of the ordinary. No signs of an explosive device, or even an accelerant. Of course, I'm not through yet."

Leigh realized she'd been holding her breath, afraid to hear that he'd found evidence of arson. Evidence that Mary was right about Zakoura. She didn't dare let her attraction to him cloud her objectivity. It was bad enough that on a subconscious level she already had. She needed to get at the truth, no matter how many fantasies it shattered.

"Did Sergeant Tsosie mention that I saw Zakoura Kree near the truck?"

"He told me you saw someone. That could have been the name. It wasn't one I was familiar with." The words had just the right ring of truth to them. It was the delivery that gave him away. His voice was tighter, and half an octave higher, than it had been two minutes earlier. And he was speaking too rapidly. No doubt Carlos had rehearsed him well—but he couldn't control the young man's nerves. To make matters worse, Dijolei kept on chattering, as if he were afraid of what she might ask him next. She almost felt sorry for him.

"I can't help wondering why anyone would have been out in that storm, unless they had a particular purpose in mind," she said when he finally paused to catch his breath.

"I couldn't say for sure, but I've known some guys who like to play chicken with lightning. A sort of Russian roulette." He chuckled unconvincingly.

"But Zakoura Kree isn't one of those guys?"

Dijolei shifted his weight from one foot to the other. "No, like I said, the name doesn't ring a bell."

Leigh wanted to tell him that he wasn't fooling her. The name most certainly did ring a bell, a whole slew of them, and every one of them a blaring alarm. But she decided to let him off the hook. He'd always been pleasant and courteous to them, and there was nothing to be gained by harassing him further. He might be nervous, but he wasn't stupid; he knew what was expected of him.

"I'll let you get back to work."

He tipped his hat to her and swallowed with a relief that sent his prominent Adam's apple bobbing up and down in his throat.

When Leigh walked into the men's camper, her colleagues were already assembled at the table. They all looked as if they needed a good night's sleep, but Hugh looked positively haggard. Half of the hair had pulled free of his ponytail and was hanging in scraggly locks around his face, his eyes were crisscrossed by a network of red veins, and the lines that bracketed his mouth were more deeply etched.

"Here's the situation," he said as soon as she took her seat. His voice was raspy, as if it, too, were worn-out. "The university won't be able to get another four-wheel drive to us for at least two days. We can't afford to lose the time, so I've made arrangements with Edward Bahe. He runs one of the tours through the canyon. He'll take us in and bring us out till the replacement arrives." He went on to detail his conversations with the university and the insurance company, then gave Paul an estimate of the additional expenses involved.

When he was finished, Alex suggested he grab a few hours sleep.

"Yeah, I think I will. Just keep an eye on Dijolei. Not that I don't trust the kid. But I want to get at the truth here, and I don't know how thorough he is."

Alex nodded. "I'll take care of it."

"I'm going to be spending the day going over the individual cassette journals," Paul said, "and I'll probably need to talk to each of you at some point. So please be available.''

Karen slammed her fist on the table. "Damn—there go my theater plans.''

Paul agreed to work on Leigh's cassettes first, so she was on her way to the Yazzi hogan by midafternoon. Neither Jimmy nor Rowdy came to escort her this time. Leigh didn't see any sign of the sheep, either, but she knew he sometimes drove them into the canyon to graze. It was probably just as well that he wasn't home. He'd been uncomfortable enough during her first visit. And this time she intended to tread less lightly, to press his grandmother for some real information. She knew she might even get booted out, though she hoped it wouldn't come to that.

She was almost halfway there when the dust devils sprang up. Initially she thought nothing of them. She'd seen plenty of these miniature tornados since her arrival here. They could irritate the eyes with the grit they threw off, and they wreaked havoc on a hairdo, but were otherwise harmless enough.

The first one was tiny, a little whirling dervish extending up only two feet from the ground. It twirled its dirt and other debris past Leigh like a ballerina pirouetting across a stage. She watched the performance, thinking that it looked like a living creature, thanks to the wind that powered it.

A moment after it was gone, two others appeared, forming right before her eyes. These columns were taller, reaching five feet in height. And more powerful. Along with dirt, dead leaves and stray feathers, Leigh could see chunks of dessicated brush and small tree limbs caught up in the swirling winds. She stopped where she was, waiting for them to blow out of her way. They headed west at first, following the path their predecessor had taken. But after several seconds they suddenly changed course and came marching straight toward her.

Leigh moved off to one side, and was uncommonly relieved when they whooshed on by her. She didn't understand why she should feel that way. Had she really expected them to follow her? Such nonsense. Yet she couldn't shake the uneasy feeling that had dropped over her like a trapper's net. She turned in a slow circle, not sure what she expected to find. Behind her in the distance, the campers crouched like alien vessels come to explore an ancient world. No one was moving around outside them. Ahead of her was the Yazzi hogan, as still and lifeless as the campers. She scanned the tops of the mesas and ridges. And then she remembered Zakoura, how he had looked standing atop the mesa after her first visit to Mary. He had seemed very like a god that evening, capable of creating dust devils, orchestrating her dreams, and worse, far worse. But he wasn't there now. At least not where she could see him. Leigh fought the panic rising in her. He was no god. He wasn't even a spirit. She was going to find out just what he was in short order, providing Mary was at home. Her brain was definitely turning to mush, and she was not going to help pummel it any longer. Resolutely squaring her shoulders, she continued on toward the hogan.

"You should not be visiting Mary Yazzi." The warning popped unbidden into her mind once again. Had he put it there, or was she simply remembering? And remembering what? A dream for goodness' sake! Yet the dreams were what complicated matters so badly. Who was the real Zakoura? The man who haunted her waking hours, or the man who held her in his arms while she slept? No matter how she tried, she couldn't reconcile the two. If he was indeed as dangerous as he appeared to be, why was she so bent on romanticizing him? And if he was somehow responsible for the content of her dreams, why was he so menacing outside of those dreams? Her brain felt as if the very neurons were hopelessly tangled around one another. She thought of what her mother would say when an issue was in dispute. "The truth lies somewhere in between." Maybe that was so, but when it came to Zakoura Kree, Leigh couldn't imagine what middle ground could exist between the two extremes.

She was still wrestling with the enigma he presented when a whole army of dust devils sprang up to her right. Within moments they had spun themselves between her and the hogan, where they remained, effectively obstructing her way. Leigh had never seen dust devils like these. They towered over her, dark and ominous, the winds at their vortex strong enough to be carrying rocks the size of baseballs, an entire bush, roots and all, even a large rabbit carcass. They twirled and twisted their debris before her like a team of synchronized jugglers. But there was nothing entertaining about them. They seemed instead to be mocking her, daring her to try to pass. As ridiculous as it sounded, she suspected that if she tried to walk around them, they would move to block her again. What was she saying—that Zakoura was pulling the strings on these marionettes of wind and dust? No, of course not. Yet she could imagine him watching and laughing as they foiled any attempts she made to outflank them.

She told herself to stop cowering, to stop letting her imagination rule her. This was no different from the haunted house of her childhood. The only thing to do was to march right through those dust devils. How much harm could they do, anyway? She put her hand over her eyes to protect them, leaving a narrow slit between two fingers so that she could see where she was going. But, to her chagrin, even as she plowed straight into the squalls, she found herself thinking that this frontal attack should certainly surprise Zakoura.

She tried to work her way between the rotating columns, but the winds tugged at her like desperate hands trying to stop her, and the grit stung her cheeks and bit at her bare arms and legs. Dust filled her nose and mouth, choking off her breath; bits of dirt as sharp as glass flew past the shield of her hand into her eyes. The thought crossed her mind that if the columns started moving they could keep her encircled and she could easily suffocate. More scared than defiant now, she lowered her head and battled her way past the whirling blades of wind. By the time she made it through their ranks, she was coughing and wheezing and her eyes were tearing so badly that everything was a blurry haze.

Behind her now, the devils were still spinning in place, as if they really had no interest in her. Not before and not now. Feeling relieved but extremely foolish, Leigh wiped her eyes, blinking until her vision cleared. She combed her hair with her fingers. When she'd made herself as presentable as she could, she started walking again. She glanced over her shoulder every few steps, and each time there were fewer of the devils. By the time she reached the hogan, every one of them had disappeared. It was as if they had never been there at all.

She found Mary in the shed, checking on the drying mutton. The elderly woman didn't seem surprised to see her. Nor did she seem pleased. She acknowledged Leigh's presence with a slight inclination of the head, then turned her attention back to the meat.

Leigh swallowed the greeting that came naturally to her lips. Instead, she said, "I've never seen so many dust devils at one time."

"Yes, so it is once in a great while." So Mary had seen them, too, and she didn't seem the least bit amazed by the number or severity of them. Leigh was relieved to hear that the whole incident hadn't been in her head, even if her imagination might have exaggerated it a bit.

"Does Jimmy have the sheep down in the canyon today?" she asked, trying to steer her thoughts back on track.

Finished with her inspection of the mutton, Mary picked up two flakes of hay from a large stack in the corner. "At his uncle's farm." She carried the hay past Leigh toward the corral.

"Can I help you with those?"

"They're not heavy."

Leigh trailed after her, feeling like a little kid trying to get in on her big brother's baseball game. "I hope you don't mind that I came to visit."

Mary dropped the hay over the railing, where the horse was already waiting, and turned to face Leigh, "It's not Jimmy you've come to see." She had an unnerving way of turning questions into statements.

"That's true." If Mary didn't like mincing words, Leigh would oblige her. "I need to speak to *you.*"

Opening a bin adjacent to the corral, Mary filled a small bucket with pellets and poured them into the feeding trough that hung on the other side of the fence.

"There's a pot of rabbitbrush tea on the stove. It will help clear the dust out of you."

Leigh followed her inside, wondering if the old woman had witnessed her ridiculous battle with the dust devils or had just noticed the veil of dirt that still clung to her. In any case, she was surprised that Mary had extended the invitation. She had anticipated far less of a welcome. Perhaps if they had met under other circumstances, without the specter of Zakoura looming between them, she and Mary could have become friends. It might not be too late even now. If Leigh didn't bring up his name this time, their relationship could take a new direction. Yet she knew that, as with the proverbial cat, her curiosity would eventually get the better of her. And in this instance, the information she sought might do more than satisfy her curiosity; it might save her sanity, and perhaps her life. Still, she regretted the loss of a friendship that would surely have enriched her.

After the brightness of the day, Leigh had difficulty seeing in the dim interior of the hogan. The sun was still too high to spotlight the room through the one window, as it had on her previous visit. As her eyes adjusted, she saw that everything looked the same, except that the rug that stretched across the loom was longer now, nearly completed. And there was no mutton stew simmering on the potbellied stove, just the kettle from which Mary was filling two ceramic mugs.

She handed one to Leigh and went to sit in her chair by the loom. Leigh decided it would be all right if she took one of the other chairs. She sipped the tea, which was different but had a nice tang, and wondered how to begin. In spite of all her plans to come here and confront Mary, she hadn't figured out exactly what she would say.

Mary broke the silence first. "Soon you will finish your work here and you will leave." It sounded like a simple statement of fact, but beneath the words Leigh heard cautionary advice.

"Yes, we will be leaving. But that won't silence the questions that plague me."

"The questions are all right. They may prick at your mind like needles, but they will not harm you. It is the answers you must forget about having. They are not for you."

"Mrs. Yazzi, I'm a scientist. For me the answers matter most."

Mary wagged her head at Leigh as if she were a recalcitrant student and drank her tea, the steam rising in a cloud around her face.

Leigh wasn't going to be put off that easily. Since Mary was far too canny for cajolery to work, she chose a direct attack instead. "Who is Zakoura Kree? Is he some kind of spirit or demigod that you can't talk about?" While she didn't believe in such entities, perhaps Mary did.

To her surprise, Mary laughed. It was a brief, gravelly laugh, heavy with sarcasm. She shook her head, and when she spoke, the sarcasm was peppered with a searing bitterness. "You make both too much and too little of him. He is no skinwalker, and he is surely no god."

Leigh knew she should be glad to have elicited even this much from the older woman. But she was mostly perplexed. She could understand all the secrecy surrounding Zakoura if the Navaho considered him a supernatural presence. But if they considered him to be nothing more than a man, why was everyone so damned tight-lipped about him?

"It's pretty clear that you don't like Zakoura," she said, hoping that anger might cause Mary to inadvertently divulge more than she intended to. "So I don't understand why you protect him."

"Protect him!" Mary came out of her seat so abruptly that the mug in her hand caught the edge of the weaving frame. It flew out of her fingers, crashing onto the hard dirt floor, tea and fragments of pottery scattering in all directions. Mary seemed oblivious of the mess. She stood before Leigh, her cheeks flushed and blotchy, her sturdy body trembling with an impotent rage.

"I do not protect him."

Leigh knew she should back off, but if she was ever going to learn anything, she had to press Mary now. "Then why won't you tell me who he is?"

Mary didn't respond immediately. Her gorge was working behind the cascade of wrinkled flesh as if she were strangling on the words that were rising in it.

"A murderer!" she choked out finally. "A murderer is what he is!" Her body was still quaking so violently that Leigh was suddenly sorry for the high-pressure tactics she'd used. Had she anticipated this violent a reaction, she never would have goaded her so.

She took Mary's arm and led her back to the chair, supporting her as she collapsed onto it. Perspiration was beaded on Mary's upper lip, and the flush was gone from her cheeks, leaving them an unhealthy gray. Leigh stayed at her side until she was breathing more easily.

"Forgive me, Mrs. Yazzi," she murmured. "I certainly didn't intend to upset you like that." Leigh was mortified that she had caused Mary such distress. Answers were important, but not at the expense of the elderly woman's health.

"You just rest there. If it's okay with you, I'll clean up the mess."

Mary didn't protest, so Leigh started picking up the pieces of the mug. The tea had already soaked into the ground, leaving a wet stain to mark where it had been. As she worked, she thought about what Mary had said. There was no doubt that she believed Zakoura was a murderer. But when someone was wanted for murder, his name and picture were typically splashed across newspapers and television screens. Wanted posters hung on post office walls, and an effort was made to alert the public so that the perpetrator could be identified and apprehended. The secrecy surrounding Zakoura made even less sense in that context.

Why would Carlos and Bill Dijolei deny even knowing his name? If he was indeed guilty of murder, it was no ordinary murder.

Once she was satisfied that she'd found every last fragment of the mug, she put the pieces on the table. She intended to find one in Chinle to replace it.

To her immense relief, Mary appeared completely recovered. Leigh knelt down next to her chair. Hoping it would not be considered offensive, she put her hand over the older woman's.

"Thank you for the tea. And I really do appreciate your speaking with me."

Mary looked directly into Leigh's eyes. "Does he frighten you?"

Leigh was taken aback for a moment by the unexpected question. She certainly owed Mary some answers of her own, but she wasn't entirely sure how to respond. While she was no longer afraid of the Zakoura who came to her in dreams, the man whom she'd last seen through the flames of the Bronco definitely chilled her blood. She decided it wouldn't be dishonest if she kept her dreams to herself and revealed only her conscious feelings.

"Yes, he frightens me."

Mary's head bobbed gently as she digested this information. "Yet you believe you love him?"

This question was even harder. Leigh supposed that she did love the man her subconscious had created. And the other? Although he scared her, she couldn't deny her attraction to him. Probably just the emotions from her dreams seeping into her waking mind. What other explanation could there be for the complicated way she felt when she was near him?

"I don't know," she admitted finally.

"Then close your heart to him if you can." Leigh felt Mary's fingers contract into a fist beneath her hand. "Perhaps you will not believe this, but I have sympathy for you. I understand better than you know."

Leigh wondered if she dared ask one last question. She didn't want to upset Mary again, but since it was she who had brought up Zakoura's name this time... Leigh decided to give it a try. If Mary balked or showed the slightest sign of agitation, she would just let it go. As it was, Leigh was almost embarrassed to say the words.

"Is Zakoura...is he Anasazi?" It was a good thing none of her colleagues were in the room, or they'd order a straitjacket for her Federal Express. While no one actually knew how or why the Anasazi had disappeared, there was no disagreement about the fact that they had. Several hundred years ago, they'd simply ceased to exist. And although it flew in the face of every scientific principle she held dear, Leigh couldn't forget what she'd seen in that dream. When she'd demanded that Zakoura tell her who he was, he'd shown her the Anasazi village.

No anger contorted Mary's face this time. Rather, an eerie, humorless smile curved her lips. "You are the scientist, Dr. Morgan. How on earth could that be?"

How on earth could she even be giving serious credence to a preposterous notion contained in a dream? Leigh sighed in frustration. "I don't know. I'm beginning to think there's a lot—" She stopped herself in midsentence when a car door slammed shut outside.

If Mary heard it, she didn't react. A moment later, there was a loud rap on the door, and a male voice called out in Navaho. Mary responded. The door opened, and Carlos Tsosie walked in. He was visibly surprised by the scene that greeted him, and he made no attempt to hide his displeasure.

"Dr. Morgan," he said curtly.

Leigh rose to her feet. "Sergeant."

Mary asked him a question in Navaho, but Carlos answered her in English. "This isn't a social call. I want Dr. Morgan to hear what I have to say. A tourist by the name of Jeremy Gates was reported missing as of 7:00 p.m. yesterday."

CHAPTER NINE

"A murderer?" Alex raised one eyebrow incredulously. "Come on, don't you think maybe she was overstating the case?"

Leigh had just finished relating what Mary had said about Zakoura Kree. "I suppose it's possible. She was so upset, she might have been letting her emotions distort the facts." Barely two hours had gone by, and already Leigh was second-guessing what she'd heard. And she knew damned well why! She didn't want to believe that the man she made love to in her dreams was capable of murder. She still hadn't learned to separate the fictitious Zakoura from the man of flesh and blood.

"It's probably just some tribal feud that's been blown way out of proportion over the years," Paul said. "Let's face it—if this Zakoura character had really killed someone, don't you think Carlos would at least know who he is?"

"I think maybe he does," Leigh said. She'd never told them about that strange triangle—Carlos watching Zakoura as he stood atop the mesa watching her.

"Then why would he deny knowing him? That doesn't make any sense." Paul's voice was rising with frustration, the way it did when he was missing pertinent information for the daybook.

"I haven't figured that out yet."

"Until we do, I think it would be wise to give our mysterious friend a wide berth," Hugh said. "That applies to you, especially, Leigh, since he seems to be avoiding the rest of us anyway."

Leigh nodded. There was no sense in arguing, although she knew that following Hugh's advice would be close to impossible. If Zakoura wanted to see her, he would find a way. He always seemed to know where she was. She didn't know how she could avoid him, short of locking herself inside the camper all day. And somehow she doubted even that would work. Besides, she had no intention of spending the rest of her time here hiding from this man. She just wished she could silence the nagging little voice in her head that kept asking her if she really would avoid him if she could.

"What do you all say to getting some sleep?" Hugh said, trying to stifle a yawn. "Dawn comes around pretty early."

Although he had originally arranged for Edward Bahe to pick them up at eight, the missing tourist had nullified those plans. Anyone with a four-wheel drive had been pressed into the search. The Navaho guide had stopped by earlier to explain the problem. He could drive them into the canyon, provided they were ready to go when the search began, at sunup, and could wait until his dinner break to be driven back to camp. He'd also passed on Sergeant Tsosie's request that they participate in the search by checking out the area of the canyon around the excavation site. Hugh had agreed immediately, but after Bahe left he'd muttered about the way events were conspiring to steal what little time they had left there. They all felt pretty much the same way, but humanitarian concerns took precedence over professional ones. They would just have to work harder, stay later at the dig each day, and hope that nothing else came along to further sabotage their efforts.

The morning was a dense, dreary gray, more like twilight than dawn when Bahe pulled up in his truck. They had to take it on faith that the sun had risen, because they couldn't see it behind the low ceiling of clouds that ran seamlessly from horizon to horizon. It was as if there were no sun, as if the night had simply worn out and faded. The bleakness only served to intensify the ominous feeling that had worked its way deep into the marrow of Leigh's bones since she'd heard about the missing Jeremy Gates. There were probably half a dozen legitimate explanations for the young man's disappearance, but she kept coming back to the one that involved Zakoura. If he was a murderer, as Mary claimed, who had he killed in the past? And could this tourist have been his most recent victim?

Bahe gave each of them a printed description of Gates and reminded them to keep an eye out for any sign of him along the way. Hugh climbed into the cab of the pickup, and Leigh and the others took seats in the open bed of the truck, where the tourists usually sat. As they drove toward the canyon entrance, Leigh counted so many police and private vehicles fanning out on the rim or heading toward the canyon that it appeared as if the entire reservation had joined in the search.

Over the microphone he used to narrate his tours, Bahe told them what he knew about the twenty-one-year-old Gates. His amplified voice had the hollow, metallic quality of a character in a bad science-fiction film.

"Gates and two friends've been bumming around the West for the summer. Sort of a postgraduate fling. Last time they saw him was day before yesterday, when he left the motel a couple of hours before dark for his daily run. According to these two, he never runs for more than an hour, hour and a quarter tops. So when it was closing in on two and a half and the sun was on its way to setting, they started getting a little edgy. Soon they had themselves a major case of the what-ifs. You know—what if he sprained an ankle or broke a leg? What if he was lying out here, easy prey for a pack of wolves or a rattlesnake? So they hopped in their car and started looking for him. The only trouble was, they didn't even know the route he'd taken. They'd seen him head out in the general direction of the canyon, but he never told them if he intended to stay on the rim or go down into the canyon itself. By the time the sun went down they hadn't found a trace of him, so they headed for the police. Tsosie and his men searched all day yesterday. No success. Not a clue. That's when they called in everyone with a truck."

Leigh was glad when Bahe hung up his microphone. The sound of that barely human voice was setting her nerves on edge. To make matters worse, when they entered the canyon they found it shrouded in a fog so thick it felt as if they were driving along the bottom of a lake. All Leigh could see of the world was the bed of the truck directly beneath her, and the faint outline of Alex, who was seated beside her. Even the cab had disappeared. Gates could be lying on the ground two feet away and they'd never know it. As Bahe slowed the truck to a crawl, Leigh could imagine Hugh gnashing his teeth at this latest obstacle.

"Great day for a search." Karen's disembodied voice floated to her on the currents of the opaque haze. "Do you think they'll ever find him?"

"Oh, they probably will." Paul's voice came from the same direction. "The real question is whether he'll be alive or not."

Leigh felt as if she were listening to a conversation among ghosts.

"The fact that they haven't found a body is a good sign." Alex's voice. "Gates may just have injured himself and one of the Navaho took him in. They don't have phones, so he wouldn't have any way of calling his friends. You'll see—he's going to turn up okay."

Leigh wished she could share his optimism. But as she peered into the impenetrable, swirling fog, she became increasingly certain of only one thing—Zakoura was out there. And he was close by.

"Listen up, guys." Hugh's disgruntled voice rattled through the microphone. "Because of this dandy weather, we're going to have to do some extra legwork. Alex and Paul, we'll be dropping you off just past the turnoff to Monument Canyon, assuming we can *see* the turnoff. You're to cover the area between there and the excavation."

"He's got to be kidding," Paul grumbled. "We're not going to find the guy unless we accidentally trip over him. And the way our luck's been going, tomorrow you'll be out here searching for us."

"I'll be taking the section of the canyon west of the dig," Hugh continued. "Leigh and Karen will cover the area between us."

It was nearly an hour later when Bahe dropped off the women. He'd had to stop several times along the way in order to reorient himself. He'd get out of the truck and walk in widening circles around it until he could make out a landmark he knew. Then he'd climb back in and they'd continue on their way.

Bahe gave Leigh and Karen each a walkie-talkie, as he had the others. Hugh reminded them that the meeting place would be directly below the excavation. No one was to attempt the climb unless the fog cleared. Then the pickup disappeared behind the curtain of clouds, and Leigh could hear the eerie theme music from "The Twilight Zone" playing in her head.

Karen, who was far too practical to be associating the fog with anything supernatural, suggested they each take a side of the wash. They would walk to the opposite canyon walls and back to the middle, meeting there after each pass so that they didn't lose track of one another. Leigh agreed, although the thought of wandering blindly through the canyon alone made her stomach knot with anxiety. She wasn't afraid of becoming lost. In spite of Paul's comment earlier, there wasn't much chance of that happening. But she couldn't ignore the certainty growing in her mind that Zakoura was out there waiting for her. While even Hugh had advised them to be wary of him, Karen would probably consider her concern overblown, maybe even paranoid. Three months ago, Leigh would have agreed. She chose not to say anything.

She walked toward the base of the cliff, trying to maintain a straight line and scan the ground as she went. After she'd gone a few yards, she looked back. Karen was no longer visible. There was nothing in front of her, nothing behind her. Nothing but the obliterating fog. She gripped the walkie-talkie more tightly in her hand.

With every step, the fog shifted and eddied around her. Its moist tendrils brushed against her face and her bare arms like the horrible silk of a cobweb. She tried to shake herself free of it, but the more she moved, the more she felt entangled in its intricate, deadly threads. A cold sweat broke on her skin, and it took all of her concentration to beat back the fear. This was fog, nothing more. Nothing supernatural. Just as the dust devils had been due to nothing more than the peculiarity of the wind, the fog, too, was a natural product of the weather. Zakoura wasn't responsible for either of them. But what she couldn't rationalize away was the notion that he might be using the heavy cover of the fog for his own purposes.

She forced herself to continue on. One step. Then another. At the rate she was going, Karen would be standing at the wash, wondering what happened to her. With visibility at zero and her head bent to examine the ground for clues, she almost walked straight into the base of the cliff before she was able to see it looming a few inches away. After that, she kept one hand outstretched in front of her as a probe.

She was on her way back toward Karen and the center of the canyon for the third time when she saw the first rift in the fog. It was off to her right. A gauzy patch of sky and ground appeared for a moment before the swirling clouds sealed off the view again. Other translucent windows opened briefly after that, granting her a glimpse of cottonwood tree, a section of muddy wash. It seemed as if the fog might actually be burning off.

"Leigh."

She stopped and jerked her head up, her heart thudding in her throat. Zakoura. There was no doubt in her mind. She tried to determine the direction his voice was coming from, but the fog was still dense enough to act like a baffle, redirecting the sound waves. Her intuition had been right when she'd sensed that he was nearby. Apparently he'd just been waiting until she was alone.

"Leigh." His voice struck divergent chords inside her. Survival instinct told her to run. Something else, just as primal, made her want to stay.

"Leigh." Strong and demanding, and nearer. She spun around, looking for him, but the fog had closed in again. The muscles in her legs twitched with indecision. She couldn't run from him—she had no idea where he was. She waited, hoping that if he called to her again she'd be able to home in on his position. A minute passed. Then two. Her pulse was as loud in her ears as the surf crashing on breakers. Nothing happened. When the walkie-talkie suddenly crackled to life in her hand, she jumped as if she'd received a jolt from a high-voltage line.

"Leigh? Are you okay?" Karen's voice was slightly garbled, like an announcement at a train station.

It took Leigh a moment to gather her wits and press the right button so that she could answer. "Yes, yes, I'm okay. I'm fine."

"Then where the hell are you?"

"I…I thought I heard someone. I went to check it out." She hoped the static masked the agitation in her voice.

"Well?"

"It was just my imagination, I guess. I'll be with you in a minute." She no longer had any choice but to move on. She reminded herself that Karen wasn't very far away, and that she had the walkie-talkie if she had to call for help. But before she'd gone ten feet, the fog in front of her dissipated and Zakoura stood there, blocking her path. Swathed in the opalescent haze, he appeared almost mythic. For a moment her heart lurched toward him as the memory of loving him swept through her. But the dark eyes that locked on hers were grim and forbidding, reminding her that she was not dreaming now. The man who stood before her was the man Mary hated, the one she called "murderer." Fear stampeded through her, trampling every other emotion in its path. She turned and ran.

"Leigh, no!" he called after her. "I must speak with you!"

She didn't know which way she was running, except that it was away from Zakoura, which also meant that it was away from the wash and Karen. She couldn't tell if he was following her. Her ears were too full of the sounds of her own footsteps and labored breathing. Remembering the walkie-talkie, she hit the transmit button. But before she could say anything, she ran smack into Carlos's arms.

"Whoa, there." He tried to hold on to her until she was steady on her feet, but she pulled away, stumbling back from him. As she stood there, trying to catch her breath and compose her racing thoughts, she noticed how calm Carlos was. He didn't seem at all startled by their near collision. It was almost as if he'd expected her to come flying in his direction. As if he'd been keeping tabs on her all morning. A ridiculous amount of effort to expend, considering the fog. How could she possibly be worth that much attention? Unless, of course, she was incidental, and Zakoura was his real quarry.

"That's not the recommended speed for conducting a search," Carlos said. Although his tone was amiable enough, his face was expressionless, and his eyes were as flat and unreadable as the mirrored sunglasses perched atop his head.

She was about to thank him for that bit of widsom when Karen's static-filled voice issued from the walkie-talkie again. Leigh explained that she'd quite literally bumped into Sergeant Tsosie and that she'd be along shortly.

"I'll let you get on with your search," Carlos said when she'd signed off.

As much as Leigh wanted to get away from the Navaho cop, there were a few things bothering her, and she didn't intend to let him off the hook that easily.

"Aren't you even going to ask me what I was running from?" That was the first question she'd have expected, especially from a police officer. The fact that he hadn't asked it told her that he already knew the answer. And, what's more, that he didn't want Zakoura's name brought up.

Carlos's face tightened as if a drawstring had been pulled, but he managed to keep his voice even. "There are many things in this place that can frighten those who don't belong here."

"Such as Zakoura Kree?"

"If you say so. As I've told you, I don't know this person."

Leigh couldn't allow the patent lie to continue to go unchallenged. She wanted to tell him that she'd seen him staring at Zakoura on top of the mesa the day she'd visited Mary, but she knew that Carlos could simply say that he didn't know who was standing up there or that he'd only been watching the flight of an eagle. She decided instead to question his abilities as an officer of the law. Sending Hugh a silent apology, she plunged ahead.

"I have to admit that it surprises me to hear you say that. According to Mary Yazzi, the man's guilty of murder. Of course, it's possible you know him under a different name." She added the last to soften the impact of her accusation. After all, she didn't want to burn all their bridges.

Carlos laughed. It was a short, brutal laugh. "Mary Yazzi is an old woman, and she's had a rough life. These days she spends as much time weaving fantasies as she does weaving her rugs."

Although there hadn't been the slightest hesitation in his reply, Leigh didn't buy it for a minute. Mary Yazzi might be old and scarred by painful memories, but she still dwelt in the real world, not in one of her own making.

"If Zakoura is her creation, then who is this man I keep seeing?"

Carlos's upper lip curled derisively. "Perhaps he's a skinwalker—a spirit angered by your presence in this sacred place."

"In that case, I guess I'd better try to stay out of his way," Leigh said with exaggerated horror, to let Carlos know she wasn't taken in by his story.

"I wouldn't dismiss the possibility too lightly, Dr. Morgan. Such entities are often unforgiving."

"I imagine they are, Sergeant. Thanks for the advice." She didn't know how much of Carlos's warning was based on personal beliefs and how much was actually a veiled threat, but she decided there was nothing to be gained by goading him further.

By the time she finished searching her section of the canyon, it was close to noon and the fog had evaporated except for a few pockets hidden in the deeper crevices of the cliffs. Within half an hour, the team had reassembled. Alex and Paul were the only ones with news, and it wasn't good. They'd come across two other search parties, and the word up and down the canyon was that there'd been no sign yet of Jeremy Gates.

Hugh hurried them through lunch. With Bahe due to return at 6:30, they had barely six hours, and far too much work to catch up on. Leigh felt as if the peanut-butter-and-jelly sandwich she'd gulped down was permanently lodged in her throat. But she couldn't place the entire blame on the speed with which she'd eaten it. Her encounters with Zakoura and Carlos had as much to do with her indigestion as anything else. What was it that Zakoura had wanted to say to her? In the panic of the moment, it hadn't seemed important, but now the question rubbed at her mind like a pebble caught in her shoe. Her hands wielded the trowel, chose the proper size brushes, tagged the fragments of pottery by rote. But her mind was stuck on the image of Zakoura glaring at her through the mist. She didn't even notice Hugh standing over her until he started to speak.

"Alex, Paul—come over here, guys." He was grinning so broadly that his eyes were scrunched into slits.

"What's up?" Leigh stood, brushing the loose dirt from her hands. Alex and Paul came up to the wall remnant that separated them from Leigh's "apartment."

"We may just have found us a treasure trove." Hugh was exuberant, his voice booming off the cavern walls. He was acting like a child who's just discovered that Christmas will be coming twice this year. "Karen unearthed a couple of magnificent necklaces, shell and lignite, completely intact. But, more importantly, she found what appears to be a shaman's rattle, also in great shape. Wait till you see it." His enthusiasm was palpable. "Who knows what else is down there? One thing's for certain, the kiva's got to be completely excavated before the end of the summer. So, here's the deal—I want Leigh to help us down there. You guys can handle the condos. Any objections?"

Alex shook his head.

Paul chuckled. "None from me. Ever since that little cave-in in Mexico, I prefer to work aboveground, thank you.

Hugh turned to Leigh. "How about you?"

"I'll have my stuff packed up in a minute." She was glad for the chance to join them. Glad that professional jealousy had never been an issue for their team, as she'd heard it often could be. Working in the kiva with the prospect of significant discoveries might even be enough to divert her thoughts from Zakoura.

Hugh helped her repack her equipment, then grabbed up the knapsack before she had a chance to close it and started back toward the kiva. He went down the ladder first, moving with the agility and speed of a fireman sliding down a pole. Leigh, who'd been in the ceremonial chamber only twice, climbed down more cautiously. When her head came level with the entrance, she looked up once more. She could see Paul's curly head bent over his work again. Alex was somewhere behind him. A hawk swooped low into the canyon, attracting her attention. It looped a figure eight, then soared upward again, drawing her eye to a wide fissure in the cliff above the scooped out cavern. Within the shadows of that breach, Zakoura stood looking back at her.

Leigh fell into bed exhausted, but she was still unable to sleep. The day had been both physically and emotionally draining. Every time she shut her eyes she saw Zakoura, remembered his words. And she thought of Jeremy Gates, still missing. Although she'd never met Gates, it was easy for her to identify with him. They were both strangers in an alien place.

After two days of searching, not a single clue had turned up. The search party had visited each little farm in the canyon and spoken with the Navaho who lived there, as well as those who lived on the rim within a ten-mile radius. It was as if the young man had simply vanished off the face of the earth. The police promised to widen the search area, but they were no longer holding out much hope. Their official comment was that Gates might have chosen to disappear; he might have run off on purpose. They'd seen it happen before. His friends refused to consider that possibility. Jeremy had a promising future, a good home life, not a problem in the world. Why would he just run off into the night, leaving all of his belongings behind?

The more Leigh thought about Jeremy Gates, the more she thought about Zakoura. For some reason she couldn't understand, the two seemed inextricably tied together in her mind. Maybe it was because Zakoura had come to her during the search for Gates. Maybe it had to do with the tone of his voice when he'd said he had to speak to her. In her fear, could she have mistaken urgency for anger?

Hours later, when she was finally drifting along the currents of sleep, his voice drew her back to wakefulness.

"Leigh, I must speak to you." The sounds had been in her head, yet she hadn't dreamed them. They had, in fact, awakened her.

"Leigh, I must speak to you." His voice again, in the same imperative tone she remembered from their encounter. The fine hair at her nape stood straight out, as if she'd been plunged into freezing water. Zakoura was outside, waiting for her. She didn't know how she'd come by this knowledge, but even in the most skeptical recesses of her mind she didn't harbor any doubts. The chill within her deepened. There had to be a logical explanation. Maybe it was telepathy. She'd read about scientific experiments that validated the concept, hadn't she? That had to be the answer. Zakoura scared her enough already. She was not going to exacerbate the problem by attributing supernatural powers to him. Thinking along rational lines seemed to blunt the fear somewhat, and she was able to weigh the possible reasons Zakoura had come to her. On the chance that it might have to do with Gates's disappearance, she decided she ought to go out and speak with him. After all, if it were she who were missing, lying out there helpless and alone, she would hope someone else would do as much for her. The thought rekindled her old stubborn courage.

She slipped on the sandals that doubled as slippers and considered waking Karen to go with her. But she quickly discarded the idea. Zakoura never approached her unless she was alone. Tonight would be no exception.

She'd worn a long T-shirt to bed, and since the night had remained warm, she didn't bother changing. As she let herself out of the camper, she tried to ignore the nagging presentiment that she could be making the biggest mistake of her life. Based on nothing but the hope of securing information, she might be placing herself in terrible jeopardy. She vowed not to go more than a few yards from the RV. Karen might not hear her scream, but the men were not heavy sleepers. Hesitantly she stepped outside.

The night surprised her. Some omnipotent hand had wiped the cloud and fog from the sky and embroidered it with thousands of stars in an intricate pattern of celestial needlepoint. For Leigh, the density of stars was more strange than beautiful, hinting at realms beyond science, and possibilities of which even her mother had never dreamed. She shook her head as if that would clear it of such nonsense. This was not the time to be falling off the scientific wagon.

Along with the stars, the moon provided enough light for her to make her way around to the back of the camper. As she rounded the corner, her courage wobbled slightly, but she took a deep breath and went on.

Zakoura was waiting for her, as she'd known he would be. And, as always, she was ambushed by her crazy attraction to him. Fear and desire—she felt as if she were tied to two horses that were pulling her in opposite directions. In spite of her confusion, she knew that only one of the emotions made sense. There was no basis for the yearning he ignited in her, other than the whimsy of her dreams. Fear of a killer who was above or beyond the law was understandable, though, and quite sane. But she'd never believed in capitulating to fear. Somehow she had to walk the tightrope between the desire and the danger. Jeremy Gates's life could be hanging in the balance.

Zakoura came toward her. Although it took all her strength to uproot her feet from where she stood, she managed several trembling steps to close the distance between them. Telepathy might tell him she was afraid, but she'd be damned if she'd let it show.

He stopped an arm's length away. She waited for him to speak. But for several uncomfortable moments all he did was look at her. His eyes roamed her body with an unabashed intensity and familiarity. And wherever his gaze touched her, she remembered precisely the touch of his hand there, or the caress of his lips. To her dismay, she felt her body responding, nipples swelling against the thin cotton of her shirt, heat flashing through her lower abdomen and thighs, and a pulsing ache deep inside, where his body had filled hers in that remarkably vivid dream. When he finally raised his eyes to hers again, Leigh had the disturbing sense that he knew the dream as intimately as she did. From what she had read of telepathy, it didn't include rummaging in another person's subconscious. Still, she felt naked before him, violated. And every bit as indignant as she was embarrassed. She had come out here tonight for one purpose—to find out what Zakoura knew about Jeremy Gates. There was no way she was going to let him ogle her and mess with her mind until *he* was good and ready to talk. The anger steadied her, and she was able to meet his eyes with a decent amount of composure.

"You've been following me all day. If you have something to say to me, I'm here and I'm waiting."

A hint of a smile plucked at Zakoura's lips and was just as quickly gone again. When he spoke, his voice was deadly serious.

"I need to know whom they seek."

Leigh was nonplussed, unable to reply immediately. She'd been so certain that Zakoura would know what had happened to Gates that his words threw her completely off balance. And what about this telepathy business—couldn't he just commandeer the information from her mind?

"Are you saying you don't know what's been going on?"

"I know the police search for someone. Is it one person?"

Leigh nodded warily. "Just what is your interest in this?"

"The same as yours."

"I doubt it."

"Does it matter that my reasons may be different, as long as I wish to help find this person?"

"If the police had wanted your help, they'd have come to you."

"No, Leigh, you are wrong. They would not come to me. But they may well need my help. Think of the one who is missing and forget about fools like Carlos Tsosie."

Although Zakoura sounded sincere, Leigh was reluctant to trust him. How could she trust a man who hid behind such a dark cloak of mystery? But the truth was that she didn't trust Carlos, either. And right now the search was going so badly that they could hardly afford to turn away any sort of help.

"His name is Jeremy Gates," she said, praying that she was doing the right thing. "He's five feet ten, weighs—"

"When did he disappear?"

"Don't you think it would help to know what he looks like?" she asked, annoyed by his interruption.

"That is not important. What I need to know is when."

Leigh sighed in exasperation. How did he expect to find someone without even the barest description? But she could tell by the hard set of Zakoura's face that he wouldn't listen to reason—her reason, anyway. "About fifty-three hours ago," she said, computing quickly. "And now that I've told you what you wanted to know, you're going to tell me something."

In spite of the bravado of her demand, she was actually surprised when Zakoura stayed there, waiting for her to continue.

"Why did you come to me about this? Why didn't you just go to Carlos or one of the other cops?" She had a pretty good idea what the answer was, but she wanted to hear what he would say.

"I did what was possible."

"Meaning that if you went to the police you'd be arrested."

"Arrested?" He repeated the word as if he found it particularly interesting.

"Taken into custody for committing murder," she said, tensed and ready to flee, in case she'd finally succeeded in shattering his imperturbable facade. But Zakoura barely reacted, except for the flash of comprehension that registered in his eyes.

"Ah," he murmured. "Mary Yazzi."

"You don't deny it, then?" Leigh had trouble keeping the dismay out of her voice. Secretly she'd held out the hope that Mary might be wrong.

"There are some questions for which there are no simple answers." There was a heaviness in his words, as if forming them required an extra effort. In spite of herself, she felt a little well of sympathy bubbling up inside her. She fought against it, sealed it off. He knew her fantasies, knew how she felt about him, and was trying to use that knowledge to his advantage. Well, it wasn't going to work.

"That's why we have a court system," she said sharply. "It helps answer those difficult questions."

Without responding, Zakoura turned to leave.

Leigh had no intentions of letting him off the hook that easily. "I'll be sure to let Carlos know that you're joining in the search," she said pointedly.

Zakoura whirled around and grabbed her by the arm so suddenly that she gasped. "This is not a game, Leigh. It is best that you stay out of it."

The anger she had expected before blazed in his eyes now. His warning hung in the air, as benign, yet as treacherous, as quicksand. But the touch of his hand seemed to reach straight into her heart, and she had no desire to pull away. They stood locked together that way for a frozen moment, while Leigh tried to summon up the will to wrench herself free, to tell him what she thought of his subtle ultimatum. But before she could react, Zakoura jerked his hand back from her like a soldier who'd just realized he was holding a live grenade. He opened his mouth as if to speak, then clamped it shut again. His jawline hard with determination, he turned and strode away.

Leigh remained where she was until she could no longer see him moving through the night. And then for a while afterward, even though a cool breeze had risen and she'd begun to shiver. She could still feel the pressure of his fingers on her skin as if his touch had branded her. Tears stung her eyes, and she rubbed them away with an angry swipe of her hand. She'd never been more confused in her life. She wanted him to come back; she wanted him to stay away; she wanted him to be the man she'd created in her dreams, and she wanted to stop dreaming of him forever.

CHAPTER TEN

Days passed. The search for Jeremy Gates was finally abandoned by the police, although his friends continued looking for him on their own. But after a while they, too, gave up and went home. Not satisfied with the reports from the Chinle police, Gates's family hired a team of private investigators to find their son. Three men who looked like retired cops arrived and interviewed everyone in and around the town, including Leigh and her colleagues. But in spite of all their legwork and paperwork, they were no more successful than anyone else had been. It was as if Jeremy Gates had never existed.

What surprised Leigh the most was that not even Zakoura had been able to find him. She'd endowed him with so much power that she'd been certain he could accomplish what no one else could. Apparently she was wrong. Or was she? Zakoura had never revealed the reason he wanted to find Gates. What had made her think that his agenda was in Gates's best interests? In spite of her threat, she'd never told Carlos that Zakoura had joined in the search. She didn't trust either man, but she had clearly allowed her attraction to Zakoura to sway her in that regard. Perhaps that, too, had been a mistake. She hadn't seen Zakoura since the night he'd come to her for information. Now she wished he would make an appearance so that she could question him. But he didn't even come to her in dreams anymore. She hadn't dreamed of him since that last encounter. She knew she should be relieved, but what she felt was a peculiar kind of betrayal, as if he'd abandoned her.

Now every night in her dreams she roamed an eerie wasteland in an endless, futile search. At first she'd thought it was Jeremy Gates she was seeking, her subconscious replaying the actual event. But then she began to suspect that it was really Zakoura she wanted to find. To confront him, or simply because she missed him. She couldn't be sure.

Worn out with worrying all by herself, Leigh finally broached her concerns to the others. They were driving into the canyon in the new black Bronco that had arrived the day before. Hugh was at the wheel, as happy as Leigh had ever seen him. The recent discoveries in the kiva, coupled with their having their own transportation again, had him literally humming as they bumped along the rutted wash. She pivoted in the passenger seat so that she could see the others in the back, then launched into a summary of Zakoura's visit, emphasizing the fact that he had planned to join in the search for Gates. She left out all references to telepathy, erotic images, and Zakoura's hostility when provoked. After all, Hugh had advised her to stay away from him.

"I don't think there's any reason to worry at this point," Hugh said when she'd concluded. "That was a pretty intensive search the police mounted. If they didn't find Gates, I doubt Zakoura could, either."

"Besides," Karen added, "maybe he really just wants to help. I mean, what diabolical motive could he have for trying to find Gates?" Her eyes twinkled with mischief. "Unless maybe he plans to boil him up in a big pot and make tourist stew."

A round of laughter followed her remark, but Leigh couldn't join in. She recalled too clearly the pain and bitterness of Mary's words, and the anger burning in Zakoura's eyes.

"No, I don't think he intends to have Gates for dinner, but I also don't believe he's harmless."

"Maybe you're taking Mary's warnings about him too seriously," Alex suggested. "Look, none of us particularly trusts Carlos, but he may have been telling the truth about her mental state."

Paul agreed. "There's no evidence to suggest Zakoura's ever done anything wrong. You saw Dijolei's official report—the man wasn't even responsible for the Bronco blowing up. It was hit by lightning, pure and simple. He was just an innocent bystander, in the wrong place at the wrong time."

Leigh shook her head. "You're all assuming we can trust Dijolei more than Carlos. Personally, I'm not convinced that we can."

"Sounds like a conspiracy theory to me." Paul grinned. "Have you by any chance been talking to Oliver Stone?"

Leigh didn't respond. She faced forward in her seat again, hoping to put an end to the discussion before the teasing had a chance to gain momentum. Apparently she was the only one who was seeing monsters in the shadows. But then, she was the only one who'd been stalked by Zakoura day and night.

The joking went on for a few more minutes. Then the conversation turned to how smooth the ride was in the new truck, and on into a debate over different makes of cars. Leigh noticed that Hugh didn't take part in any of it. He was staring straight ahead, his brow furrowed in concentration the way it was when he was trying to identify an unusual fragment of pottery.

"Something wrong?" she asked.

"There's one thing about this disappearance that's been bugging me."

"What's that?" Leigh was immediately attentive. Hugh wasn't the type to imagine problems that didn't exist. If something was bothering him, it was bound to be a legitimate concern. There was a time when she'd felt that way about her own instincts, but since meeting Zakoura Kree she no longer felt that she could trust them.

"It was something Bahe said the day we were helping in the search. Remember, I was sitting up in the cab with him, and while we were chatting he made an interesting comment. He said, '*This* time Carlos is really shook up, Gates being a tourist and all.' When I asked him what he meant by that, he got flustered, like he realized he'd spoken out of turn. He made up some stupid answer that didn't explain anything."

"'This time,' huh? That sure makes it sound as if disappearances aren't all that unusual around here."

"Exactly what I've been thinking."

Although this was hardly good news, Leigh was heartened by the fact that she was no longer alone in her belief that everything was not what it seemed to be at Canyon de Chelly. They had come here seeking answers to ancient mysteries, and had found themselves in the midst of a modern mystery. One that had the potential to be deadly.

"The next time we're in Chinle, I'm going to check out the police records and see just how many people have been reported missing in this area in recent years," she said.

"Just don't go getting on the wrong side of any cops. I wouldn't want to be thrown out of here with half the kiva left to excavate."

They had reached the site by then. Hugh nosed the Bronco into the base of the cliff, and they all strapped on their packs and began the climb up to the cavern.

Inside the kiva, Karen lit the propane lamps while they waited for their eyes to adjust to the dimmer light. The underground chamber had been designed so that sunlight streamed in through the open hatchway nearly all day, illuminating even the farthest recesses of the room. But the amount of light, while adequate for most purposes, wasn't enough for the detailed work of archaeology. Leigh and Hugh started unpacking their equipment within their individual sections of the grid. Marked off by lengths of string, the squares always reminded Leigh of adult sandboxes.

Karen brought them their lamps, then stepped over the string borders into her own work space. But instead of settling right down to work, she stood there, hands on her hips, a puzzled expression on her face.

Leigh asked if she'd forgotten something.

Karen shook her head. "This is going to sound a little strange, but I think someone else has been digging in here."

"You sound like one of the three bears." Hugh laughed, but he pushed himself to his feet and joined her in her square. "I don't see anything out of the ordinary. But then, you were the one working here, so you're probably the only one who'd notice if anything was different."

"I don't remember doing any work over there." She pointed to the far right corner of the lot, to an area that didn't appear as uniformly packed down as the ground immediately surrounding it.

Hugh went over to the spot and roughed up the soil with his fingers. "Dirt does seem a little looser here, as if it had been dug up and then tamped down again." He stood, brushing his hands clean. "It's hard to say for sure. I think it would be a good idea to stay alert to the possibility, though. Let's take a good look at our sections before we leave at night so we'll have a real means of comparison."

"If someone has been down here, it's quite a coincidence that they came only after we started finding the more valuable pieces," Leigh remarked.

"I'll say." Karen was looking around the kiva, trying to determine if anything else seemed amiss. "But how would anyone even know about the discovery?"

"With the search going on that day, there were people all over the canyon," Hugh said. "Anyone could have been near enough to hear us discussing it. Odds are, in my enthusiasm, I was too damned loud."

The memory flashed through Leigh's mind of Zakoura half-hidden in the crevice of the cliff as she climbed down into the kiva. From where he was, he might have heard Hugh. But so might a lot of other people, including Carlos. There she went—trying to protect Zakoura again. Wouldn't she ever learn that he was not the man she wanted him to be? If he was capable of murder, he was certainly capable of stealing a few historical treasures.

"I did see Carlos near here that day. Zakoura, too." She tried to keep her voice impartial, but it was difficult. Despite all that had happened, saying Zakoura's name out loud still quickened her heart unreasonably and reminded her how much she yearned for his arms at night—even if those arms were nothing more than figments of her imagination.

"Trouble is, we can't exactly question either one of them," Hugh said. "So I guess we're just going to have to be more vigilant. And if there is an intruder, maybe he'll slip up."

Nothing else was said about the issue, but Leigh couldn't pull her mind away from it for the rest of the day. When she was twelve years old, her house had been burglarized and the thieves had rummaged through all of her things. She'd felt violated and vulnerable then, and she felt much the same way now, even though she knew the circumstances were vastly different. The longer they stayed at Canyon de Chelly, the more questions begat questions and mysteries begat mysteries. And Zakoura Kree remained the greatest mystery of them all.

When Sunday rolled around, Hugh was faced with a dilemma. He wanted to make up the time they'd lost due to the truck fire and the search, but supplies were running low and laundry was piling up. Leigh offered to drive the rest of them over to the site and go into Chinle herself. Everyone was agreeable—work was preferable to those onerous chores. Only Hugh seemed aware that Leigh's offer wasn't completely altruistic.

"Remember, don't step on any big cop toes," he said as he jumped down from the Bronco and slung his knapsack over his shoulder.

Leigh made the police station her first stop, thinking she would count herself lucky if she didn't bump into Carlos. She parked next to Graffiti, who was nibbling on a patch of grass that was growing through the cracked macadam.

The station was deserted, except for one officer who was stuffed behind his desk, dunking a donut into a mug of coffee with one hand and swatting at flies with the other. Leigh thought she'd seen him at the dig at least once, but the nameplate on his desk didn't sound familiar.

"Excuse me, Officer Joe," she said, thinking that the Navaho certainly had the oddest collection of last names she'd ever encountered, "I'm Leigh Morgan, one of the archaeologists working in the canyon." She thought of holding out her hand until she realized that his was covered with chocolate icing.

Peter Joe bobbed his head and stuffed the last of the donut into his mouth. "What can I do for you?"

"I wonder if you could help me out with some information."

He washed the donut down with a large swig of the coffee. "Sure will try to. What is it you need?"

Leigh explained that she was doing a profile on the area as part of their work there, and that it would be helpful if she could see the police records for the past couple of years.

Fortunately, Peter Joe didn't know enough about archaeology to question the need for such data.

"Don't see why not. They've got everything on computer over in Window Rock, but we keep copies of the reports here, too."

Leigh tried not to be too profuse in her thanks. No point in letting on just how important this was to her. Joe brought her a stack of manila folders and showed her to a vacant desk. Now, as long as Carlos didn't walk in ... The thought was enough to tug her nerves a notch tighter. She tried to put the possibility out of her mind and concentrate on the papers in front of her, but she couldn't help feeling like Marie Antoinette awaiting the fall of the guillotine blade. Every sound made her jerk up her head and lose her place. When Joe came up beside her to offer her a donut, she jumped several inches out of the chair. Luckily, he was too busy selecting his next donut to notice how jittery she was.

An hour later, she was heading for the door, relieved that her mission had been so easily accomplished, but more perplexed than ever. In the past two years, Chinle had seen its share of robberies, rapes, stabbings, shootings and drunk-and-disorderlies. There had even been two murders—the full repertoire of crimes that plagued civilization. But there wasn't a single report of a missing person other than the one on Jeremy Gates.

Only two things could account for this peculiarity, she reasoned as she walked back to the Bronco. Either there hadn't been any missing people, or the reports of them had been deleted from the records. Intuition, coupled with Bahe's comment, pointed to the latter. Now the million-dollar question was "Why?" Why were the police altering records to hide such disappearances?

She was trying to work her way through the spreading maze of questions when Carlos stepped out from behind the Bronco, barely a foot away from her. Her heart leaped into her throat, choking off a startled scream.

"Didn't mean to scare you," he said amiably, but the angry set of his face said something very different.

Leigh managed a little laugh. "I must have been daydreaming."

"Police station's a strange place for daydreams."

"Yes, I imagine it is." Looking into the mirrored curve of his glasses, Leigh could see her own distorted reflection, as if she were peering into a fun-house mirror.

"Was Officer Joe able to help you?"

There was nothing to be gained from subterfuge. Carlos would ask Joe, and Joe would tell him exactly what she'd been after. Her only recourse was to be consistent. She repeated the story about needing data for a background report.

"None of the other archaeologists that came around here ever needed that kind of information," he said, resting his hand on the butt of his gun.

Leigh wondered if the posture was meant to intimidate her. She certainly didn't intend to let it. "You know how it is," she said lightly. "Every year, more requirements, more paperwork."

Carlos wasn't buying the story. "Gates isn't your concern, Dr. Morgan. Young fool's probably off somewhere laughing at all of us, so just let it go."

Leigh wanted to ask him outright why the missing-persons reports were absent from the files, but she'd promised Hugh that she'd be diplomatic. So she thanked him for the advice, filtering out the sarcasm as best she could.

The afternoon was half-over by the time Leigh finished the laundry and the shopping and stopped for a quick slice of pizza. Back at the camp, she tossed the dairy and meat into the refrigerator, splashed cool water on her face and was on her way to the dig.

The first section of the canyon was clogged with tourists. She could do little more than crawl along at a pace that would have had Hugh gnashing his teeth. But once she was past the White House, the crowds had thinned out, and by Spider Rock she was quite alone, except for a few stray sheep. Today the solitude didn't trouble her. Zakoura hadn't been around for days. And if he chose to make an appearance, well, that would be fine with her. She had more than a few questions to ask him.

As she came around the curve before Bat Canyon, he was standing directly in front of her. She pulled the truck to a stop and waited to see what he would do. Now that he was actually here, her bravado was slipping. It was easier to stand up to Carlos; there was no wrestling with conflicting emotions. Around Zakoura she always felt muddled. In fact, the anxiety that was shooting adrenaline into her blood was interlaced with a maddening flush of relief because he hadn't deserted her after all.

Zakoura came up to the side of the truck. A fine sheen of perspiration coated his chest and arms, highlighting the muscles there, which were standing out as if they'd recently done strenuous work. In spite of the circumstances, in spite of her questions, Leigh found herself wanting to touch him, to let her fingers trace the hard swell of those muscles across his chest and down the flat plane of his stomach. She bit on the inside of her lip to stop her mind from following that particular path any farther.

Zakoura was studying her the way he always did, and she didn't know how well he could read her thoughts. But if he knew what she'd been thinking, he gave no sign of it. There was no amusement in his eyes this time, no sly triumph, and when he spoke his voice was grave.

"The one you seek is in the storage cave where you have worked."

Leigh's heart pitched like a small boat caught in a sudden squall. She had hoped that Carlos was right, that Gates had simply taken off. "He's dead, then."

"Yes."

The distress that enveloped her was completely out of proportion to the situation. She'd never even met Jeremy Gates. Then, in an instant of clarity, it came to her—she'd wanted Zakoura to bring him back alive, because in the illogical recesses of her heart that would have vindicated him. A killer would not go out of his way to save a life. She would have been able to dismiss Mary's accusations against him. She would have been able to justify the powerful feelings she had for him.

"Did you kill him?" The words spilled out before she even knew she was going to say them; the dam holding back all her questions had finally burst.

For a moment, Zakoura's guard dropped, and Leigh could see beyond the darkened windows of his eyes. But she couldn't identify the emotions she saw there. It was a brief glimpse into chaos. There was far too much for her to make sense of. She moved her hand to the gearshift in case she needed to make a quick getaway. Accusing a potential—no, a probable—murderer in a deserted canyon might well be the stupidest thing she'd ever done.

"He went where he could not be," Zakoura replied.

"Is that a reason to kill someone?" In for a penny, in for a pound. Her foot hovered above the gas pedal. Whatever else Zakoura could do, he couldn't outrun a Bronco.

"I did not kill him. His death was an accident."

Leigh wanted to believe him, but she wasn't sure what he considered accidental. Did it include execution for accidental trespassing?

"If you choose not to believe me in this, I have no way to convince you," he said, as if she'd already voiced her doubts.

She knew that trying to probe further would be futile. Zakoura had told her all that he intended to. "I'd better tell the police where to find Gates," she said, putting the truck in gear.

"Leigh, there is one thing more. You and your people must stay out of the kiva. It is not safe."

Not safe? she thought. In the same way that Gates's death had been *accidental?* Knowing what they'd discovered, Zakoura probably just wanted to keep them away so that he could take the rest for himself. No doubt he was the one who'd been digging down there.

"That's ridiculous," she said, looking him straight in the eye. "The kiva is perfectly fine. But if you're concerned, just don't go there anymore." She spun the Bronco in a tight U-turn before he could reply and sped back in the direction of Chinle.

It might have been easy to believe that Zakoura and Carlos were working together, hiding the same secret— Zakoura killing off everyone who went where "they couldn't be" and Carlos deleting their names from the files.

Yet the antipathy between the two men was genuine. She'd take bets on that. No, whatever they were covering up, they had their own methods and their own motivations.

When she told Carlos where to find Gates's body, he didn't seem particularly pleased. In fact, he looked disturbed and, at the mention of Zakoura's name, even a little angry. Leigh had the distinct impression that he would have preferred *this* body to remain missing. Because of his reaction, she was determined to get a look at Gates's body before the police had a chance to whisk it away. Maybe the cause of the young man's death would be readily apparent.

She drove back to the dig as fast as she dared, grabbed one of the lanterns and practically dragged Hugh out of the kiva to accompany her to the cave. Two perspectives would be better than one. Besides, she really didn't want to have to view the body alone. Skeletal remains of people who'd died centuries before were not at all the same thing as what was likely to be a partially decomposed corpse.

She explained the situation to Hugh as she hurried him along the ledge, all the while listening intently for sounds of a vehicle approaching along the rim or down in the canyon. Even before they reached the cave, it became clear that Zakoura had told her the truth. The stench of death formed an invisible moat around the entrance, keeping them back and causing Leigh's determination to waver.

"Well, Nancy Drew, we've come this far," Hugh said, "and you've gotten my curiosity into an uproar. I say we hold our breath and go for it."

Leigh nodded and turned on the lamp. "Remember—we can't touch anything."

He smiled wryly. "No problem."

Leigh counted to three, and they took a deep breath and headed inside. Gates was lying on his back, several feet beyond the entrance, still wearing the running gear his friends had described. His body appeared to be intact, but it was badly bloated, the skin discolored and oozing unidentifiable fluids. There were no signs that he had been attacked by an animal, and no gashes on his head, although they couldn't turn him over to make sure, and no bullet wounds. Yet his death had not been a peaceful one. Dried blood caked his ears and nose and formed a gory mask around the lower half of his face. And although an attempt had been made to close his eyelids, they only partially covered his eyes, which seemed to have swelled nearly out of their sockets like water balloons filled to the bursting point.

Leigh felt her stomach contract, the bile rise in her throat. She turned and fled the cave, gagging and gasping for air, with Hugh right behind her. They didn't stop to catch their breath until they'd passed the first curve of the ledge. A minute later, Carlos and Bill Dijolei found them there, Hugh leaning against the cliff, dripping with perspiration, and Leigh doubled over, trying to wrestle her stomach into submission.

Carlos was livid; not even the sunglasses could camouflage the extent of his anger. In a venomous tone, he told them they'd had no business trespassing at a crime scene, and he guaranteed they'd be arrested if he found even the slightest indication they had tampered with the evidence.

After dinner Leigh apologized to Hugh for having put the team's work there in jeopardy. She found him in his lawn chair, balancing the medicine rattle between his hands and watching the sunset. Nudging his feet aside, she made a space for herself on the edge of the chair. The entire western horizon was torched with scarlet flames. At another time the scene might have enchanted her, but after the events of this day it looked to her as if the door to hell had cracked open and was spewing out its fire.

Hugh was silent until the blaze had died to a smoldering pink crown on the darkened ridges. "You didn't put a gun to my head, Leigh. Although trying to outmaneuver Carlos probably wasn't the wisest thing we could have done." His voice was low and distracted, as if the sunset had drained the fire out of him, as well.

"You know, when I told Carlos where Gates was, he denied that that cave was ever searched."

"We all saw Dijolei go to check it out. Besides, if the body had been there all this time, animals would have gotten to it—it would have been picked clean."

"It's pretty obvious he doesn't want us wondering how the body suddenly showed up there. Do you think we'll ever find out where Gates really died, or how?"

Hugh shook his head. "There'll be an autopsy, but who knows if they'll tell us the truth? I think what we've got to do is put all these questions behind us and try to remember we're archaeologists, not private eyes."

"Easier said than done," Leigh said with a sigh. Because of Zakoura, she had a much higher emotional investment in the answers.

"*This*," Hugh said, holding up the medicine rattle, "should be the focus of our questions. Ever since Karen dug this thing up, it's been haunting me."

So that's why he'd seemed so removed from the discussion.

"Anything in particular?" she asked.

"You know I've always held with the theory that the Anasazi just moved on—the ground was depleted, the water was drying up. But now . . ." He shook his head. "Now

I'm not so sure anymore. Why would they leave behind a sacred ceremonial rattle?''

Leigh was chagrined that the question hadn't even occurred to her. She'd been as vocal a proponent of that theory as Hugh. But she'd allowed herself to become so mired in thoughts of Zakoura, what he was hiding and how he made her feel, that she'd forgotten her purpose in coming to Canyon de Chelly.

"Maybe it was just overlooked," she suggested, trying to reel her brain back into line.

"I don't think so." His voice was becoming more animated. "We're finding too many other important pieces there."

"Then you're hopping on Paul's bandwagon and saying they were killed off by an invading tribe?"

"No. No, I still can't subscribe to that one." Hugh pushed himself out of the chair, too agitaged to stay seated any longer. "There are no bones. You've gotta have bones when a whole civilization's wiped out, lots and lots of bones." He was pacing up and down, waving the rattle in the air for emphasis. "So tell me—" he spun on his heel to face Leigh again "—where the hell are the damned bones?"

"But if we eliminate both of those theories, all we're left with is the legend," she pointed out.

Karen had stepped out of the camper, hair wet from the shower, in time to hear Leigh's comment.

"I'm afraid the Navaho they-were-whisked-off-to-a-higher-plane theory just doesn't cut it in the better scientific circles. Any coffee left, Hugh?"

"Enough for a cup."

"Look, guys," she said as she crossed behind them to the men's RV. "Don't wear out your brain cells over this. Someday the answer will turn up, and we'll all wonder how we could have overlooked it for so long."

Hugh shrugged. "She's right. I've never had enough patience for this career. For now I'll have to say that I don't support any current theory."

"I still don't think that what we found has to negate the migration theory," Leigh said. "The Anasazi just forgot to pack a few things. I know I always do."

"Touché," Hugh chuckled. "And now it's time to lull myself to sleep with some Stephen King."

That night sleep came more easily to Leigh than it had in days. Talking about the legend had made her think of the dream canyon that was so different from the canyon as she knew it. Even though she hadn't thought about that old Indian tale for years, her subconscious must have dredged it up to use as a setting for the dream. Now it made sense. Zakoura had had no telepathic hand in it. She'd created the alien place all by herself, from bits and pieces of folklore. She drifted off, relieved that at least one of her troublesome questions had so simple an explanation.

She watched the last of the sun's light flicker below the horizon like a sputtering candle snuffed out by the night. She and Zakoura were on top of the mesa where she had once seen him standing. But even before the sunset, when she could see from horizon to horizon, there had been no sign of Mary Yazzi's hogan, nor of the campers. Just the wide expanse of green she remembered from that other dream, and a band of wild horses settling down for the night.

"Tell me about your family," Zakoura murmured into the silence, which seemed denser now that the light was gone. Leigh was sitting within the naked arc of his body, her back against his chest, her legs pressed to the inside curve of his legs, her arms folded beneath his at her waist. He was like a cloak around her. When the wind gusted, his hair danced across her bare shoulders and the tops of her breasts. She could feel the tiniest quivering of his muscles, the slightest quickening of his heart. She felt as closely joined with him now as when they'd made love.

"You don't need me to tell you anything," she said with a laugh. "You can read my mind."

"It is only your strongest thoughts I hear."

"Why do you want to know about my family?"

"You are their child. I want to know them, so that I will know you better."

She started by telling him how different they were, the man of science and the woman of "possibilities." She talked about little things, like the trip to the planetarium, when her father explained about black holes and her mother had wondered which star systems might be home base for the UFOs. And big things, like the day her collie Samson had died and her father explained that Sam wouldn't be gone as long as they remembered him and her mother told her that people brought back from the brink of death had seen their pets waiting for them in the afterlife.

"Whose words brought you most comfort when your Samson died?" Zakoura whispered, his mouth close to her ear, his breath causing a frisson of desire to reawaken in her body.

Leigh had to take a moment to rein in her truant thoughts. "My mother's, I guess. But I was only eight years old," she added quickly.

"Age is of no significance. You are very like your mother, though you wish not to see this."

Leigh tossed her head gently against his cheek. "I've always been exactly like my father. Everyone who knows us says so."

"Everyone is wrong. They look at what is easy to see, and no further. Your mother has an openness of mind that frees the spirit. This I see in you, though you work hard to hide it—most of all from yourself."

Leigh didn't debate the point. If Zakoura wanted to believe she was some New Age guru, she'd let him. They didn't have time to waste on silly arguments. She wasn't sure how she knew that their time together was limited, but she did. And she didn't want to squander even one minute of it. She snuggled deeper into his embrace.

"I'm so glad you came back," she said. "I missed you."

Zakoura brushed the hair away from the side of her face and kissed her gently on the neck and cheek. She angled her head back so that he could reach her lips. He cradled her chin with one hand, while the other played across her breasts as lightly as the touch of a breeze. Her nipples rose up, aching to increase the contact.

She trailed her fingers down the length of his legs as far as she could reach and then up along his inner thighs, which hugged her on either side. She found the rough welt of the scar that stretched for several inches up to his groin. He'd told her it was the result of a fall down a mountainside when he was ten. She traced the edges of the scar, trying to imagine him as a boy. It seemed almost impossible that he could ever have been anything but the man he was now.

"I came looking for you every night that you were gone," she said, her voice low and breathless as she arched her body to meet his touch. But instead of the pressure of his fingers on her skin, she felt his body tense, his hands drop away from her.

"No," he said harshly, pushing himself to his feet and walking away. "You must *never* try to find me. You must *never* come looking for me."

Leigh felt as if she'd been physically slapped. Tears stung her eyes. Tears of confusion and anger and loss. One moment he was loving her so tenderly, and the next he only wanted to be away from her. What had she said that was so terrible?

She turned in his direction, but the darkness hung like an impenetrable curtain between them; she couldn't see him at all. "I don't understand the harm in wanting to be with you." She tried to keep her voice even and strong, but her emotions overwhelmed her. The words quavered badly in spite of her efforts.

"I pray you never know the harm," Zakoura said, his tone rock-hard, as if he'd sealed himself off from his heart and from her.

Leigh got up and walked blindly toward the sound of his voice, too distraught to consider that she might step off the edge of the mesa. Zakoura put his hands out to let her know where he was, then quickly pulled them away again.

"Go back, Leigh. You don't belong here. I have no right to you."

"I give you the right," she said, determination steadying her. She'd never loved anyone in her life the way she loved this man. She didn't understand why or how, and it didn't matter. Nor did it matter if he remained a mystery forever. All that was important was that he love her in return. And she suspected that he did. She wasn't going to let him out of her life without a fight. Giving up had never been her style.

She twined her arms around his neck and put her lips to his throat, where she could feel the beating of his pulse.

"It is my fault for starting this," he said, wrenching himself out of her embrace. "I don't know how I ever thought it would be safe. I was wrong."

"I don't care about what's safe or sane," she said, bringing her mouth up to his. But he was unyielding in her arms, and he refused to return her kiss. What if you can't change his mind? a nagging inner voice taunted her. What if you can't make him admit that he needs you? No, she wouldn't even consider that. She kissed him again, plying his lips with her tongue and pressing her body along the length of his. With a rush of relief, she felt him responding, growing full and hard against her lower belly. She ran her fingers down his chest, down his stomach, down to that part of his body that had betrayed him.

He moaned softly. "Leigh, no... You do not know... what you are doing."

"I have a pretty good idea," she whispered, her lips nipping at the broad expanse of his chest, following the trail her fingers had already blazed. When she knelt and drew him into her mouth, she felt the tremor that swept through his body.

With a strangled cry of desire and defeat, he lifted her into his arms and carried her to the fur rug where they'd been sitting. He laid her on her back, and when she reached up for him he took her arms and placed them above her head, deliberately, as if he wanted her to leave them just that way.

Leigh didn't protest, although she wanted to bury her hands in his wind-tangled hair. She knew that if she was patient there would be time for everything.

Zakoura kissed her throat and her shoulders, brushing his lips across the tender skin of her upturned arms. With his tongue he traced the circumference of each breast and each nipple, sucking the peaked tips into his mouth. He worked his way down her stomach, between the wide flare of her hips. Using his hands and lips, he caressed the delicate skin of her inner thighs, and then, finally, the wet, burning core of her.

Leigh could barely lie still. She dug her hands through his hair now, her body aching with a pleasure that was close to pain.

Zakoura scooped her off the ground and placed her on top of him. Straddling his hips, she sank onto him, moaning softly as he opened her and filled her. She moved slowly on him at first, her muscles gripping him inside her, molding to him as if they would remain cast just that way forever, accommodating no other man for the rest of her life.

They moved together, the rhythm of passion and sensation building, until Leigh was beyond thought, and the borders of consciousness had opened to deeper places in her mind, places she'd never touched before.

Zakoura cried out first, and as his warmth and wetness filled her, Leigh felt her body tense, then shatter into a million pieces around him, like crystal struck by a perfect note. They stayed together that way until Zakoura felt her start to shiver in the cooling night air. Then he drew her down into the crook of his arm and pulled the fur rug over her like a blanket. She curled against him, wishing time would stop right then—if she had to live one moment forever, this was the one she would choose.

"I never believed that love at first sight was possible," she whispered.

"It is not possible in the way that you mean it," Zakoura replied.

"Then how can you explain the way I've been drawn to you from the first moment I ever saw you?"

"What you call love at first sight is not mysterious." He ran his finger along the curve of her cheek. "It is only the soul recognizing its mate, its missing half."

Only the soul recognizing its mate. He spoke about such things as if they were incontrovertible scientific principles.

Yet, in spite of herself, Leigh found that she believed him. No other explanation made as much sense. Maybe science didn't have all the answers. Maybe it needed to guard its borders less closely. And maybe, just maybe, she was more like her mother than she'd ever wanted to admit.

CHAPTER ELEVEN

The cause of Gates's death was listed as a massive myocardial infarction. The team heard the news from Edward Bahe when his path crossed theirs as they were leaving the canyon a week later. Bahe's pickup was filled with tourists, but he pulled over to talk to them anyway. As Leigh listened to the Navaho guide delivering the official line, she stole a glance at Hugh. She could tell by the way his mouth was pursed that he didn't believe it any more than she did. The body they'd seen hadn't died of anything as uncomplicated or as common as a heart attack—unless, of course, his heart had literally exploded.

Catching her eye, Hugh gave an almost imperceptible wag of his head, the meaning implicit. "Keep your mouth shut and don't say a damned thing." For once she agreed. Nothing would be gained by arguing the matter with Bahe. He was only the messenger, repeating the gospel according to Carlos. Paul could tease her all he wanted, but Leigh was more convinced than ever that Carlos was guarding a mystery of some kind, and that many—if not all—of the Navaho in the area were in league with him. She was equally certain that Zakoura Kree was at the center of whatever they were trying to hide. And Gates's death might just be the loose thread that could unravel it all. If only she could discover how he had really died . . . But she'd never be able to. Carlos would see to it that they were run out of Canyon de Chelly before he would let that happen. Besides, her prying and snooping had already done irreparable damage to the team's status there. She had no right to take a chance on making matters worse. But although she could accept the situation on a pragmatic level, the questions kept nagging at her as if they had a will of their own. During the remainder of the ride back to camp, frustration worked its way into her like a cactus barb. The harder she tried to free herself of it, the more securely entrenched it became. But it wasn't long before she had a more immediate concern to occupy her mind.

They'd only been back for half an hour when Hugh came thundering out of the men's RV. Leigh was outside with the rest of the team, finishing up their reports so that Paul could enter them in the daybook. They all looked up at the banging of the camper door.

"It's gone!" Hugh shouted, bright welts of anger highlighting his cheeks. "The medicine rattle's gone!"

"What do you mean, 'gone'?" Paul said, rubbing his eyes as if clearing them would help him hear better.

"Vanished, disappeared, no longer here, *gone!*" His voice was growing more strident with every syllable.

Leigh had never heard Hugh this angry, this out of control. "It was stolen?" she said, her mind already weighing who the perpetrator might be.

"Unless one of you borrowed it," he said without humor.

There was a murmur of denials.

"In that case, short of the rattle growing feet and walking away, my best guess is that it was stolen."

"Was anything else taken?" Alex asked.

"I don't think so." Hugh's shoulders slumped as the anger burned off and the magnitude of the loss settled in.

Paul volunteered to check the rest of the inventory against his records.

"Okay," Karen said as Hugh collapsed onto one of the chairs. "Let's consider who might have taken it."

The names that had come immediately to Leigh were Carlos and Zakoura. They were also the names Hugh listed first. Alex pointed out that it would be hard to eliminate anyone on the reservation, since they all considered the canyon their property.

"It could even be Jimmy," Karen added. "He might have wanted to play with the rattle. That would explain why nothing else was taken—the other pieces wouldn't be as interesting to a kid."

Leigh didn't think Jimmy would ever break into a locked camper, but she really didn't know him well enough to vouch for him.

Paul returned and reported that all the other important pieces were accounted for, which only made the issue more bewildering. Why would a thief go to the trouble of breaking into the camper just to take one piece?

"All right, this is how it's going to be," Hugh said, his voice gruff, but his composure somewhat restored. "I'm going to report the theft to Carlos. Not that I think he'll be of any help in finding the culprit or the rattle, but I want to see his reaction. He may just do or say something that will give him away. Leigh can speak to Jimmy—she knows him best. Even if he didn't take the rattle, he might have an idea who did. As far as Zakoura goes—I don't think there's much we can do. I don't want you going after him yourself, Leigh. I mean it."

Leigh nodded, but she didn't make any promises. If no other clues turned up, she would have to seek out Zakoura. The rattle was too precious a discovery to lose without a fight.

Hugh waited until the morning to drive into Chinle. He wanted to be sure that Carlos was on duty when he reported the robbery. Before dropping the others off at the excavation, he stopped at the Yazzi hogan so that Leigh could speak to Jimmy. The sheep were still there, but when she knocked on the door, Mary told her that Jimmy was out riding. Leigh debated asking the old woman if she'd seen a medicine rattle in Jimmy's possession, but decided against it. She might get the boy in trouble when he hadn't done anything wrong. Instead, she just asked Mary to have him stop by to see her when he could.

Leigh and Karen spent the morning working in the kiva, but their hearts weren't in it. Not even Leigh's discovery of a pipe bowl could do much to lift their spirits. What was the point of all their work, if the artifacts they unearthed could be so easily stolen? Less than two weeks remained of their tenure in the canyon, and it wasn't likely that the rattle would be returned to them or that they would find anything else of such significant value.

"Dr. Leigh." Jimmy's smiling face peered down at them from the hatchway.

"Hi there. I'll be right up." Although she suspected he would probably like to join them in the underground chamber, she didn't want to question him in front of Karen. He might not be as forthcoming around a stranger.

"My grandma told me you wanted to see me," he said once Leigh had emerged onto the plaza, blinking and squinting in the sharp sunlight.

"I do, but you didn't have to come all the way out here to find me."

"That's okay, Skywalker brought me." He pointed down into the canyon, where the mare was busily cropping grass.

Leigh sat down on the roof of the kiva and motioned for Jimmy to join her. "I have a really important question to ask you, Jimmy."

He nodded, his face at once solemn and eager, honored to be helping out.

"Have you been inside the campers when we weren't there?"

"No." He seemed puzzled by the question, and disappointed. "Is that all you wanted to know?"

"Not exactly. You see, we found a rattle in the kiva, the kind a medicine man might have used. We were keeping it in one of the campers, but now it's missing, and I needed to know if maybe you had borrowed it to play with."

She saw the painful realization register in the boy's eyes.

"You think I went into your camper and took it."

His reaction was so immediate and uncontrived that Leigh was certain of his innocence and sorry that her accusation, even as carefully phrased as it had been, had hurt him.

"No, I didn't think that," she told him honestly. "But we're questioning everyone in the area, no exceptions."

"Oh." He seemed placated, but his forehead remained scrunched with thought.

"Now this is the part we need your help with," she continued. "Will you let us know if you hear anything about the rattle or who might have it?"

Jimmy nodded hard. "But I know—" He stopped himself short.

"You know what?"

"Nothing." He shrugged and picked up a pebble, pretending to inspect it. "I forgot what I was gonna say."

Leigh pressed him. It was exactly this kind of uncensored comment she had hoped to elicit from him. Children were simply not as practiced in deception as adults were.

"If you're going to help us, Jimmy, you can't hold anything back."

He thought about that for a minute. "Okay," he said reluctantly, tossing the pebble over the edge of the cliff. "I was just gonna say that Zakoura might be the one who stole it."

Leigh almost wished she'd let it go, even thought Jimmy hadn't told her anything she hadn't already told herself. "What makes you think it was Zakoura?"

"Because he does whatever he wants." There was a bitter twist to his words.

"Does he? Well, if he is guilty, he's not going to get away with it this time," Leigh said, with more assurance than she felt. "I'm going to have a little talk with him."

"Oh, no, Dr. Leigh. No." Jimmy's head was shaking so fast he seemed to be trembling. He put his hand on her arm as if he could physically stop her from going after Zakoura. "You can't. I shouldn't have told you. It'll be all my fault." Tears streamed down his face, Leigh could tell that he really had begun to shiver.

"It's okay, Jimmy. Remember the last time, when you were so worried because I went to see him? Nothing happened to me."

Jimmy couldn't be reassured. "That doesn't matter. Just because he let you go then, that doesn't mean you'll be safe this time."

"You don't know that for sure." She was getting off the subject of the rattle, but she had to find out why the boy was so deathly afraid of Zakoura, and he might just tell her this time.

"Yes, I do. I do know it." He was crying out loud now, deep, wrenching sobs that shook his whole body. "He...he killed my mother."

His mother— Oh, Lord. Leigh shut her eyes for a moment to steady herself. No wonder he was so terrified. No wonder Mary was so consumed with anger and hatred. Although she'd steeled herself to hear the worst, Leigh found herself unprepared for it. Suspecting Zakoura of murder had been relatively easy, but having that suspicion so passionately confirmed was unbearable. In spite of everything, her heart had never let go of the irrational hope that he might yet become the man she'd invented, the man with whom she'd fallen in love.

"And it didn't happen the first time she was with him," Jimmy was saying between hiccups of breath. "It didn't happen right away."

Leigh put her arm around his narrow shoulders and hugged him against her side. Had she known the cause of his anxiety about Zakoura, she would never have pushed so hard to get past his defenses. A hundred questions whirled in her head, but they would have to wait, and she would have to find someone else to answer them. All she wanted to do was to quiet the grieving child beside her. But Jimmy needed to talk.

"I saw her when they brought her home. They didn't think I did. They thought I was playing out back with Rowdy, but I was in the shed and I saw her. I remember. I remember. She didn't even look like my mother, except she was wearing the same clothes. Mostly she was okay but not her face. All bloody, like the blood had all spilled out of her. And her eyes were popped out, almost, and—and she was so pretty. What happened to her? I heard them talking about Zakoura. I heard my grandma say it was his fault. She kept saying it over and over, 'He killed my Ruby, he killed my Ruby.' And I knew who she meant, 'cause I saw my mother with him once. He was angry with her, and—and I wished she would stay away from him. I told her to stay away from him, but she didn't listen to me. She should've listened to me, 'cause he killed her." Jimmy fell silent, the emotional torrent ending as abruptly as it had begun. His head dropped back against Leigh's shoulder. She rocked him gently, and after a while his sobs grew softer and his breathing became regular again.

Leigh was as drained as Jimmy, limp inside. She couldn't even imagine the horror this child had experienced, seeing his mother that way. But she knew how she'd felt after seeing Gates's body, and she'd never even met that young man. And along with Jimmy's tragedy, there was another, more personal loss for her. The loss of hope. Ruby had died in the same strange manner as Jeremy Gates, and Zakoura seemed to be the common link. He was not the man who held her in his arms at night; he never had been, and he never would be.

She wasn't sure how long she'd been sitting there with Jimmy when she realized Hugh was talking to her. All at once she became aware of the steamy intensity of the sun, and the cramping in the arm that cradled the boy.

"Everything okay?" Hugh asked. Jimmy sat up with a start, as if he'd suddenly been awakened.

"Yes," Leigh said. "Jimmy's going to let us know if he hears anything about the rattle." She didn't add anything about Zakoura or Ruby. Maybe she would tell the others later. Right now she didn't have the energy to talk about it, and Jimmy certainly didn't need to be around to hear his words repeated. He'd been through enough for one day.

Jimmy stayed to have lunch with them, and by the time he'd finished his sandwich and lemonade he'd bounced back to his usual good spirits. Leigh watched him scramble happily down the cliff, wishing she had the resiliency of a child. Distracted by her own despair and an impotent anger, she had a hard time keeping her attention focused on Hugh as he explained what had happened in Chinle. He'd reported the theft to Carlos, and although he wouldn't bet his life on it, he was pretty much convinced that Carlos had known nothing about it.

Leigh wasn't the least bit surprised. The thief was Zakoura. "He does whatever he wants," Jimmy had said. She kept her thoughts to herself, though, because Hugh would make her promise not to go after the Indian. And that was precisely what she intended to do.

As she worked through the afternoon, she tried to figure out exactly how she might contact him. She could go for a walk this evening—he often came to her when she was alone. But he probably wouldn't be anxious to see her after he'd just burglarized the camper. Mary might know how to find him, but Leigh didn't think she'd be willing to tell her.

She was labeling a bag to hold an arrowhead when it came to her. She would find Zakoura in the rocky alcove beyond the cave, where they'd met once before. The image of him in that place flashed in her mind. Once. Then again. She tried to ignore it at first, but it wouldn't let her be. It came again. And again. And again. Until finally she realized that it might be more than just a nagging memory.

She told Hugh she was going for a walk to stretch her legs and get some fresh air. For safety's sake, she would have liked to tell him where she was going, but it wasn't worth the argument that would ensue, and she didn't know how long Zakoura would wait for her. If he was there at all. Psychic premonitions, telepathy—her father would tease her unmercifully; her mother would applaud. But neither one of them would want her to go after a murderer alone. She slipped her pocketknife into her hand when no one was watching. It wouldn't be much protection, but it was better than nothing.

By the time she was halfway to the cave, she could no longer hear the occasional comments being bandied between Alex and Paul while they worked in the condos. The canyon was quiet. Unnaturally quiet. There was no humming of insects, no rustling of trees. Even the wind was still. In contrast, her footsteps resounded sharply, announcing her progress to whoever might be listening. Leigh told herself she was imagining things; her nerves were playing tricks on her. She forced herself to move on. She passed the cave. The odor of decay was gone. Gates was gone. Ruby was gone. But nothing was going to happen to her. If Zakoura wanted to harm her, he'd had ample opportunity in the past. Besides, someone had to stand up to him. She clutched the knife more tightly in her hand, positioned her finger on the switch that released the blade. She had reached the last curve. If the images in her mind had been right, she would see him once she came around that bend.

Zakoura was leaning against the cliff wall. And, as always, she was unprepared for the intensity of her response to him. For a moment her purpose in coming there fled her mind and all she could do was look at him. Her gaze slid from his face, down his chest, to where the breechcloth hid the inner part of his thigh. She remembered the scar she'd seen there in her dreams, and she wondered if it really existed. And, if it did, how had her subconscious known about it?

"I don't believe you have come here just to stare at me," Zakoura said without humor.

Leigh was nonplussed. She hadn't realized she was being that obvious. "You're right," she said briskly, hoping her cheeks weren't as red as they felt. "I was just lost in thought."

"Why is it you need to speak to me?"

He wasn't here by sheer coincidence—he'd come because she'd wanted him to, because she'd called to him in her mind. And he didn't seem particularly pleased to be here. She reminded herself that he was the one who should be on the defensive. It was time to straighten out their positions.

"Why did you steal the medicine rattle?" she asked without preamble.

Zakoura's expression didn't change. "I stole nothing," he said evenly.

Someone who was innocent would at least have shown surprise at such an accusation, if not outright indignation. "I don't believe you."

"It is not possible to steal that which is already yours."

"What are you saying—that the rattle belongs to you, since we found it on Navaho land? Because if that's your argument, you can forget about it. First of all, we have permission from the tribal government in Window Rock for this excavation and secondly, Mary Yazzi told me that you're not even Navaho."

"This is all true, and what I have told you is true, as well."

"Right. And up is down and east is west. Are you going to return the rattle, or do I have to go to the police?"

"It is not their business," Zakoura said roughly. He pushed away from the cliff wall and came toward her as if he'd tired of their conversation and decided that action was required.

Leigh was at the edge of the cliff. No room to back up. All she could do was turn and flee back to camp. But he would catch her easily. She wasn't accustomed to running on the narrow, rocky ledge, and he was no doubt as surefooted as Carlos and Jimmy. She decided to stand her ground. The weight of the knife in her hand provided some small comfort.

"The same way Gates's death wasn't their business?" she said contemptuously. "The same way Ruby's death wasn't their business?"

Zakoura stopped abruptly a few feet from her, the color draining from his face, at the mention of Ruby's name. Leigh could see him working to regain control of his emotions. In those strange, silent moments, Leigh wondered what would come next. Had she pushed him too far this time? According to Jimmy, Zakoura and Ruby had been arguing not long before she was killed.

When Zakoura spoke again, his voice was low, and too carefully measured; the turbulence that was roiling just below the surface was unmistakable. Leigh found it far more frightening than if he had shouted at her. "Go from here, Leigh. Do not call to me. Do not even think of me. And stay out of the kiva. What you seek will destroy you."

"And if it destroys me, why would you care?" She wasn't sure what kind of answer she expected, but she couldn't help asking. His concern just didn't jibe with his attitude toward her. In fact, the closer they'd become in her dreams, the more openly hostile he'd become in reality.

"Remember what I have told you," he said, turning and walking away from her.

"I want to know, Zakoura," she called after him. "I want to know why you try to scare me off, and why you're concerned about my safety. I want to know why you sought me out to begin with. Why not Karen, or Hugh, or the others? Why me?" She was shouting with frustration now, but her own echo was her only reply. Zakoura was gone. She thought of following him, trying to find out where he went when he left her. But she'd been gone too long already. The team would be packing up soon. They'd be worried about her.

When she told them about her conversation with Za-koura, Hugh reminded her that she'd been instructed not to go after him alone, and she reminded him that Zakoura never came to her unless she was alone. And at least now they knew who the thief was.

"In spite of what you may think," he said, "you are more important to me, to us, than that damned rattle."

"The guy must be psycho," Alex said. "It sounds like he's claiming to be some kind of direct descendant of the Anasazi. That's the only way the rattle would belong to him."

Paul laughed glumly. "Yeah, well, I'll believe that right after I start believing in the tooth fairy."

Leigh also relayed Zakoura's warning about the kiva. Although she considered it just a bluff, a way to keep them from the rest of the treasures buried down there, they each had a right to make their own decision where their safety might be concerned.

Neither Hugh nor Karen was willing to be scared off so easily. Karen was especially vehement in her response.

"No way am I giving in to that kind of threat," she said without hesitation. "We have little enough time left, and I don't want to leave behind even one pottery shard more than we have to. It sickens me to think about him stripping the site once we're gone."

On Sunday, Hugh accompanied Leigh into Chinle in the morning to take care of the chores. Alex offered to take Leigh's place, since she'd gone the week before. Leigh thanked him, but declined. She had an agenda of her own. Ever since her talk with Jimmy, she'd wanted to find out the official cause of Ruby's death. She'd considered asking Mary, but quickly discarded that idea. Not only would it be insensitive of her to stir up those memories again, but Mary had formed her own conclusions even before a medical examiner performed the autopsy. And those conclusions were badly tainted by emotion. Of course, there was no guarantee that the police reports would be any more credible, but it was her only other option.

Hugh had agreed to half a day's work. Since they'd discovered the treasures of the kiva, the day of leisure had been reduced to the morning of leisure. And that suited everyone just fine. After they returned from Chinle, the team would spend the afternoon hours at the excavation.

Leigh dropped Hugh off at the Laundromat to get the clothing started, then went on to the police station. Officer Joe was on duty again. He greeted her warily. No doubt Carlos had reprimanded him for allowing her access to the files the last time. When she asked to see the file on Ruby, he pretended that he didn't even know whom she meant.

"What's the last name?" His eyes skittered past her; he seemed to be looking toward the door for reinforcements.

She was about to say, "Yazzi," when she realized that Ruby had already been married at the time of her death. But the question was ridiculous to begin with. Peter Joe knew who Ruby was. He knew everyone in Chinle and Canyon de Chelly, and probably on most of the reservation, as well. But he was afraid of being the target of Carlos's wrath again. Given the circumstances, she was going to have to play along.

"I'm afraid I don't know her married name, but she was Mary Yazzi's daughter."

"Dennetsonne," Carlos said.

Leigh turned to find him standing in the interior doorway. She hadn't even heard him come in.

"Her married name was Dennetsonne." He came to join her in front of Peter Joe's desk. Joe was noticeably relieved, his face relaxing back into jowls now that the cavalry had arrived.

"Is this more research, Doctor?" Carlos inquired with a sardonic smile.

"Curiosity," Leigh said.

"It's no secret. She died of a heart attack. You don't even have to take my word for it—if you want to see her file, I'll show it to you."

Leigh thanked him and told him that wouldn't be necessary. If Carlos was that willing to show her the file, there wouldn't be anything useful in it, anyway.

"So she died just like Gates," she said, as if she'd just realized the link between the two.

"Just like Gates." His tone dared her to challenge the autopsy reports.

"Don't you find it strange—two young people dying of heart attacks like that?"

He shook his head. "It's rough country here. Rougher than you know. Count yourself lucky that you'll be leaving soon."

But Leigh didn't count herself lucky. The thought that she might never see Zakoura again should have filled her with relief, but it only produced an aching emptiness. It's just the dreams you don't want to give up, she'd told herself over and over, disgusted with her obstinate heart. You can take your damned dreams with you. But somehow that logic didn't make her feel any better.

"Maybe you should add a health disclaimer to your tourist information," she said. The words were out before she could consider their long-term effects.

"If it were up to me, there would be no tourists in Canyon de Chelly. No archaeologists, either."

Leigh thanked him for his help. It was definitely time to leave.

* * *

When she and Hugh returned to camp, Alex and Paul were ready to go, but Karen was nowhere in sight.

"She was going stir-crazy just waiting around for you guys," Paul explained as they jumped into the Bronco. "So when Bahe drove by with a truckload of tourists, she flagged him down and begged for a ride."

Hugh frowned and shook his head. "She knows the rules—no one works alone."

"She's a big girl, *Dad*," Alex told him with a laugh. "She'll be fine. Besides, she knew we'd be along in a little while."

Ordinarily Leigh would have come to Karen's defense, as well, but a cold premonition had slithered into her mind when she heard that Karen had gone to the site alone. Too many threats. Too many mysteries. She wished Hugh could drive faster along the winding canyon floor.

CHAPTER TWELVE

Leigh was the first one up the cliff to the cavern. She hauled herself up over the ledge and nearly stumbled headfirst into the gaping chasm where the roof of the kiva had once formed the plaza. Her screams brought the rest of the team scrambling up beside her. For one moment, they all stood in stunned silence around the jagged opening, trying to absorb what had happened. Leigh recovered first, calling out Karen's name. The others took up the cry. There was no answer except the hollow echo of their voices bouncing off the cliff walls.

Leigh took a few steps closer to the lip of the crater. The remains of the stone plaza cracked menacingly beneath her feet.

"For God's sake, be careful!" Hugh shouted at her. Now that the initial shock had passed, he was back in charge, his voice grim with determination. "Paul, take the Bronco into Chinle and get us some help. We'll do what we can with our shovels. Time is critical—we've got to try to get to her."

Leigh hunkered down at the edge of the crater, trying to see past the dirt and debris, but the floor of the chamber was completely obscured. If Karen had been down there when the roof collapsed, she could have been buried alive. And they had no way of knowing how long ago the cave-in had occurred.

In spite of their urgency, they had to move slowly. The perimeter of the hole was clearly fragile. Too much pressure could cause it to collapse even more and send them all crashing into the kiva. Hugh and Alex crawled to the edge so that their weight would be more evenly distributed and less likely to cause further damage. Once they were assembled at the hole, Alex helped ease each of them down to the top of the rubble. He handed down the shovels, then he lowered himself over the edge.

They worked cautiously, but still the fallen debris kept shifting beneath them, and they were afraid they could be compacting it on top of Karen, cutting off any air that might be reaching her. They considered stopping and waiting for Paul to return with help, but time seemed even more important than caution.

Leigh continued to call out to Karen, hoping to hear even a whimper, a groan, in response—anything to let them know she was alive, to let them know in which direction to look for her. They'd been working for half an hour when she finally heard something. The sound was so faint that she thought she might have imagined it at first. She waved to the others to be still and listen. When it came again, they all heard it. A single word—''Here.'' Leigh's heart soared. It was Karen, she would swear to it. But, strangely, the sound seemed to be coming from outside the kiva.

The climb out of the kiva was frustratingly slow. Every time they reached for a handhold on the edge, the brittle rock broke off in their hands, causing small avalanches of dirt to shower down on them. Finally Alex located one section that hadn't been as badly undermined by the cave-in, and they were able to haul themselves out.

''Karen?'' Leigh cried again once she was outside.

''Over here.'' The reply was clearer this time, stronger. It was coming from the area of the condos. They found Karen inside one of the rooms where the overhanging cavern blocked out the sun and kept the air cooler. She'd angled herself up against one of the wall remnants. Aside from a few bruises and cuts that appeared superficial, she seemed fine, though a little dazed. Leigh poured her a glass of iced tea from their thermos.

"What happened?" Hugh asked when she'd finished drinking.

Karen shook her head, wincing with the motion. "I don't know. One minute I was working merrily along, and the next, pieces of ceiling were crashing down on me, with no warning at all. In seconds the dust was so thick that I couldn't see, I could barely breathe. I remember thinking I might die down there." Her mouth curved up in a wry smile. "And that Hugh would be really angry with me then. It's funny what goes through your mind at a time like that." She paused, and the smile dissolved into a frown. "I don't remember anything else. How did I get out of there? Did you guys—?"

Leigh shook her head. "We didn't even know you were safe over here. Until we heard you calling, we were digging through the rubble for you."

"Well, either she just doesn't remember getting herself out of there," Alex said, "or whoever started the cave-in rescued her."

"How can you be so certain the cave-in was engineered by someone?" Leigh knew there was a good chance he was right, but she thought she should point out the possibility that it might have been an accident. Maybe she just wanted to believe that Zakoura's warnings had been given in good faith and were not the threats they'd seemed.

"I'm as certain as I need to be. And the two best suspects are your mysterious Indian friend and our benevolent police sergeant."

"If you're right, whoever collapsed the roof didn't know I was down there until they heard me scream," Karen said.

"I guess they pulled me out because they didn't want a death on their hands."

Her last remark made Leigh think that perhaps the culprit wasn't Zakoura. Why would he care about one more death, when he was already responsible for two others? And yet how had he known they were in danger, if he wasn't the source of it? Nothing in this strange place had a simple answer.

"Whoever did this, if their intention was to keep us from working the kiva, they were mighty effective." Hugh sounded more defeated than Leigh had ever heard him. "It would take all our remaining time to clean the place out again." He brushed the hair out of Karen's face and managed a crooked smile. "I'm just glad that whoever did this was humanitarian enough not to leave you in there to die, kiddo—even if you don't know how to obey rules."

They had to table any further discussion then, because Paul had returned with Carlos, Bill Dijolei, and his cousin, Dr. John Dijolei. "Graduated from Cornell Medical back east," Bill said with pride as he introduced him.

Karen insisted she was fine and didn't need any medical attention, but Hugh said she wasn't going anywhere until she'd been checked out. While they stood outside the condo, waiting for the doctor to complete his exam, Leigh noticed something silvery glinting in the mix of dirt and pebbles near Hugh's feet. She made her way around to him as casually as she could so that no one's curiosity would be aroused. But once she was close enough to realize what she'd seen, she gasped out loud and had to camouflage her reaction with a sudden fit of coughing. The thunderbird pendant Zakoura always wore lay exposed on the ground. Apparently they'd all been too preoccupied to notice it before. She quickly put her foot on top of it and didn't budge until Dr. Dijolei emerged and everyone started milling around again. Then she managed to drag it under her shoe to the edge of a wall remnant, where she shuffled a layer of dirt over it.

Dijolei gave Karen a clean bill of health. He'd bandaged her cuts, but couldn't find anything else wrong with her, except for some sprained muscles in her neck and leg. He told them the signs of concussion to watch for and instructed her to take it easy for twenty-four hours, which elicited a sardonic smile from Hugh. No one would be able to keep Karen away from the dig for even one day.

Carlos expressed his dismay over the cave-in and promised a complete investigation into the cause, but no one on the team believed they would ever learn the truth from him. In fact, Leigh had the distinct impression he was hardpressed to mask his pleasure over the entire incident.

Alex and Hugh helped Karen down the cliff. Leigh trailed behind, reluctant to leave Carlos and the Dijoleis up there where they might find the pendant. She wasn't even sure why that mattered so much to her. She told herself it was because they were likely to suppress the evidence and deny its existence, even as they'd denied knowing Zakoura. But she knew she had other, more complicated motives, as well, because she couldn't even bring herself to tell her colleagues what she'd found.

She hadn't wanted to believe that Zakoura had killed Ruby or Jeremy Gates, and now she didn't want to believe that he was responsible for the cave-in. She had some crazy hope that if she confronted him with the pendant, he would have a credible explanation for having lost it there. Even as she toyed with this idea, she was also wondering just what it would take to convince her once and for all that Zakoura was the monster Mary and Jimmy claimed he was. Perhaps nothing short of her own death at his hands.

* * *

It was still light out when the team finished dinner, though the days had grown noticeably shorter now that summer was on the wane. Leigh told Hugh she wanted to borrow the Bronco to pay Mary a visit; she was too worn-out to walk. He didn't question her, which was just as well, because the Yazzi hogan wasn't her real destination. She didn't like lying, had never been very good at it, but since she wanted to go back to the dig alone, she had no choice.

As she drove into the wash, day immediately plunged into evening, the cliff walls blocking out the sinking sun as effectively as the horizon. Shadows, slick and viscous as oil, seeped down the rock face, pooling in corners and crevices and reshaping the canyon into an alien place. The red sandstone escarpments that were so magnificent in daylight had become dark sentries looming over her, watching. The deeper she moved into the canyon, the more they seemed to be closing in around her, blocking off any chances of escape. Suddenly this little expedition of hers didn't seem like such a good idea. Maybe she should turn back. Climbing down the cliff once it was fully dark was going to be tricky and dangerous, even with the propane lamp she'd smuggled into the truck. Besides, there was a good chance Carlos had already found the pendant, in spite of her discreet efforts to hide it. He and his friends must have scoured the area after the team left. The last thing Carlos wanted was for the team to uncover evidence that would require further investigation. No clues, no cause to pursue the matter. He could claim that the collapse of the kiva's roof was the result of hundreds of years of stress upon the stone, and that Karen had suffered some minor amnesia after the trauma of dragging herself out of the hole. He could probably even persuade Dr. Dijolei to concur.

Leigh stopped the Bronco in the middle of the wash and tried to decide what to do, while the shadows blotted up more and more of the light around her. Although reason told her to turn back, instinct urged her to see her plan through. Once the logical part of her mind would have won out easily, but since her tenure in Canyon de Chelly, logic was no longer her master. She put the truck into gear again and headed deeper into the dusky twilight of the canyon.

Parking at the base of the site, Leigh began the treacherous climb. She moved cautiously, depending on the lamplight to help her place each foot. She was nearly there, congratulating herself on her agility, when the howling of a pack of wolves startled her. Her heart started banging in her chest and her legs became rubbery and useless before she realized that the sounds were muted; the wolves were far away. She slumped against the cliff wall until the rush of adrenaline subsided and she was steady enough to go on. Had she not been so close to the top, she might have turned back right then. But she was only a few steps away, and the climb down was too long to consider in her current state.

When she finally pulled herself up onto the lip of the cavern, she thought about sitting down to rest for a while. But with every breath the light faded another degree. She had to keep going.

Staying at the outermost rim of the plaza, where the footing was more stable, she made her way around the collapsed kiva. In the descending night, the chasm looked unnervingly like the gaping maw of a subterranean beast waiting for her to take one wrong step. Leigh wished she could put her imagination on hold. There were enough real dangers out here to scare her; she didn't need to invent any additional ones.

When she reached the cavern where the condos were situated, she stopped, suddenly unsure near which wall she'd hidden the pendant. Beneath the overhanging rock, night had already settled in, and everything looked different. In addition, since she was now relying completely on the light from her lamp, she could see only one section at a time, which altered her perspective.

She tried retracing her movements as she remembered them from the afternoon, starting with the room where they'd found Karen. But although she thought she knew the right one, once she was within it she was no longer certain. This room was small, too small for them all to have stood here together. The next one seemed a better size. She went back outside to the area where they would have been waiting with Carlos and Bill and tried to visualize where everyone had been standing. She was concentrating so hard that she jumped at the unexpected sound of something scrabbling around in the dirt and crushed sandstone. She listened carefully for a few moments, but all she heard was her own shaky breathing. She told herself it was probably just some small nocturnal animal surprised to find a human there and eager to make its getaway.

She found the wall where she remembered Hugh standing and knelt down, running her fingers through the loose dirt. Almost immediately they brushed across the hard, smooth surface of the thunderbird. With a sigh of relief, she picked up the pendant and stuffed it into her shirt pocket. But when she rose to leave, she found Zakoura directly in front of her, blocking her path.

A cry of shock swept up her throat, but she cut it off before it could reach her mouth. She wasn't going to give him the satisfaction of knowing how completely he'd surprised her. But she couldn't disguise the trembling that was causing the lantern to bob about in her hand. The wobbling light made him fade in and out before her, as if he were a ghost who might vanish at any moment.

"I believe you found something that belongs to me," he said.

Leigh withdrew the pendant from her pocket and held it so that the light reflected off its highly polished surface. "I guess it fell off while you were destroying the kiva," she said, pleased with the sharp edge she'd managed in her voice.

"I warned you that the kiva was dangerous."

"And what engineering degree brought you to that conclusion?"

"There are ways of knowing—the rock itself has a voice, if you know how to listen."

"Since you're so good at listening, how is it that you didn't hear Karen working down there?"

"I knew someone was in the kiva."

"So you simply didn't care—which doesn't surprise me. But then why bother to rescue her after the fact?"

"It is this fact that you have wrong. The cave-in was not caused by my hand. But neither was it ever in question. Only the exact hour was unknown to me."

Leigh looked straight into his eyes, but found no signs of guilt or dissimulation there. He returned her gaze evenly. But as much as she wanted to believe him, there was a large hole in his logic that had to be dealt with.

"From the beginning you've made it crystal-clear that you don't want us around, so why would it have mattered to you if one of us, or all of us, had been killed down there?"

If his calm demeanor had been a facade, she'd managed to shatter it now. The wavering lantern light accentuated the tension that gripped his handsome features and the angry frustration that burned within his eyes. But his loss of control lasted only a moment. When he spoke, his face was once more composed and unreadable.

"This I cannot answer."

"Will not answer," she said tartly.

He held out his hand for the thunderbird.

"A trade," she said. "The pendant for the medicine rattle." There was no reason he should agree, but Leigh couldn't resist trying to win something from him anyway.

With a wry smile, Zakoura grabbed for the hand that held the necklace. Leigh pulled it back and moved away from him. She knew she should just hand it over. After all, there was no place she could run for sanctuary up here, and he could overpower her with no trouble. But she couldn't bring herself to give up the pendant so easily.

Zakoura came toward her. She backed away, sidestepping so that she wouldn't wind up corralled against the wall of the cavern. For several minutes they circled around the ruins, like partners in a strange, ritual dance. Then, suddenly, he lunged at her. She managed to keep her hand out of his reach, but he grabbed her around the waist and pulled her to him, so roughly that she nearly dropped the lantern. She cried out in protest, but he held her tightly to him, his arm like a vise around her so that she couldn't wriggle free. The worst part was that she wasn't sure she wanted to. She'd never been this close to him before, except in her dreams, and the pressure of his body against hers was stirring her blood with an excitement that was rapidly overpowering both anger and fear. She looked up at him and saw a wild confusion mirrored in his eyes, as well. She couldn't tell if he was going to kiss her or kill her—the one seemed as plausible as the other. If she waited for him to make the next move, she might wind up as dead as Ruby. But even as she was mustering the will to fight her way free, he pried the pendant out of her fingers and thrust her away with such force that she staggered backward, barely managing to remain on her feet.

"The kiva is gone," he said gruffly as he slipped the silver chain over his head. "There is little else for you and your people here."

"We'll be gone soon enough," she replied, in a tone harsh enough to match his. Even if the kiva hadn't collapsed, they would have had to leave in another two weeks.

"It is the only way. You don't belong here."

Leigh thought she detected a peculiar note of sadness behind the words. Perhaps it was just wishful thinking on her part, or perhaps he mourned the loss of her as an adversary. Who would become his prey when she was gone?

As she watched him walk off in the direction of the supply cave, she had the feeling that she might very well never see him again, and the thought produced a hollow ache deep inside her. She shook her head in exasperation. Maybe once she left this place she'd become herself again.

She held her watch to the lamplight. She'd been gone over an hour, and she didn't dare rush the climb back down to the canyon floor.

Half an hour later, she was just passing the halfway point, having navigated the steepest part of the descent, when an owl sailed by her, its wing skimming her arm. Without thinking, she jerked away, and the movement cost her her balance. For several terrifying moments she teetered on the side of the cliff like an amateur tightrope walker, her heart pounding so hard in her throat that it cut off her breath. The lantern flew out of her hand. Seconds later she heard it crash to the canyon floor. And then she was falling through the pitch darkness, grappling frantically for a handhold on outcroppings of rock as she tumbled downward. She seemed to be falling forever. Sandstone raked her hands and tore at her clothing. She kept expecting the shattering impact that would kill her. But there was only a hard, jarring thud, and then she wasn't moving anymore. Pain as hot as a branding iron exploded in her hip, and she heard herself cry out.

Struggling to hold on to consciousness, she felt around herself in the blinding night. The cliff face was still on her left, but her hand fell off into nothingness a few inches to the right of where she lay. A narrow ledge of rock had broken her fall. The pain was becoming a torch that flamed through her entire leg now, pulsating in rhythm with her ragged heartbeat. Her head was spinning as if it weren't properly attached to her body; her stomach churned with nausea. And although the night was warm, she was shaking so hard that her teeth clanked against one another.

The blackness around her was starting to seep into her head; she could feel it pulling her down...down into a soothing velvet tunnel. She wanted to let go, to escape from the pain, but she fought it with every ounce of strength she still had. If she passed out, she might topple off her narrow perch.

Gingerly she shifted her body to throw as much of her weight as possible against the cliff wall; she had to make gravity work for her. Every movement brought with it another concussive wave of agony. She didn't know how much longer she could hold on to consciousness. When she'd done all she could to secure her position, she was as exhausted and out of breath as if she'd run a marathon. She let her head drop against the rough stone surface, indifferent to the minor discomfort it produced. She was cold. So... cold. And her eyelids...were so...heavy. She could barely... keep...

The first thing she felt was the heat. Even before she opened her eyes. It reminded her of first summer days at the beach, the warmth of the sun burning right into the marrow of her bones, casting out the chill of winter. The image confused her—the last thing she remembered was being gripped by intolerable pain and numbing cold. The cold was gone, and the pain— She waited for it to come roaring back now that she was awake. But all she felt was a muted ache that receded with every breath.

Her eyelids were still awfully heavy, but she forced them open. She had to make sense of what was happening to her. But what she saw confounded her even more and sent a shock of fear spiraling through her. Zakoura was kneeling at her side, his hands opened flat and poised just above her injured hip. A deep, iridescent blue light flooded the space between his hands and her body. Illuminated by the glow of that peculiar light, he looked like a phantom, or an alien creature.

"What...what are you doing?" She tried to shrink away from him, but she was already against the cliff face.

"Do not move," he commanded, without moving his eyes from the light beneath his hands. "You must be still."

Leigh didn't argue. His tone made it clear that he was deadly serious. And she didn't have the strength to spar with him, anyway. She watched his hands play above the light, moving it slightly this way or that as if he were a master puppeteer. The intensity of the blue kept increasing, becoming more and more brilliant, until it made her eyes tear to look at it. But she was too fascinated to turn away. She wasn't even aware of the exact moment when the pain stopped.

"How do you feel?" Zakoura asked without shifting his focus.

"Fine," she said tentatively, surprised to find that she really did feel all right. Not only was the pain gone, but the lethargy was lifting, too. "I feel fine."

He drew his hands back from her slowly, and as he did the blue light diffused and faded until it had vanished completely.

Zakoura rose and held his hand out to her. "Try standing."

Although the pain was gone, Leigh was wary of putting weight on the leg so soon. The remembered agony was too fresh in her mind.

"It is healed. Do not be afraid," he said, understanding her reluctance.

There was a gentleness to his voice that Leigh had never heard before. For one wild moment, she wondered if she was still unconscious and this was just another dream from which she would soon awaken to find herself alone in the canyon and badly injured.

"You must do it now. You have to return to your camp." The harsh edge had returned to his voice, and for once Leigh was glad to hear it. She was awake, and she was all right. Had he been just a pain-induced hallucination, there was a good chance she would not have survived the night. Even if she hadn't tumbled off the ledge, she would have been easy prey for a pack of hungry wolves. She had no idea why he had come to help her, but since he had, it seemed reasonable to trust him.

Pushing off with her free hand, she eased herself up from the ledge. At first she leaned most of her weight on the uninjured leg. But when she didn't experience even the slightest twinge of discomfort, she mustered her courage and stood straight. There was no evidence that she had ever been hurt.

"How on earth did you do that?" she asked incredulously. Her mother had books on psychic healing, but Leigh had never even bothered to look through them. The subject had seemed like nothing more than New Age quackery.

"Hold on to me," Zakoura said, ignoring her question. "You will never find your way in this dark."

She followed him down to the canyon floor, holding tightly to his arm. He moved with uncanny assurance, although there was no light to see by and the path was difficult enough to navigate in daylight. When they reached the bottom, he walked her to the Bronco. Leigh withdrew her hand, reluctant to break the contact.

"I still don't understand why you came to help me, or why you rescued Karen, or a dozen other things," she said as she opened the door on the driver's side, "but thank you."

If Zakoura nodded or smiled, she couldn't tell in the darkness. But she felt the void as he walked away, in the empty air around her, as well as in her heart. She climbed behind the wheel and switched on the headlights, hoping to see him one last time. But he was already out of sight, and she was alone in the canyon.

CHAPTER THIRTEEN

The last days went by in a kind of slow motion. The team was just marking time. The death of Jeremy Gates, the loss of the medicine rattle and the collapse of the kiva had all taken their toll. Their energy and drive were gone. They performed their jobs with proficiency, but without enthusiasm. Leigh was the only one who suffered mixed feelings about leaving Canyon de Chelly, and these she kept to herself. None of her colleagues would understand the pang of loss she felt when she thought about Zakoura Kree. She didn't understand it herself, but she sensed it had to do with regret over lost opportunities. There was a powerful connection between them whose source eluded her completely, a connection that seemed to anger him even as it lured him back to her time after time. She knew that if she was to stay, her relationship with him might end in tragedy, even as Ruby's had. Still, it was not going to be easy to leave.

She and Karen spent the remaining time working with the two men in the condos. Hugh chose to work in the storage cave. Leigh suspected that he just wanted to be alone. She understood the feeling. Conversation was an effort.

She kept looking and listening for a sign that Zakoura might be watching her, but there was none. She even prowled around the camper one night while everyone else slept. Had he wanted to come to her, he would have come then. But she waited for an hour, staring at the arcane shapes of the mesas in the moonlight, before she gave up and returned to her bed. She spent most of her free time trying to make sense of why he'd threatened her, then rescued her, and why she couldn't let go of him.

All that remained of him were the dreams, as lush with detail and sensation as ever. When morning came, she crawled out of bed feeling as if she were leaving the best part of her life behind and secretly counting the hours until she could be with him again. Although she couldn't deny the pleasure she derived from these games of her mind, she worried that they were becoming an unhealthy obsession. Not that it mattered. She'd never had any control over them anyway.

The team spent the last day packing up. Paul completed the entries in the daybook and excavation register. Hugh concocted a huge, eclectic meal from the supplies that remained in their pantry, but nobody had much of an appetite. And when Karen made a toast to "next year," they obediently clinked glasses and echoed her words without any real passion. There was little chance that they would be returning.

Jimmy stopped by with Rowdy to say goodbye.

"Maybe I could dig out the kiva before next summer so you could come back and work there," he offered.

Leigh hunkered down so that she was at eye level with him.

"No, Jimmy. You've got to promise me that you won't even go near the kiva. That whole plaza is unstable now. If we come back, we'll bring the proper equipment to do the job safely."

"*Will* you come back?" His voice quavered.

She wanted to tell him that they would, but it was too close to an outright lie. Financial realities, and the problems they'd encountered this summer, made their return unlikely.

"I don't know," she said, trying to stop Rowdy from lapping at her face. "But I still need your promise."

Jimmy took a deep breath. "I promise, Dr. Leigh," he said solemnly.

"Okay." She stood up to get out of the range of Rowdy's sandpaper tongue. "Do you think maybe you could write to me?"

Jimmy's face lit up. "Sure I could. And you'll write back?"

Leigh said that she would, and she asked him to say goodbye to his grandmother for her.

They left at dawn the next morning, looking like a modern-day wagon train. Karen and Alex drove the campers; Hugh and Paul were in the Bronco. Leigh sat in the passenger seat beside Karen, trying not to look back. She focused on the road that stretched to the horizon, straight as an airport runway. She was determined to put all the mysteries of Canyon de Chelly behind her, to purge Zakoura from her heart and mind, and to move on with her life.

By the end of September, she was traveling back along that road, alone. She and her colleagues had finished cataloging all the artifacts for the university in Tucson. After a bittersweet farewell dinner, the other four had left to return to their teaching positions. Leigh was scheduled to fly back east at the end of the week to pick up her dogs and start hunting for a job. She'd planned to spend her last few days in Phoenix relaxing and doing some shopping, but it quickly became apparent that she didn't have the patience for either. Zakoura filled her mind completely. While she'd had the wrap-up work to keep her busy, she'd managed to keep thoughts of him under control; now that she was idle, they'd taken over, occupying her every waking minute. But not her dreams. Since she'd left Canyon de Chelly, the dreams had stopped. She knew that she should be grateful, that it was a sign that she was returning to her old self, but she couldn't help feeling a little cheated.

It was after yet another fruitless expedition through a mall where she couldn't find a single item of interest that she made up her mind to go back to Chinle. Just for two days. Just to see the canyon one last time. Just to stop in and say a proper goodbye to Mary, see how Jimmy was enjoying the new school year. Who was she kidding? She was going back to see Zakoura.

She rented a Jeep with a towing hitch and a compact camper to haul behind it. She didn't need much for a couple of days. To allay the concerns of her more practical nature, she swore to herself that no matter what, she'd be on that plane home on Friday.

It was almost dark by the time she reached Chinle. She stopped at the motel for dinner, which she found she was too anxious to eat. The cafeteria-style restaurant was almost empty. The tourist season was nearly over now that schools throughout the country were back in session. She was glad she didn't bump into Carlos or one of his cronies. They were sure to ask what she was doing back here, and she hadn't worked out a reasonable answer as yet.

The cashier was the same young woman Leigh remembered from the past few times she'd eaten there. She smiled at Leigh with patent curiosity as she took her money. By morning, everyone would know Leigh was back. Probably even Zakoura. She didn't know what she intended to say to him if he did show up. None of their past encounters had been particularly pleasant or illuminating. The truth was that she would be content just to be near him again.

She set up camp in the same place where the team had stayed. Since it was already too dark to wander around, she tried reading by the light of a propane lamp. But she gave up after an hour, unable to concentrate. Lying down on the thin mattress, she listened to the hooting of the owls and the howling of the coyotes and the wolves. She wasn't going to get any sleep tonight.

Yet she must have eventually fallen asleep, because sometime after midnight Zakoura's voice awakened her. At first she thought she was hearing him in her mind, as she had on that other occasion. But after coming fully awake, she realized this was not wishful thinking. Nor was it telepathy. He was calling to her from outside the camper.

"Leigh," he called again, in a tone that left no question about his displeasure in finding her there.

For the first time since deciding to return, Leigh wondered what the hell she was doing. Fear was wedged in her throat like a thick bone that kept her from breathing or swallowing properly. If she didn't go out to him, he might just barge right into the camper. She quickly combed her fingers through her hair and straightened her clothing.

He was waiting a few feet from the door. Although she'd only been gone a month, her memory of him had already become distorted. His hair was thicker, blacker, than she remembered, the angles of his face more chiseled and regal, the fire behind his eyes more intense. How would she ever manage to hold on to any semblance of him? At the end of a year, he would be no more real than a grainy old picture in an archaeology text.

She set the lamp on the ground and walked over to him.

"Why are you here?" he demanded. If he was at all glad to see her, he was hiding it well.

"I didn't know I needed your permission to come back."

Zakoura didn't respond. He just stood there studying her until she felt obligated to say something more.

"My flight isn't for a couple of days, and I never had a chance to say goodbye to Mary."

"You came back to see Mary Yazzi," he said, with the snap of sarcasm that always infuriated her.

"Are you saying that I'm lying?"

"A half-truth is sometimes no truth at all."

"You're not exactly the right person to be giving lessons on honesty," she said sharply. With each exchange she could feel the air between them thickening, crackling with an emotional current as volatile as lightning. It was only a matter of time before a full-blown storm would erupt.

"Tell me you didn't come back to see me, and I will leave," he said.

Coming from another man, such a statement would have been laughably self-absorbed. But this was Zakoura. He probably already knew why she was there. Even so, she didn't find it easy to reply. She'd never been comfortable admitting her feelings, especially in the face of imminent rejection. But she'd come all this distance to confront him, and that would take some honesty on her part, as well.

"And if I did come to see you?" she said, her chin thrust out defiantly. It wasn't exactly a confession, but it was the best she could manage under the circumstances.

"Then you have made a bad mistake." He hadn't raised his voice, but each word sizzled with a blistering anger.

For the first time since she'd emerged from the camper, it occurred to Leigh to check him for a weapon. Although the light reaching them from the lantern was dim, she could see that there was nothing in his hands, and nothing tucked into the top of his breechcloth. Not that he really needed a weapon. He could snap her neck with his fingers.

She debated running back into the camper, bolting the door and grabbing a steak knife for protection. But she stayed where she was. If he'd meant to do her harm, he wouldn't have rescued her on the side of the cliff. He was just trying to scare her away, she'd stake her life on it. With an involuntary shudder, she realized she might be doing exactly that. Well, she'd played the game out this far—she was going to see it through.

With no warning, Zakoura came toward her. In spite of her decision, she faltered and fell back a step. Before she could change her mind and run, he closed the space between them and grabbed her roughly by both arms.

She started to scream, but his mouth came down upon hers, hard and hungry. It was less a kiss than a punishment. For a moment she was too stunned and confused to respond. Her mind told her to get the hell away from him, but her heart was entrapped, and her body already enflamed. She kissed him back, her lips soft and pliant beneath the bruising pressure of his. She wanted to wind her arms around his neck, but his hands were still gripping her, holding her away, as if he were fighting the desire that consumed him. They stood locked that way, in an embrace that was a battle of wills, until passion began to melt his anger. His mouth grew more tender, although no less insistent. He folded his arms around her and drew her body tight to his, tighter and tighter, as if he wanted to absorb her right into his soul.

Finally—this was the man she'd known in her dreams. All her crazy, inexplicable feelings for him hadn't been one-sided after all. She still didn't understand how she could have fallen in love with a man she didn't know, a man who was so alien, but she no longer believed that such a thing was impossible. The word *impossible* no longer existed for her. But her joy was short-lived. As suddenly as he had grabbed her, Zakoura now thrust her away.

"You should not have come back here," he said heavily. "There is no good way for this to end."

Leigh struggled to clear her mind, which was still muddied with desire. She wished she could argue the point, prove him wrong, but she had no idea what he meant, what it was that troubled him so. All she could do was object in a voice that was weak with yearning and bewilderment.

"I don't believe that. I won't accept it."

"Do not push me too hard." He turned on his heel. "I know what must be done."

Leigh snatched up her lamp and started to follow him. Not this time. He wasn't going to simply walk off and leave her bewildered and alone. This time she was going to find out where he went when he disappeared.

He wheeled on her, his eyes as vicious as those of a cornered animal.

"If you follow me, you will find your truth, and you will die for it as Ruby died, and Gates, and others you know nothing of."

Leigh wasn't sure if he was bluntly admitting to murder or hinting at something more insidious, but there was no doubt in her mind that he was serious. Maybe it was a flash of psychic insight, or just basic survival instinct, but she knew that his words were not an idle threat. No matter what he might feel for her, if she pursued him, she would die.

She stopped where she was and let him go. But she wasn't giving up. She was determined to have some answers before she left. If Zakoura wouldn't supply them, Mary might still be able to.

She waited until the sun had been up for a few hours before setting out for the Yazzi hogan. Although she'd been awake most of the night, she was afraid it might be considered impolite to go visiting too early in the morning.

When she arrived, Jimmy was leading the sheep out of their pen, while Rowdy raced around them, barking, as if he were in charge. They were both thrilled to see her. The dog did his usual mad dance, punctuated by occasional leaps to try to lick her face. Jimmy bubbled over with questions about why she was there and what she'd been doing since she left. She answered them as briefly as she could, because Mary was looking on, clearly not as overjoyed by her appearance.

Jimmy begged his grandmother to let the sheep wander around on their own, but Mary was adamant. There wasn't enough for them to eat on the rim. They had to be taken down into the canyon. Leigh tried to ease the situation by promising to spend some time there with him. Appeased, Jimmy told her where they'd be, and he and Rowdy headed the sheep out.

Leigh turned to Mary, ready to explain that she'd come to say goodbye, but the older woman spoke first.

"You are a fool," she said wearily. "You got away, you were safe. You should never have come back."

Leigh knew she was thinking of her daughter, who hadn't been lucky enough to get away. What could she say that Mary would understand? The truth was all she had. "I couldn't help it. I can't seem to let go of him."

Mary wagged her head. "Come inside. There's still some tea from breakfast."

"How can I find him?" Leigh asked once they were seated with steaming mugs in their hands.

"Even if I wanted to help you find him, I couldn't. He is not of this place. He comes and goes as he pleases."

"What does that mean—'he's not of this place'? Who is he? Where *does* he come from? Please, Mary, at least let me know what I'm up against."

Mary sipped her tea, her brow furrowed deeply, as if she were weighing a difficult choice. "I have already said more to you than I have the right to say."

"Who decides what you're allowed to say?" Leigh knew she was dangerously close to crossing the line into behavior that would be considered intrusive and therefore intolerable. But this was her last chance.

Mary seemed surprised that she would ask such a question, but not particularly angry. When she didn't answer, Leigh pressed forward.

"I don't mean to pry, but has someone ordered you not to talk about Zakoura?"

"You *are* prying, and you are well aware of it," Mary scolded gently. "But the answer is no. No one has ordered me not to talk. It has to do with an understanding among the people of this reservation. I would be breaking a trust."

It was Leigh's turn to be surprised. She would have sworn that Carlos had demanded Mary's silence for reasons of his own. Apparently he was not the leader of this conspiracy of silence; he was merely another player.

"I promise you that anything you tell me I will hold in the strictest confidence."

"I think it is best that you go now," Mary said, starting to push herself out of the chair.

Time to play her last card. "I know Zakoura Kree is Anasazi," Leigh said, with more conviction than she felt. If she was wrong, Mary would think her an absolute fool. But if she was right, the older woman might just decide that there was no longer any point in guarding the secret.

Mary sank back down heavily. The color had drained from her face, leaving it as sallow as dried parchment. She didn't have to say a word; her reaction told Leigh enough. The impossible was true. Zakoura was part of an Indian tribe that had disappeared without a trace eight hundred years ago. The other questions she'd so carefully prepared were temporarily blown out of her mind.

A wobbly "How—?" was all she could manage.

"If you tell anyone about this, we will deny everything," Mary said gravely. "We will hold you up to ridicule, and you will lose face in your profession and among your family and friends."

Leigh nodded, leaning forward in her seat, straining to hear the words, the explanations, that hadn't yet been uttered.

"This world of ours has many levels. The one we know is not the only one, and it is not the highest. There are many beyond ours. The Anasazi lived for hundreds of years in peace and in harmony with nature. Their reward was to be lifted to the next plane."

Leigh's mind was reeling. This was nothing but a fantastic story, a legend told around campfires. How could she possibly believe that an entire tribe of people had suddenly been zapped into another dimension? Yet Anglo science had never been able to come up with a better explanation. Maybe that was because it refused to look outside its comfortable circle of knowledge. But even if she accepted Mary's theory, there were a lot of unresolved questions, including why Zakoura was still here.

"He should not be," Mary told her. "But after the Anasazi were raised to the next level, a doorway remained open, a portal connecting our two planes. It has stayed so for all these years. To this day we are not certain where it lies. Only the Anasazi know its exact location. They come and go as they please. My grandmother used to tell stories about the ancient ones who would mysteriously appear and then vanish, but I had never seen any of them, until Zakoura came.'' Her lips curled with bitterness, and she paused to take a long swallow of her tea, as if that could wash away the loathsome taste of his name.

''Now you understand why we must keep this a secret from the outside world.''

''You'd be overrun with scientists, the media, curiosity seekers,'' Leigh murmured, imagining the hoardes who would descend on Chinle and the canyon. Followers of every religion and cult, as well as hucksters and con artists from all over the globe. And if the federal government ran true to form, it might even try to take the land away from the Navaho. It certainly wouldn't be the first time. The ramifications of this knowledge, and of the portal itself, were mind-boggling, but there was no doubt that it had to remain a closely guarded secret. The world wasn't ready for such a revelation. From what Leigh could tell, it might never be.

She sat there trying to absorb the impact of it all, her teacup growing cold in her hand. Mary didn't interrupt her thoughts. She waited for the inevitable questions to come, while the silence settled around them like a fine layer of dust.

Finally one question separated itself from the maddening tangle of them in Leigh's head. ''The clothing Zakoura wears is so primitive. How is it that after all these centuries there's been virtually no change?''

''Their clothing serves its purpose, I'm sure. Do not judge the Anasazi by the simplicity of their dress. There are many ways of living. What you Anglos call progress has not earned you a higher level of existence.''

Leigh had to admit that that was certainly true. Innovations and technology had brought them closer to extinction than to heaven. It was just difficult adjusting to the idea of a society that was both primitive and more advanced. But then she remembered Zakoura's telepathic abilities, and his healing powers. Apparently the Anasazi had their own measure of progress. They'd made incredible strides in realms that she and her fellow scientists still dismissed as quackery and fiction. She wondered if those advances included virtual immortality.

"Has Zakoura been alive since the twelfth century?" she asked.

Mary shook her head. "The Anasazi are as mortal as you and I. They simply live out their lives on another plane ... and bring misery to us on this one," she added heavily. Her eyes grew dull, glazed, as if they were focused on another time.

"I know about your daughter," Leigh said. "I'm so sorry." If Mary hadn't alluded to the tragedy, Leigh would not have brought it up, even though she wanted desperately to know more about Ruby's relationship with Zakoura.

"It was seven years ago." Mary's gaze settled on Leigh again. Her voice had a harder edge to it now. "Seven years. The pain was finally becoming bearable under the layers of so many days. Then you archaeologists came to dig up our canyon. And you, Dr. Morgan, came to dig up my memories. Now they are stripped clean again, like a grave dug up by the wolves. And they are as painful as ever."

Leigh felt a sharp pang of remorse. "It was never my intention to hurt you."

"If I had thought it was, I would not have invited you into my home. It is just your way—to look for answers. Now that you have them, do you truly believe it will be any easier?"

"I don't know."

"Zakoura has charmed you, bewitched you, as he did my Ruby. If you follow this path you are on, you will die as she did. I see it happening all over again."

"Ruby was in love with him?"

"Beyond all wisdom. She'd been alone since Jimmy's father ran off, a few weeks after she gave birth, and Zakoura was handsome and mysterious." Mary's body tensed; she gripped the arms of the chair. "I should have known. I should have warned her. It's a mother's duty to see these things."

"There's no way you could have known," Leigh said. "You can't blame yourself. Believe me when I tell you that Ruby would not have listened to you, even if you had had proof that he would harm her. Look at me—I've been warned, and I still can't walk away from him."

Mary took a deep, quaking breath, and the rigidity seeped out of her. "Thank you. Thank you for that."

Leigh rose and put her mug on the table. It was time to go. Time to let the healing begin again for this poor woman. Perhaps she would never have all her questions answered; she'd have to learn to live with that. After all, it was one of the liabilities of her profession.

Mary walked her to the door. She moved slowly, as if their conversation had taken a toll on her. "I wish you would take the advice I didn't have for Ruby."

Leigh couldn't bring herself to make a promise she might not keep. Instead, she hugged Mary to her.

"You are welcome here," Mary said, clearly flustered by the unexpected display of emotion. "But understand that I hope I don't see you here again."

Leigh nodded and left; she'd never become accustomed to goodbyes without the actual words. Jimmy was waiting for her, no doubt wondering what was taking her so long. Since she'd walked to the hogan, she decided to continue on into the canyon by foot. Her thoughts were in such turmoil, she needed the time alone to think.

Zakoura Kree was Anasazi. The legend was true. A doorway existed into another dimension. This time and place in which she existed was only one of many. The neurons in her brain were firing so rapidly, it felt like an explosion in a firecracker factory. She'd been given the knowledge of a lifetime, but she couldn't share it with anyone. Well, she would have to be content with satisfying her own scientific curiosity. If fame and fortune had been her goals, she never would have become an archeologist to begin with. In spite of the jumble of ideas cramming her head, her thoughts kept circling back to Zakoura. From the first time she'd seen him, she'd known he was somehow different. Her instincts had been right. She stopped dead in her tracks as a new realization struck her. The place Zakoura had taken her in her dreams—it had to be the other plane. That would explain so many of the strange things she'd seen there. And his contention that the medicine rattle belonged to him made sense now. It could easily have been his ancestors'. More and more of the puzzle was falling into place. But there was still too much she didn't know. Like why Zakoura would kill Ruby and Gates. Why he would be so loath to admit he cared for her. Why he had caused the cave-in and then rescued Karen, and on and on, including the pivotal question of whether her life was actually in jeopardy when she was with him. If she could confront him just once more with her knowledge of the portal, perhaps he would finally be willing to reveal the rest. But she still didn't have the vaguest idea of how to find him, or where to begin looking for this portal. And she had only until the morning. After she finished visiting Jimmy, she'd start her search. If she concentrated hard enough, Zakoura might even come to her.

CHAPTER FOURTEEN

As Leigh made her way into the canyon, it occurred to her that Jimmy might unwittingly have a bit of information that could help her find the portal, or at least narrow the area of her search. According to Mary, only the Anasazi knew its precise location, and that was most likely true. But Leigh suspected that over the past few hundred years the Navaho must have developed some idea of its general vicinity, if only by observing where their Anasazi visitors most frequently appeared or disappeared. She knew she could never hope to glean such information from Mary. The old woman was no doubt already regretting all she'd revealed. But there was a good chance that she'd alerted Jimmy to the spot, in hopes of keeping him away from Zakoura and the danger she was so sure he represented. If Leigh was careful about the way she approached the subject, Jimmy might just pass that information on to her.

She spent close to two hours with him, listening as he kept up a constant string of chatter, segueing smoothly from movies to horses to the stupidity of sheep, including the latest jokes circulating on that subject, and on into a list of the places he wanted to travel to when he got older, and the stories he'd heard from other citizens of Chinle who'd traveled beyond the borders of the reservation. Through all that time, he barely paused to take a breath, as if he were afraid she would leave if he didn't keep her entertained.

As anxious as Leigh was to squeeze in her question and start searching for the doorway and Zakoura, she didn't have the heart to interrupt him. She kept thinking how lonely and boring it must be for the child to look after a flock of sheep day after day with only Rowdy for company. Unlike his East Coast peers, he probably looked forward to the beginning of the school year as a reprieve, a chance to be with other children.

Just when it seemed that he would never run out of words, his voice became scratchy with wear and the rhythm of his monologue slowed, like a clock winding down. He dragged out a basket he'd had stashed in the shade of a cottonwood tree and offered her half of his mutton-and-fry-bread lunch.

Leigh declined. Although she hadn't eaten since her corn muffin at dawn, she didn't have the slightest interest in food. Rowdy, on the other hand, abandoned the sheep at the first whiff of lunch. He loped up to Jimmy and lay down with his big head in the boy's lap, hoping for handouts.

Jimmy bit into the oddly shaped sandwich, mutton gravy dribbling down his chin. He wiped it away with the back of his hand. Realizing what he'd done, he blushed with embarrassment and groped around in the basket until he found a napkin. Leigh pretended not to notice. This was as good a time as any to try her luck.

"I'll bet you know every nook and cranny of this canyon," she said, as if the thought had just come to her.

"Pretty much." He took another hearty bite, napkin in hand.

"When I was a kid, there were a lot of places I wasn't allowed to go by myself. You know, where my parents thought it might be too dangerous for me. I guess that's how parents are. Are there places that are out-of-bounds for you, too?''

Jimmy frowned at her as he continued to chew, a wary look in his eyes. A moment later, his brow unfurrowed. "I'm not allowed to go into Wild Cherry Canyon," he said once he'd swallowed.

That was easier than Leigh had expected. And fortunate, because Wild Cherry Canyon wasn't far from where she and Jimmy were sitting. It branched off the main canyon just before Spider Rock. She and the team had passed it every day on their way to the dig, but they'd never driven through it. More than once they'd talked of taking a day to explore the smaller canyons, but somehow they'd never found the time. Well, today she would. Wild Cherry *had* to be the site of the portal. Why else would Mary have warned her grandson to stay away? For the first time since hearing of the remarkable doorway to another plane, Leigh thought she actually had a chance of finding it. She felt mildly guilty about having tricked Jimmy into revealing the information, but since she had no sinister agenda, she told herself she hadn't done anything all that terrible.

She kept him company until he'd finished his lunch. Then, renewing her promise to write, she hugged him, gave Rowdy one last scratch behind the ear and set out to start her search.

Wild Cherry Canyon was much like the other sections of Canyon de Chelly. It followed a branch of the Chinle Wash, winding and weaving until it came to a forked cul-de-sac that resembled the business end of a scorpion. Leigh started on the right side of the wash, moving back and forth between the shallow stream and the red sandstone cliffs in order to cover as much ground as possible. Even so, she knew she might miss the doorway. She could pass an inch from it and never know it. Or it could be somewhere up in the cliffs themselves. Or directly in front of her. That thought shot a bolt of adrenaline straight into her heart. What would happen if she actually found the portal and stumbled across the threshold, like Alice in Wonderland? The idea was as frightening as it was exciting, but her footsteps didn't falter for a moment. She might not know what would happen if she tumbled into another dimension, but if she left tomorrow without even trying to find the portal, without trying to see Zakoura again, she would never forgive herself. Of that she was certain. But when she saw a limb from a cottonwood tree lying across the wash, she picked it up as a compromise with good sense. Held out in front of her, it might at least provide some warning if she was about to step into the portal.

Exploring the entire canyon, including the two dead ends, took considerably longer than Leigh had anticipated. By the time she made her way back to the main branch of Canyon de Chelly, the sun was well on its way to setting and she was frustrated and exhausted from the trek and the constant tension of not knowing if her next step would take her into an alien world.

She trudged toward the exit through the lengthening shadows, trying to console herself. After all, she'd had no guarantee that she'd find the doorway. If it was easy to find, the Navaho would have found it themselves by now. And Jimmy had never really *told* her that it was in Wild Cherry Canyon, she'd just assumed... Suddenly she remembered the wary look on his face when she'd asked if there were places he wasn't allowed to go, and then his reply, almost too quick and eager. She didn't know whether to laugh or scream. He'd outsmarted her. He'd known immediately what she was after, and he'd sent her on a wild-goose chase, no doubt to protect her. And she'd felt guilty for taking advantage of *him!*

It would have been funny if her time there hadn't been so limited. But the day was gone now; there was no time to explore anywhere else. She'd be lucky to make it back to camp before dark. She told herself it didn't matter. If she'd spent the day following her intuition, she wouldn't have had any better success. Finding the portal in this vast land was tantamount to finding a needle in a whole warehouse full of haystacks. Somehow the logic didn't make her feel any better.

Once she was up on the rim again, she paused for a moment to rest and catch her breath. The straightest route back to the safety of her camper would be directly past the Yazzi hogan. She could see it from where she stood, smoke rising from the chimney hole, lamplight already glowing in the window. Jimmy had probably driven his sheep up the wash and home while she'd been busy hiking through Wild Cherry Canyon. If she stopped by, Mary might even invite her to join them for dinner. The thought of food caused her stomach to grumble irritably. But she ignored it. Standing there, she'd realized there was one more place she wanted to check before giving up—the dwarf mesa where she'd first encountered Zakoura. It seemed only right that she should end her search for him and for the portal where it had all begun, at the dwarf mesa. Unfortunately, that would mean going out of her way by half a mile at least. It would also mean making the last part of the trip back to camp in utter darkness, because she didn't even have her pocket flashlight with her. She looked toward the horizon. The sun seemed to wink at her as it started its plunge behind the western ridge, daring her to outrun it. She glanced the other way, at the tiny humped forms in the distance that were her car and camper. She knew the dangers, the snakes and the predators that waited for the night, the distinct possibility that she wouldn't be able to locate her camp on this vast plain, that she could spend the night wandering aimlessly, with the temperature dropping and no protection. The sensible thing to do was to go back to camp now, but she'd stopped being sensible weeks ago. All she could focus on was visiting that spot once more. A decision had to be made—she was wasting precious time and light. Tired as she was, she started jogging toward the mesa.

By the time Leigh reached it, she was out of breath and a little dizzy. But there was no time to rest. The sun was almost gone. Dusk was throwing its sheet of gray over the world; it was no longer possible to distinguish land from sky. She gave herself fifteen minutes. Fifteen minutes to walk around the mesa in widening circles. At the end of a quarter hour, whether or not she'd found anything, she would head for camp. She'd left the cottonwood branch back in the canyon, and there were no trees nearby to provide a new one, but fatigue and disappointment had combined to give her a fatalistic attitude. She'd deal with the consequences if and when she actually fell into the other dimension. Legs aching with fatigue, she began the first circle. The mesa was small enough that she made it around in thirty seconds. At the end of each circuit, she paused to reorient herself by the dim light from Mary's window. As long as that lamp burned, she could find her way back to camp.

Twilight was giving way to deep night when Leigh heard the first wolf howl. Before a second passed, another took up the cry. Then another. She told herself they weren't near, but the feral sounds scared her, reminding her how vulnerable she was. What had she been thinking to stay out here after dark? Zakoura wasn't going to come to her, he'd made that clear. And did she really expect to find the portal, when no one else had? Goose bumps rose on her arms.

She didn't know if they were from the wind that had picked up, or from the hungry wailing of the wolves.

She looked for Mary's light and felt a moment of panic when she couldn't locate it. She pivoted. There it was, behind her. Walking in circles had thrown off her sense of direction. Even though her fifteen minutes wasn't quite up, it was definitely time to leave. The wolves howled again. Closer now. Probably just her nerves playing tricks on her perceptions. She started walking quickly, using Mary's light as a beacon, eyes straining to see through a darkness as impenetrable as steel. She didn't see the red eyes burning like hot cinders until the last minute. The wolves had raced ahead of her. Three of them stood blocking her path, snarling. Her heart stopped; her blood froze. Her mind refused to work. She had to think. She had to decide what to do. If she stayed where she was, they would attack her, tear her to pieces. She tried to remember what she knew about wolves, but all that came to her was that they traveled in packs and were loosely related to dogs.... You weren't supposed to run from dogs, you were supposed to move slowly. Okay. She started backing up, one trembling step at a time. The wolves kept snarling. She could hear the saliva gurgling in their throats. But they stayed where they were. A few more steps back. She hadn't come that far. The mesa should be near. She didn't know if it was high enough to offer much protection, but it was her only option. A few more steps. The red eyes started moving, three pairs of them. Moving toward her. She glanced over her shoulder. It was so damned dark she couldn't see the mesa. The wolves were still coming. She had no choice but to run now and hope she could reach it before they were on her.

She ran with one arm out in front of her so that she wouldn't slam headfirst into the mesa. Although she was pumping her legs as fast as she could, she seemed to be moving in the maddening slow motion of a dream. There was no way she could outdistance them. She kept expecting to feel the sharp rip of pain as jaws clamped down on her leg.

Her foot rammed into an outcropping of the rock and sent her sprawling, hitting the ground hard. The wolves came to a stop a few feet away. They closed ranks around her. They were near enough for her to smell their hot, foul breath. She grabbed two handfuls of dirt and stones and threw them at the eyes that hovered before her like satanic fireflies. She must have hit her mark, because one of the wolves yelped, and the others drew back. During their few moments of confusion, Leigh managed to scramble up onto the mesa. When the wolves realized she'd gotten away, the snarling began again, more intense, anger mixing with their hunger. They weren't going to give up. They leaped at the rock, their nails clawing for purchase on the sheer sides. One made it halfway up before losing his balance and tumbling to the ground. It wouldn't be long before they found a way to the top and her.

There was nothing left for her to do; she was too numb with fear even to think. The wolves kept coming. Higher. Falling off. Coming again. She heard Zakoura telling her to stay where she was. Fear was making her delusional.

For some reason she couldn't fathom, the wolves suddenly stopped hurling themselves at the mesa. They hadn't left, though; she could still hear their menacing growls below her. She crawled over to the rim and peered down, trying to figure out what was happening. Their glittering eyes were no longer focused up at her. They were fixed instead on something to their right. Leigh couldn't see what had captured their attention, but she had the sense of another presence, of movement like ripples in the darkness. She wanted to call out, to ask who was there, but she knew instinctively that her voice could change the balance of power in the tense standoff going on below her.

Minutes passed, each as long as an hour. Then one of the wolves lunged toward his new prey. A powerful howl ruptured the night, making the air vibrate and penetrating right to the marrow of Leigh's bones. It was a wolf sound and yet not a wolf sound, and its effect was immediate. The aggressive animal fell back. The growling and snarling of the others faded to a bewildered whimpering. From her perch, Leigh saw their eyes blink out as they turned and slunk away into the night.

She was still huddled at the edge of the mesa, trying to make sense of what she'd witnessed, when she heard someone moving beside her. Before she had time to question who it was, strong arms were drawing her up into a tight embrace.

"Are you all right?" Zakoura's voice whispered through her hair, heavy with emotion.

Leigh nodded. The hopeless terror of her situation and the sudden, overwhelming relief of rescue had left her shaking so violently that she couldn't manage words.

He rocked her gently in his arms, murmuring words in a language she'd heard only in her dreams. His lips brushed across her forehead, down the side of her cheek. Little by little, her quaking subsided.

"Why are you still here?" he said, as much to himself as to her. "Why do you refuse to listen?"

She didn't answer. They both knew why she was there.

"Do you not know the danger you were in? You might have died here tonight." His voice had risen with each word, but where last night there had been the whiplash of anger, now she heard only raw frustration.

She tilted her head up. She couldn't see his face, but she could feel the fire burning in his eyes.

"If I had been a minute later..." He didn't finish the sentence. Instead, his mouth found hers in the darkness. He seemed frantic with the horror of what had almost happened and a desire over which he no longer had any control. Holding her face between his hands, he kissed her hard and deeply, tasting every part of her mouth, a ragged moan issuing from his throat. His hands swept down her neck and shoulders, across her back to her tiny waist, and up along her rib cage to cover her breasts, as if to assure himself that she was really there with him and safe.

Leigh didn't flinch from the possessiveness of his exploration. This was the first time they'd come together in this way, and yet it wasn't. The dreams might have been only a product of her subconscious, yet somehow, because of them, he wasn't a stranger, but a lover she already held in her heart.

Aching for his touch against her bare skin, she pulled her sweatshirt over her head and slid open the clasp on her bra. Zakoura knelt in front of her. In the cooling night air, his tongue was hot on her skin. She shuddered as his teeth rasped across her hardened nipples, jagged bolts of pleasure ripping through her body. He tugged open the snap on her jeans, and before she could reach for the zipper he'd yanked the two halves apart. With his help, she wriggled out of the clothes. Before she could straighten up, his tongue was trailing down her stomach and sliding within the cleft between her legs, taking her breath away. All the dreams that had seemed so incredibly real at the time had only been hazy abstracts of this. When her knees gave way, he caught her and laid her down on the flat tableland.

She tried to untie the rawhide strip that held the breechcloth at his waist, but he pulled it open himself, flinging it aside impatiently. The desire he had fought so desperately to deny, to subjugate to his will, was now the master. When

Leigh reached out to touch him, he was hard and slick in her hand. All she wanted was to have him moving inside her as she had imagined on so many nights.

She guided him between her legs, arching upward to meet him as he thrust inside her. The thunderbird dangling from his neck rode up and down between her breasts, a metal finger warm from the heat of his skin. She drew his head down to kiss him, and his tongue plunged into her mouth, stroking it in rhythm with his hips, consuming her in the fury of his passion. The rock beneath her was hard and rough, but she didn't feel it. He'd taken her far away from such discomforts, to a wild, primordial place, to a time when men and women had been one, before they were cleft in two and left to roam the earth seeking their missing halves. And then farther still, to a higher realm where they would be one again and forever.

From such a height, when the crash came, it was shattering. Her heart had barely started to slow from its violent pounding and her thoughts were still spinning in dizzying circles when he withdrew from her, so abruptly that she ached with the suddenness of the loss. She reached out, needing to hold on to him, needing to be held in his arms. But he had moved away from her. She heard the soft rustlings as he picked up the breechcloth and retied it, slid his feet back into his sandals. Reality was not like the dreams after all. She sat up and fumbled around in the darkness for her clothing, tears of confusion and betrayal welling up in her eyes and spilling down her cheeks. Why had he made love to her with such a burning passion, only to reject her the very next moment? She didn't want to give him the satisfaction of knowing how completely he'd devastated her, but she couldn't let him leave without demanding some sort of explanation.

"Tell me what it is that I've done to displease you so," she said, struggling for a semblance of composure.

"You have done nothing wrong. Except to be here." His voice, devoid of emotion, came to her like the voice of the darkness itself. His desire spent, he was once again in absolute control. Did she mean so little to him?

"Then I don't understand what's happening between us."

"What has happened should never have happened. For that I blame myself completely. I will see you safely to your camp. Tomorrow you will leave, and that will be the end of it, as it should be."

His words ripped into her as savagely as the wolves nearly had. Tomorrow would come, and she would leave, but that would not be the end of it. Not for her. She would never know a day of peace or happiness unless she could understand why he rejected her, why their union was so unthinkable to him. And if she was to be honest with herself, she couldn't leave without trying everything in her power to change his mind. Nothing mattered in her life but to stay with him.

She no longer worried about angering him with her questions. Even if he hadn't healed her on the cliff that night or protected her from a pack of hungry wolves only an hour ago, she would know she didn't have to fear him. No man could love a woman as he had loved her unless he was driven by much more than simple lust.

"It is not that easy, Zakoura," she said. "I know who you are, and I know about the portal."

"Mary Yazzi," he murmured.

"You owe me some answers before I go."

She felt the air move as he came up beside her. "I owe you more than that. Answers will not keep you safe."

"I know Mary blames you for Ruby's death, but I don't believe you killed her. And I don't believe you killed Jeremy Gates, either."

"If I had not come here, Ruby would be alive."

"Why did she die?"

"She tried to follow me back through the portal. No one from this plane has ever survived the crossing."

Her instincts had been right. He was not guilty of murder; he probably wasn't even capable of it. "Then why do you hold yourself responsible?"

Zakoura took her hand and drew her down to sit beside him. His voice was weighted with resignation, as if he had made a difficult decision and wasn't certain it was the right one.

"In all the generations since my people were moved on, only the shamans have been able to withstand the stress of passing through the portal again. Others have tried and found themselves weakened, their life spans shortened. The shamans themselves may only stay on this plane for short periods before their lives, too, begin to fail. As for the people here—I have never heard of anyone who survived the crossing for more than a few minutes."

"Gates must have stumbled across it during his run," Leigh murmured. The theory had been brewing in her mind since Mary revealed the secret of the portal to her.

"He was already dead when I found him on the other side. There is no one to blame for it, except the gods. But Ruby's death was no accident. She knew of the portal. All the Navaho know. Yet when I told her she could not cross it with me, she would not believe me. Perhaps she thought I wanted to be rid of her. I never lied to her. I told her from the beginning that I did not love her, but she would not let it be. It is my fault that I failed to see how deeply she had come to feel for me, how desperate she was to follow me."

Zakoura's voice trailed off; he didn't speak for several minutes.

Leigh allowed him the silence; she needed time, too, to absorb what she'd heard. Poor Ruby. She felt a surge of compassion for the young woman, abandoned by her husband, living in such utter isolation with her little son and elderly mother. It was easy to understand Ruby's heart. In her own way, and for far less reason, she had pursued Zakoura just as recklessly.

"After she died, I tried to stay away from the portal," he went on. "But the curse of a shaman's curiosity drew me back here again and again. I was careful, though. I stayed away from contact with anyone on this side. For years. Until you came. From that day I have been drawn to you in ways I cannot fight. And I have seen the same forces at work in you. How could I encourage those feelings? How could I allow you to know about the portal? I could not be responsible for your death, as well."

He did love her. Hope seeped up again through the battered chambers of her heart. The pieces were finally falling into place in this convoluted puzzle she'd been living.

"So you tried to scare me away," she said. "The explosion in the truck, the collapse of the kiva . . ."

"No. Only in my manner did I try to frighten you. I would never put your life in the slightest jeopardy."

"But I saw you there when the truck was burning, and I found the thunderbird after the cave-in."

"Carlos told you the truth—lightning hit your truck. I came only to assure myself that you were safe. As for the kiva—I knew the roof was weak and would fall. I tried to warn you, but you wouldn't believe me. You wouldn't stay away. I came there whenever I was able, hoping to save you if I could."

"Only Karen was alone down there when it happened."

"Yes."

"I haven't been right about anything, have I?"

"I did take the medicine rattle," he said, and she heard a smile in his voice. "It belongs in my family. And now all your questions are answered."

"No, there's one more. I don't understand how it's possible, but I've been dreaming about you since I came to this canyon, even before I ever saw you." She hesitated, fumbling for the right words. In spite of the intimacy they'd shared, it was awkward to admit to her erotic fantasies about him. "And these dreams, they don't feel like ordinary dreams. They're very... intense. At times they even seem to be out of my control."

"As they are out of mine," he said ruefully. "There are layers to the mind, to the soul, that are difficult to master. In sleep it is the hardest. I did my best to stay away from you when awake. Asleep, I sought you out in dreams." His fingers stroked her cheek. "I know I have not made this easy for you in any way."

Leigh took his hand and pressed the palm to her lips. In all the clutter and confusion of her mind, only one thing seemed perfectly clear. He loved her. All the time she'd spent fighting what she'd felt for him was over, meaningless. He loved her, and she was finally free to return that love without constraint. But since he could only withstand short visits to this plane she would make the canyon her home so they could be together as much as possible. She thought he'd be pleased when she said this to him, but he pulled his hand away from her and rose to his feet.

"No. I thought you understood. I cannot live here with you, and you cannot come with me."

Leigh jumped up and stood before him. "I do understand. Whatever time we can have together will be enough."

"That is no way for you to spend your life. I will not allow it."

"It's not your choice, it's mine."

"I will make it mine. I will not come back, Leigh," he said with steely determination. "I make this vow for your sake, and for your sake will I keep it. You will go back to your home and go on with your life. This time will fade in your mind. It will fade for both of us."

"And if I stay on in Canyon de Chelly anyway?"

"You will stay on alone." Without another word, he took her arm and guided her down from the mesa. She went without further argument. Her heart ached, and her mind railed against the injustice of his edict. But there were no arguments left.

Mary's lamp had been extinguished, and although the moon had finally risen, it was only a dull smudge of light behind a layer of clouds. By herself, Leigh would never have found her way. But Zakoura led her back unerringly.

He brought her to the door of the camper. Then he turned and walked away into the night, as he had so many times before. No last kiss. No final words. Not even a goodbye. She wanted to call out to him. To beg him to come back. To stay just until morning. But she knew that he wouldn't. That he wouldn't dare give her any hope that he might change his mind. And even if she could convince him to stay, in the end morning would come anyway, the sun would rise and he would go, and the ache would rush back to fill her heart in the way that air rushes to fill a vacuum.

CHAPTER FIFTEEN

The next morning Leigh packed up the few things she'd brought with her, checked the trailer hitch and slid behind the wheel of the Jeep. There was just enough time for the drive back to Sky Harbor Airport in Phoenix to catch her flight home. She turned on the engine and sat there, unable to go.

After a half hour paralyzed by indecision, she made a deal with herself. She would stay a little longer, but not more than a week. In case Zakoura changed his mind and came back. She tried not to think about the uncompromising finality of his words.

She phoned her parents and told them she'd decided to do some sight-seeing before she returned. She called the airline and rescheduled her flight. Then she stocked up on canned goods that didn't require refrigeration, since she didn't have the luxury of a generator this time.

She spent the days exploring the canyon as she'd always wanted to. Since the university's permit had expired, she no longer had the right to roam through it at will. But the tourist season was essentially over, and Edward Bahe offered to be her guide. At first he refused to let her pay, but Leigh insisted, so they worked out a reduced rate that suited them both.

Carlos came by, wanting to know why she'd returned. She recited her sight-seeing story for him. But it was clear he didn't buy it, because wherever she went, either he or

Dijolei or Joe seemed to be watching her. She would have liked to tell him that they were wasting their time; she already knew all about the portal. It would have been satisfying to watch that inscrutable mask of his crack. The words were poised at her lips, but fear kept her mouth shut. Who knew how far he might go to keep her from leaving the reservation with that secret?

Zakoura was always on her mind. She looked for him wherever Bahe took her—on every ledge, in every cavern, in the shade of every stand of trees. Still, the days passed swiftly in the Navaho's company. The nights were a different matter, endless and lonely. She slept fitfully, waiting for the dreams to bring Zakoura to her. But the only dreams she had were the ordinary patchwork variety, with little sense or substance. Somehow he was even managing to keep his subconscious from straying. He meant to honor his promise this time. The realization, as painful as it was, made it possible for her to leave when the week was over.

Her parents met her at the airport, thrilled to see her after so many months. Butch and Sundance were ecstatic. They weren't holding it against her that she hadn't phoned much lately. They settled back into her apartment in New York as if they didn't even miss the open spaces of Connecticut. Leigh had a harder time adjusting. She went through the motions of living, but she didn't feel any real attachment to her life. It was amazing to her that she had been so happy before she met Zakoura, and that now that same life brought her no joy.

Since professorships in archaeology were still impossible to find, she took a job with a company that published college textbooks, doing everything from clerical work to line editing to acting as a technical adviser on manuscripts in her field. At night she took courses that would enable her to teach at the secondary level. The busier she was, the less she hurt. She kept waiting for her memories of Zakoura to fade, but they seemed to grow more potent with time, more deeply etched in her soul.

By the time summer rolled around again, she'd made her decision. She was going back to Chinle. To live. She wasn't entirely sure why. Maybe it had to do with being closer to him, though she might never see him again. Maybe it had to do with a spark of hope that he would return someday and see that she'd chosen to live there even without him. On impulse, she'd contacted the Navaho school and been told that, yes, they needed teachers. That had clinched it. The pay wasn't terrific, but then, living expenses out there weren't close to what they were in New York, either.

When she told her parents what she intended to do, David Morgan shook his head and left the room with a bewildered expression, unable to understand what had become of his sensible daughter.

"What's his name?" her mother asked once they were alone in the kitchen.

A wry smile tugged at Leigh's mouth. "Have you been taking more of those classes guaranteed to improve your psychic abilities?"

"I'm a woman and I'm your mother. I don't need any extraordinary talents to see what's been troubling you since you got back. I just haven't wanted to pry."

"His name's Zakoura Kree."

"Native American."

"Yes."

"Even so, it's a strange name. Is it Navaho?"

"Not exactly." Leigh didn't like lying, but she'd promised Mary she wouldn't reveal the truth to anyone. She had no right to make exceptions whenever she chose.

"Does this man want you to come back?" Psychic ability or not, somehow her mother always managed to see straight to the heart of things.

"He isn't there anymore."

"Will he be back?"

"I don't think so. But I just need to be there for now. I know it doesn't make much sense...."

Nina nodded.

"Thanks for understanding and not asking a million questions that I can't answer," Leigh said, leaning over to kiss her mother's cheek. "I'm afraid Dad thinks I've gone off the deep end."

"Don't worry about it." Nina grinned. "Living with me all these years, he's learned how to tread water."

When the school year started in September, Leigh was settled into her new home, a small prefab ranch house with two bedrooms, a bath, a kitchen and an all-purpose living room/dining room/den. She'd purchased it with money her parents had loaned her, and with the reluctant permission of the Navaho council, she'd had it erected on the plain that led to Canyon de Chelly. The council understood that she needed a place to live if she was going to be teaching in Chinle, but they were suspicious of her motives for wanting to settle there. The agreement they had her sign made it clear that their permission could be revoked at any time and for any reason they deemed just.

The location they agreed on was close enough to the main road into Chinle for electrical and telephone lines to be drawn in and for water pipes to be laid at a reasonable cost. While Leigh was willing to brave the relative isolation of the area, she had no intention of learning to live like a pioneer.

The dogs seemed a little confused at first by their new surroundings. Her parents' two acres hadn't prepared them for these vast open spaces. Leigh introduced them to Rowdy, who was overjoyed to have some canine friends. The three raced around maniacally whenever they were together, thoroughly exhausting themselves, until they collapsed in a heap of panting fur.

Jimmy was equally pleased that Leigh had come back, but Mary welcomed her gravely, the old sadness welling up in her eyes. When Jimmy went outside to feed the mare, Leigh tried to explain to her that Zakoura had not killed Ruby and that he posed no threat to her, or to anyone for that matter. The danger resided solely in the portal, over which he had no control. Mary's features tightened at the sound of Zakoura's name, but she listened quietly, her hands continuing to knead the dough for the fry bread she was preparing.

"I know what I know," she said firmly once Leigh had finished.

Until that moment, Leigh hadn't realized how badly she wanted Mary to understand that it wasn't Zakoura's fault, how much she wanted the older woman to understand how she felt about him. But Mary was clearly determined to hold Zakoura responsible, as determined as Zakoura himself was. Jimmy returned from his chore then, so Leigh couldn't pursue the question of his mother's death. She wasn't sure she had a right to, anyway. Mary needed someone to blame.

Instead, she asked if either of them had seen Zakoura while she was away.

"Nope," Jimmy responded, with obvious relief. "We think maybe he's gone for good."

Leigh tried to hide the disappointment that twisted her heart, but Mary saw through the pretense and fixed her with a disapproving stare. "So, that is not what you wish to hear. Yet you say the reason you returned was because you want to teach." She wiped her hands on the cloth that was tucked into the waistband of her skirt. "You say that you missed the land, the quiet of life here."

"And us," Jimmy chimed in.

Leigh managed a smile for him. "What I said is true."

"And what you have not said is true, as well," Mary murmured, so that her grandson wouldn't hear.

They talked of other things then, the year Leigh had spent away, the rugs Mary had sold, Jimmy's school term. Mary invited her to stay for dinner, and Jimmy prevailed upon her to accept.

After that day, Leigh fell into the pattern of having dinner at the Yazzi hogan on Sundays. Sometimes it would just be the three of them sitting around the small table. Other times, there would also be a cousin or niece or nephew who'd stopped by to visit. When she was with them, she felt as if she were actually beginning to belong there. But Carlos was always around to remind her that she was an outsider, to be tolerated for the time being, but never to be allowed into the fabric of the tightly knit community.

On the day Leigh moved into her new home, he was her first visitor. He made it clear that he didn't agree with the decision of the council to hire her as a teacher and to allow her to live on the reservation. And he didn't understand why she'd chosen to be there.

"I would have thought that after all the misfortune you and your people suffered here the summer before last, this would be the last place you'd want to live," he said, walking around the perimeter of the house as if he were inspecting it for some problem or violation.

"I guess we archaeologists are just a resilient bunch," she replied crisply, following him to make sure he didn't create any problems. She wouldn't put sabotage beyond him.

Carlos stopped in his tracks and wheeled to face her. "As far as the Navaho Nation is concerned, you are no longer an archaeologist. You have no current permit to exacavate the canyon, and if I find you so much as digging up a stone I'll have you thrown off this land before you can pack up your belongings."

"I'll be sure to keep that in mind," Leigh retorted.

"You may have been able to fool the council, Dr. Morgan, but I don't for a minute believe that the only reason you've come back here is to teach. I'm going to make it my business to find out what you're really up to."

Leigh fought back her rising anger. Carlos was just trying to protect his people and their land, by guarding the secret of the portal. His motives were basically good, even if his methods were those of a petty tyrant.

"You ought to be more careful about your paranoia, Sergeant Tsosie," she said smoothly. "You wouldn't want me to think that there *is* something worth hiding around here."

Carlos's posture became rigid; his brows snapped together in a dark ledge over the rims of his sunglasses. He studied her for a long moment, as if he were trying to read the subtext of her words.

While she had him slightly off guard, Leigh decided to try to tease some information from him. Although neither Jimmy nor Mary had seen Zakoura since she'd left, that didn't necessarily mean he hadn't been back. Mary rarely left her hogan, and Jimmy's travels were somewhat circumscribed by school and the grazing areas of his sheep. If Zakoura had returned, Carlos and the other police were more likely to have spotted him in their wider travels through the canyons.

"By the way, I haven't seen Zakoura Kree since I've been back. Has he been around here lately?" She spoke off-handedly, as if she were inquiring about the amount of rainfall last month.

Carlos's frown dissolved. His face became a smooth mask again and when he spoke there was mocking humor in his voice. "Still chasing figments of your imagination, I see."

If Zakoura had been around during the past year, her question would probably have elicited more concern from Carlos. The relaxed confidence of his response probably meant that Zakoura had indeed kept his vow. Well, she had come here knowing that she might never see him again. Nothing had changed, nothing but her level of hope. Still, she felt tears building around her eyes. She tightened her jaw against them. One thing was certain—she wasn't about to cry in front of Carlos.

"Should I take that to mean that you haven't seen him?"

"You should take that to mean that he doesn't exist, except maybe in your mind."

"I think we both know that's not the case," she replied with acerbity. "Now, if you'll excuse me, I have lesson plans to finish." At the front door, she stopped and glanced back at him.

"You know, it really is pointless for you to keep denying that you know him." She let the door slam shut behind her. Let him wonder just how much she knew.

Leigh discovered that she enjoyed teaching high school more than she had anticipated. Of course, she fully intended to keep looking for a position in the archaeology department of a university, and she still hoped to join other digs, but for now she was satisfied that Chinle was where she belonged. Her days developed a routine that she found comforting. There had been enough upheaval in her life to last her a while. The hours she spent in the classroom flew by. After school there was always someone who wanted to stay for extra help, or to hang around just to talk. When Leigh got home, she'd take Butch and Sundance out to run. Then, before sunset, she'd go out to the dwarf mesa to watch night arrive. It was the one concession she made to her hope that Zakoura might yet return. She wanted him to know that he could find her there every evening, in case he ever changed his mind. She always took the Jeep. She'd learned her lesson about how quickly darkness fell out here, and how dangerous it could be.

She never missed a day through that first fall and winter. Not even when she had the flu and was running a fever that left her shaking one minute and sweating the next. And when a foot of snow blanketed the area, she blazed a trail to the mesa with the snowplow she'd bought for the front of the truck. By spring, the trek had become more of a ritual than a pilgrimage of hope.

She was sitting on the hood of the Jeep at her usual spot, near the end of a particularly beautiful day in early June, when she saw the dark silhouette walking toward her from the west. At first she thought it might be Carlos, coming to tell her she couldn't loiter there anymore. He'd tried every other means of harassing her. But as the figure drew closer, she noticed the breadth of the shoulders, the long hair whipping in the wind. She eased herself down to the ground and took a few hesitant steps forward, afraid to believe that what she was seeing was real and not a hallucination. She'd spent so many evenings imagining what it would be like to see him again that her mind might have conjured up this mirage to placate her. But when she was close enough to make out the detailed etching of the thunderbird hanging against his chest, close enough to see her pain and hope mirrored in his dark eyes, her doubts dissolved. She ran to him, her feet nearly skimming across the ground. Zakoura stopped where he was and opened his arms to her. Leigh flew into them, his name catching in her throat like a cry.

EPILOGUE

Leigh opened the door and Butch and Sundance bounded into the house ahead of her. The clots of snow in their fur caused a miniature shower when they shook themselves. Leigh unzipped her ski jacket and pulled off her boots and the knitted hat and gloves she was wearing. The weather had turned sharply colder overnight, ushering in the first real snow of the season. Christmas was only a week away.

The house was cozy and warm and fragrant with the holiday smell of turkey cooking. Leigh put the candied sweet potatoes and rolls into the oven and set the vegetables on the stove to steam. She'd covered the table with a white linen cloth before going out to play with the dogs. Now she laid out the place settings, three of them. While she worked, she listened to a Navaho station on the radio. Over the past six years, she'd developed a passable fluency in the language.

Butch and Sundance, aware that company was expected, were too agitated to sleep. They paced around the house, cocking their heads and barking at every sound. When someone finally knocked, they tripped over each other racing to the door. Leigh had to push them aside to open it.

Edward Bahe and Jimmy were outside, holding a six-foot evergreen in their arms.

"That looks great, guys. Thank you," Leigh said, trying to keep the dogs from jumping all over them.

"In the usual place, right?" Jimmy asked, already steering his end toward the living room window. At sixteen, he was still determined to become an archaeologist, and under Leigh's private tutelage his schoolwork had improved dramatically. With a scholarship a real possibility, he spent hours poring over college catalogs, trying to decide where he wanted to apply. For the past two summers Leigh had even arranged for him to assist her and the team she'd assembled in the continuing excavation of Canyon de Chelly.

"Sure smells terrific in here," Bahe said as they set the tree in the stand Leigh had waiting for it.

"You know you're both welcome to join us."

Bahe shook his head. "Thanks anyway. But in this case, three's company and five's a crowd."

"Besides—" Jimmy shrugged "—you know how my grandma is."

Leigh smiled ruefully. Mary had never changed her mind about Zakoura. In spite of all the evidence to the contrary, she still blamed him for her heartache. But she loved Leigh without qualification and doted over their daughter as if she were another grandchild.

Before Jimmy and Bahe left, Leigh gave them each a loaf of the fruitcake she'd baked. She handed Bahe an extra one and asked him to deliver it to Carlos for her. Over the years, her relationship with the policeman had undergone a metamorphosis so gradual, so subtle, that she couldn't point to one time or event when they had stopped being enemies and started being friends. Although Carlos still maintained a wary distance from Zakoura, he treated Leigh with a grudging respect and had even come to trust her. She supposed she'd earned that trust by keeping the secret of the portal as well as any Navaho. And once Jandi had been born, she clearly had a vested interest in making sure the outside world never intruded.

After Jimmy and Bahe left, Leigh dragged out the three cartons of lights, tinsel and ornaments and left them near the tree; they would decorate it after dinner. Jandi had two Christmases every year, complete with trees and presents. One she celebrated with her parents in Canyon de Chelly, the other she celebrated in Connecticut with her grandparents.

With the council's permission, Leigh had told her mother and father the truth about Zakoura and the portal just before Jandi's birth. Her father, in typical fashion, had smiled through her recitation and, when she was finished, looked as if he were still waiting for the punch line. When none came, his face had collapsed into a frown.

"You're not being *serious?*" he'd muttered.

"Of course she is," Nina had said, half dazed herself by Leigh's revelation.

"That kind of thing just isn't possible . . . is it?"

Leigh had felt sorry for her father. The world he'd known for over sixty years was suddenly not what it had seemed to be. The scientific principles that had provided the unshakable basis of his life lay pretty much in ruins. If he had been wrong about the structure of the world, how much else had he also been mistaken about?

In spite of her open-minded belief in "possibilities," Nina had been nearly as nonplussed as her husband. But after the initial shock had worn off, she'd bombarded Leigh with a barrage of questions, interrupting herself as new thoughts occurred to her. David Morgan had sat and listened in silence, his face as gray and slack as if he'd just come through major surgery. And now, five years later, he still had trouble accepting the fact that his granddaughter could travel into a dimension whose existence was completely beyond the knowledge of the scientific community.

At three o'clock, Leigh combed her hair and changed out of her jeans and sweatshirt into a soft sweater and a long skirt. Grabbing her jacket, she climbed into the Jeep and set out for the meeting place that Jandi had named the Baby Mesa.

While she waited there, she recalled the first time Jandi had crossed through the portal, and an awful chill swept through her, even though the heater was on full blast. She and Zakoura had decided not to tell their daughter about the doorway into his world until she was old enough to understand that she must never try to cross through it. With no way to determine how the passage might affect her, they had to assume it might be fatal. But Jandi hated the times when her father had to be away, and one evening when she was barely three she'd stolen out of her bed and followed him. Although she couldn't match his pace, she'd managed to keep him in view until the moment when he suddenly vanished. Ten minutes later, she'd found the portal herself. Zakoura had discovered her the next morning, frightened and hungry, but otherwise sound, and brought her back to Leigh, who was nearly hysterical with worry. Jandi had her father's ability to move between the dimensions. Now she shuttled back and forth between the two planes as if she were simply commuting from one town to the next.

When Leigh saw them coming across the snowy plain, her heart contracted with happiness. Unable to wait another moment, she slid out of the truck and hurried toward them. In deference to the weather, Zakoura wore a robe of fur and leggings of feather cord. Although Jandi was also wrapped in furs, Zakoura carried her to keep her dry and to speed their progress. But as soon as she saw

Leigh, she begged to be allowed down, and she ran to her mother as if she'd been gone for months instead of weeks.

Leigh scooped her up in a fury of hugs and kisses. A moment later, Zakoura caught them both in his arms, kissing Leigh with a passion as hot and reckless as the first time, until Jandi complained that she was being squashed. Then they all piled into the Jeep and headed back to the house to celebrate an early Christmas and another home-coming.

* * * * *

SILHOUETTE *Shadows*·

Join award-winning author Rachel Lee as

CONARD COUNTY explores the dark side of love....

Rachel Lee will tingle your senses in August when she visits the dark side of love in her latest Conard County title, **THUNDER MOUNTAIN, SS #37.**

For years, Gray Cloud had guarded his beloved Thunder Mountain, protecting its secrets and mystical powers from human exploitation. Then came Mercy Kendrick.... But someone—or something—wanted her dead. Alone with the tempestuous forces of nature, Mercy turned to Gray Cloud, only to find a storm of a very different kind raging in his eyes. Look for their terrifying tale, only from Silhouette Shadows.

Three new stories celebrating
motherhood and love

Birds, Bees and Babies '94

NORA ROBERTS
ANN MAJOR
DALLAS SCHULZE

A collection of three stories, all by
award-winning authors, selected
especially to reflect the love all
families share. Silhouette's fifth annual
romantic tribute to mothers is sure
to touch your heart.

Available in May,
BIRDS, BEES AND BABIES 1994 is a
perfect gift for yourself or a loved one
to celebrate the joy of motherhood.

**Available at your favorite
retail outlet.**

Only from 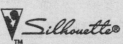 *Silhouette*®

—where passion lives.

CAN YOU STAND THE HEAT?

Silhouette
™

SUMMER

Sizzlers

'94

You're in for a serious heat wave with
Silhouette's latest selection of sizzling
summer reading. This sensuous collection
of three short stories provides the perfect
vacation escape! And what better authors
to relax with than

ANNETTE BROADRICK
JACKIE MERRITT
JUSTINE DAVIS

And that's not all....

With the purchase of *Silhouette Summer
Sizzlers '94*, you can send in for a FREE
Summer Sizzlers beach bag!

SUMMER JUST GOT HOTTER—
WITH SILHOUETTE BOOKS!

Silhouette Books
is proud to present
our best authors, their best books...
and the best in your reading pleasure!

Throughout 1994, look for exciting books
by these top names in contemporary
romance:

JULIE ELLIS
The Only Sin in May

FERN MICHAELS
Golden Lasso in May

DIANA PALMER
The Tender Stranger in June

ELIZABETH LOWELL
Fire and Rain in June

LINDA HOWARD
Sarah's Child in July

*When it comes to passion,
we wrote the book.*

BOBQ2

Fifty red-blooded, white-hot, true-blue hunks
from every State in the Union!

Look for MEN MADE IN AMERICA! Written by some of
our most popular authors, these stories feature fifty of
the strongest, sexiest men, each from a different state in
the union!

Two titles available every other month at your favorite
retail outlet.

In May, look for:

KISS YESTERDAY GOODBYE by Leigh Michaels (Iowa)
A TIME TO KEEP by Curtiss Ann Matlock (Kansas)

In June, look for:

ONE PALE, FAWN GLOVE by Linda Shaw (Kentucky)
BAYOU MIDNIGHT by Emilie Richards (Louisiana)

You won't be able to resist MEN MADE IN AMERICA!

Rugged and lean...and the best-looking,
sweetest-talking men to be found in the
entire Lone Star state!

Diana Palmer

LONG, TALL TEXANS

In July 1994, Silhouette is very proud to bring you
Diana Palmer's first three LONG, TALL TEXANS.
CALHOUN, JUSTIN and TYLER—the three cowboys
who started the legend. Now they're back by popular
demand in one classic volume—and they're ready to
lasso your heart! Beautifully repackaged for this
special event, this collection is sure to be a
longtime keepsake!

"Diana Palmer makes a reader want to find a Texan
of her own to love!"   —*Affaire de Coeur*

**LONG, TALL TEXANS—the first three—
reunited in this special roundup!**

**Available in July,
wherever Silhouette books are sold.**

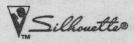